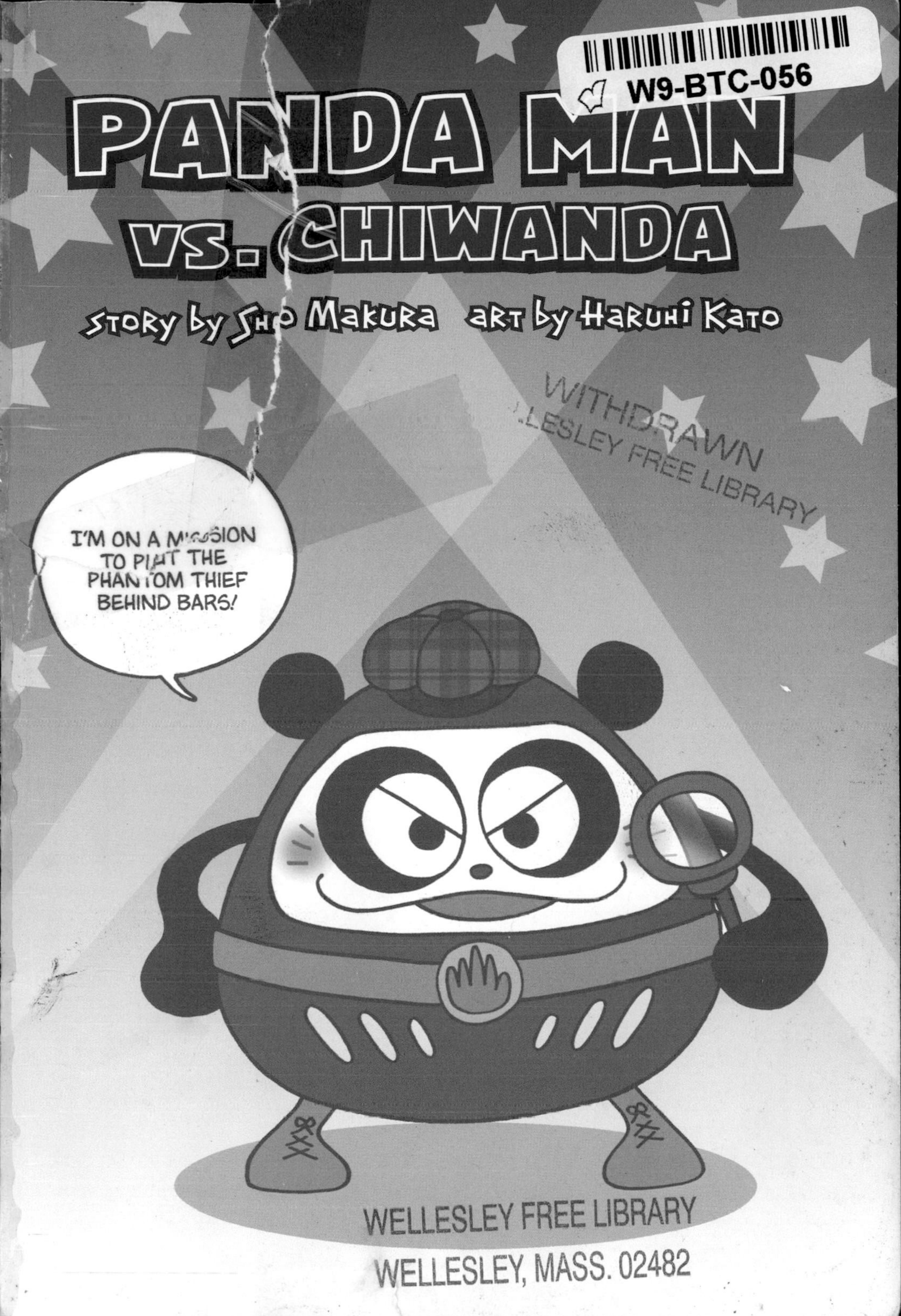
PANDA MAN
VS. CHIWANDA
STORY BY SHO MAKURA
ART BY HARUHI KATO
I'M ON A MISSION TO PUT THE PHANTOM THIEF BEHIND BARS!

One cold winter day, while training in the mountains, Panda Man ran out of food. He went down into town to get some.

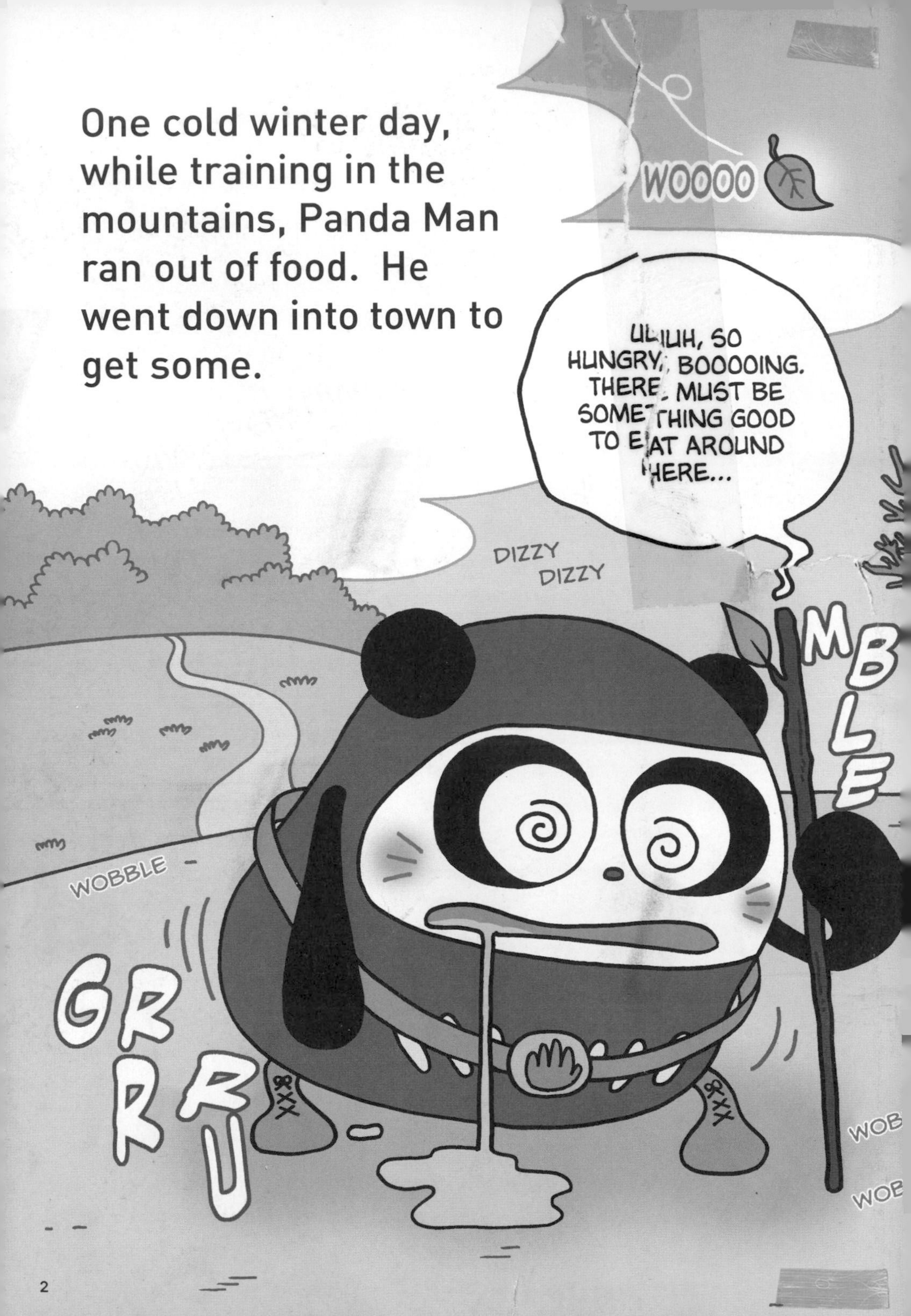
WOOOO
UHHUH, SO HUNGRY, BOOOOING. THERE MUST BE SOMETHING GOOD TO EAT AROUND HERE...
DIZZY
DIZZY
MBLE
WOBBLE
GRRRU
WOB
WOB

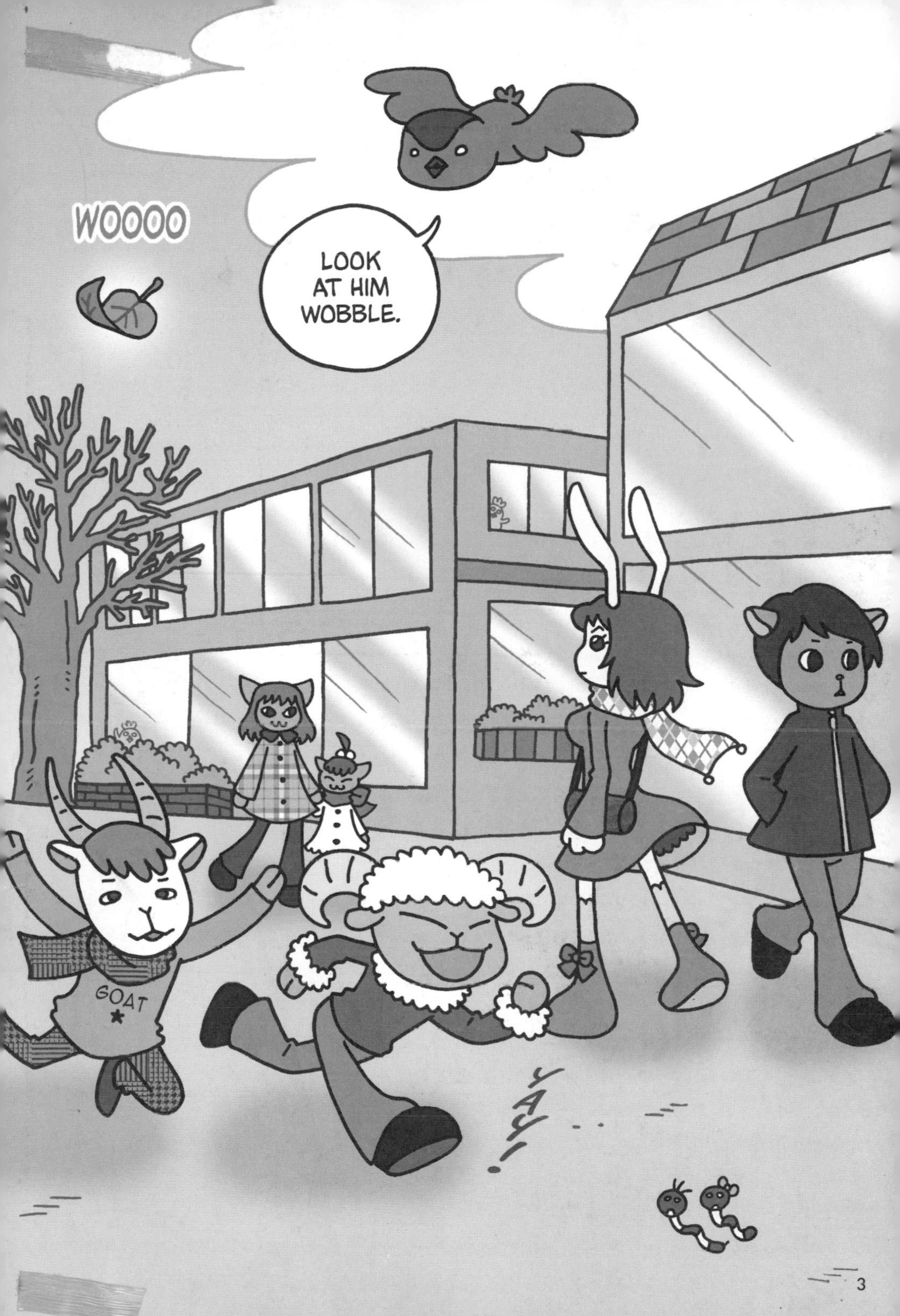
WOOOO
LOOK AT HIM WOBBLE.
GOAT
YAY!

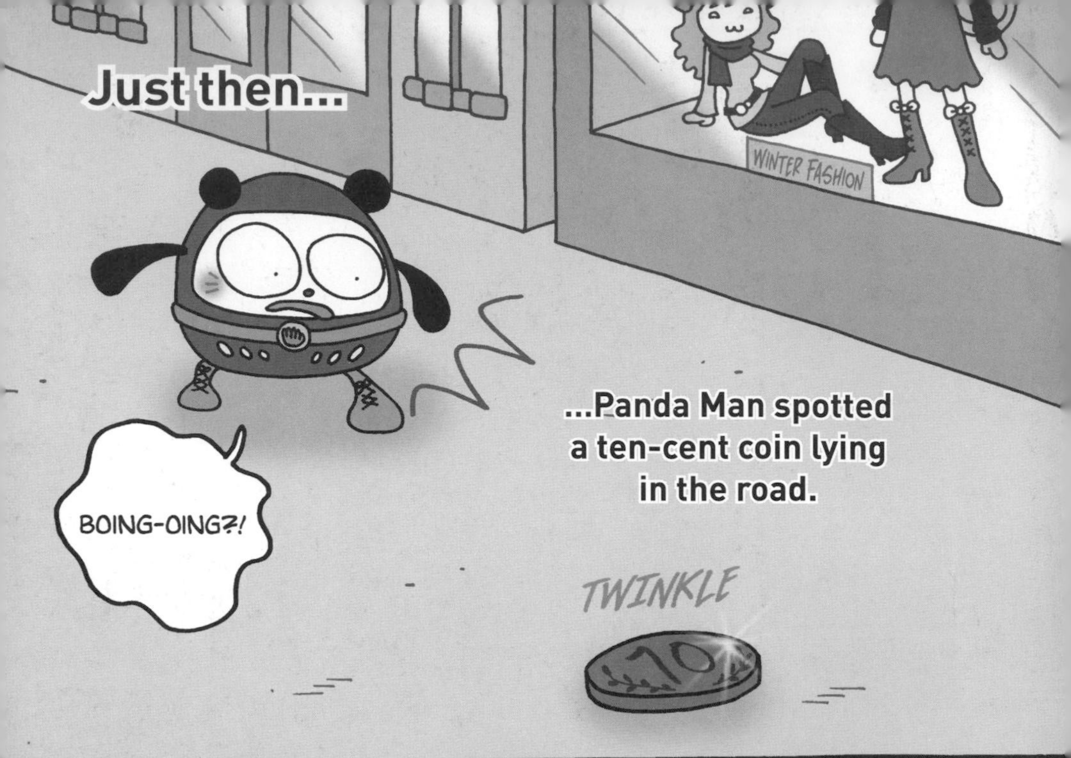
Just then...
BOING-OING?!
WINTER FASHION
...Panda Man spotted a ten-cent coin lying in the road.
TWINKLE
10

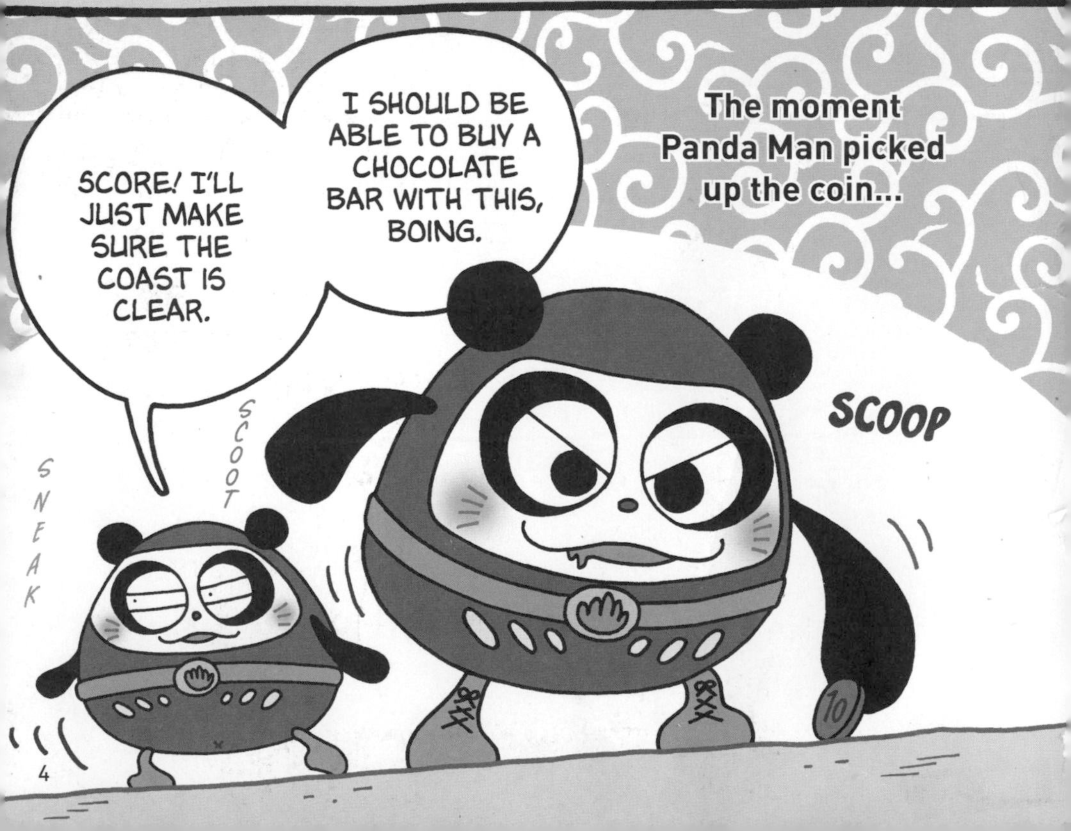
The moment Panda Man picked up the coin...
SCORE! I'LL JUST MAKE SURE THE COAST IS CLEAR.
I SHOULD BE ABLE TO BUY A CHOCOLATE BAR WITH THIS, BOING.
SNEAK
SCOOT
SCOOP
10

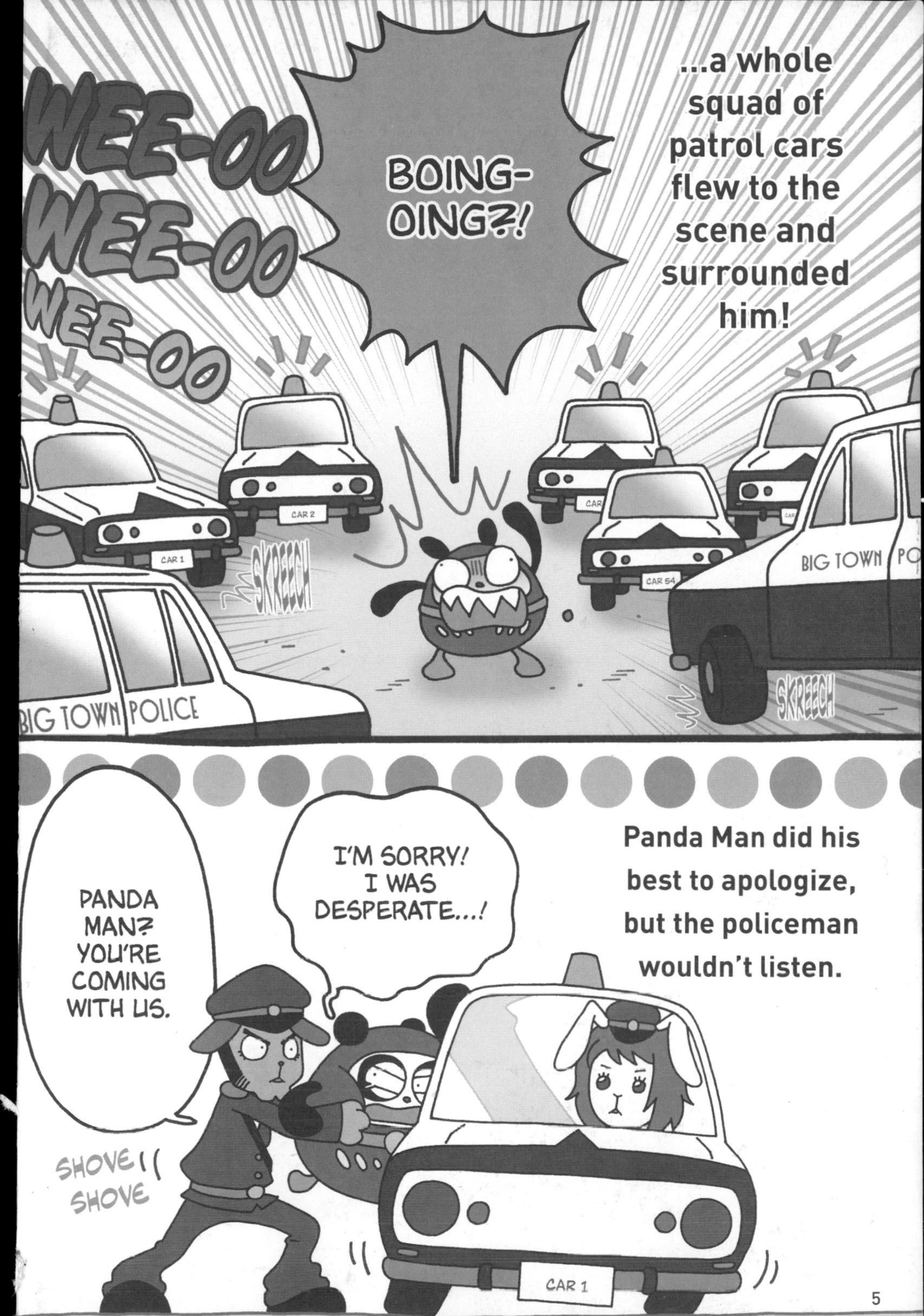
...a whole squad of patrol cars flew to the scene and surrounded him!
BOING-OING?!
WEE-OO WEE-OO WEE-OO
BIG TOWN PO
CAR 54
SKREECH
CAR 2
CAR 1
SKREECH
BIG TOWN POLICE
Panda Man did his best to apologize, but the policeman wouldn't listen.
I'M SORRY! I WAS DESPERATE...!
PANDA MAN? YOU'RE COMING WITH US.
SHOVE SHOVE
CAR 1

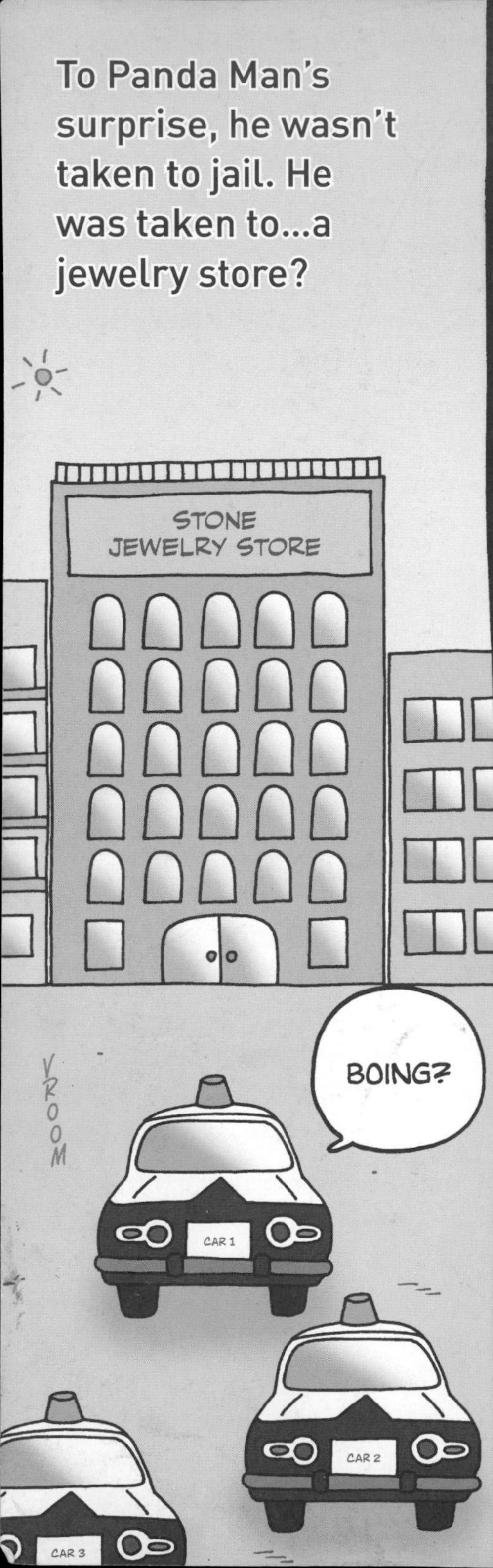
To Panda Man's surprise, he wasn't taken to jail. He was taken to...a jewelry store?
STONE JEWELRY STORE
VROOM
BOING?
CAR 1
CAR 2
CAR 3
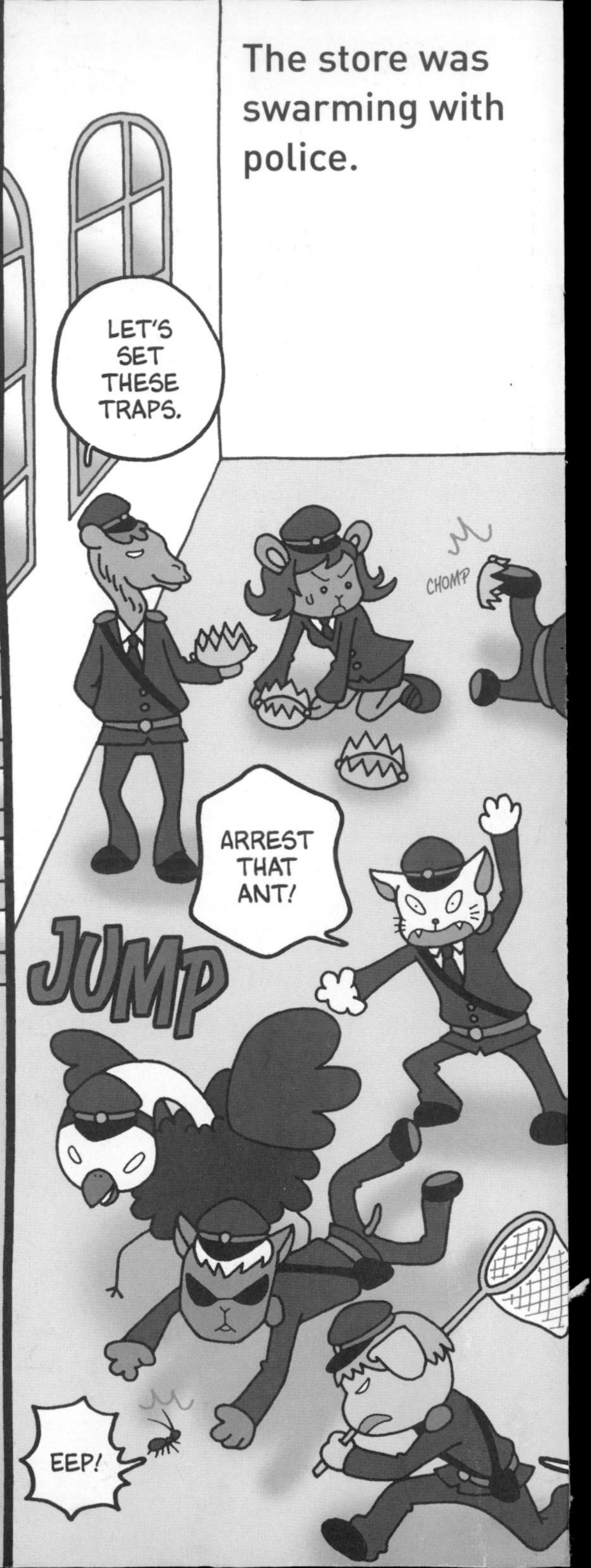
The store was swarming with police.
LET'S SET THESE TRAPS.
CHOMP
ARREST THAT ANT!
JUMP
EEP!

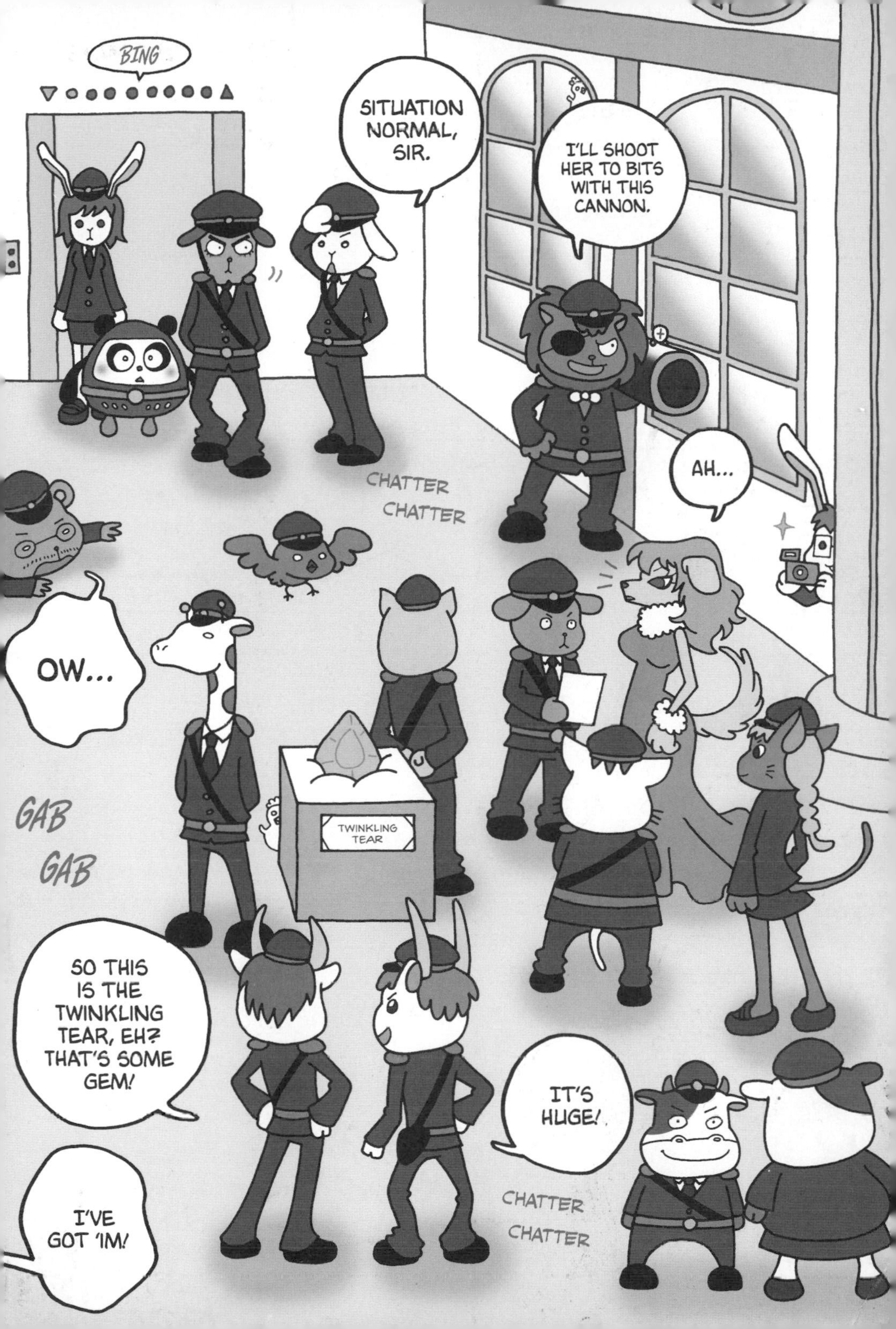
I'LL SHOOT HER TO BITS WITH THIS CANNON.
SITUATION NORMAL, SIR.
BING
AH...
CHATTER CHATTER
OW...
TWINKLING TEAR
GAB GAB
IT'S HUGE!
SO THIS IS THE TWINKLING TEAR, EH? THAT'S SOME GEM!
CHATTER CHATTER
I'VE GOT 'IM!

Once he was inside, a very elegant woman approached Panda Man. "I am Madam Stone," she said. "And this is my jewelry store. I've read all about you, Panda Man. The *Really Big Book of Heroes* says you're the world's greatest martial artist. Is that correct?"

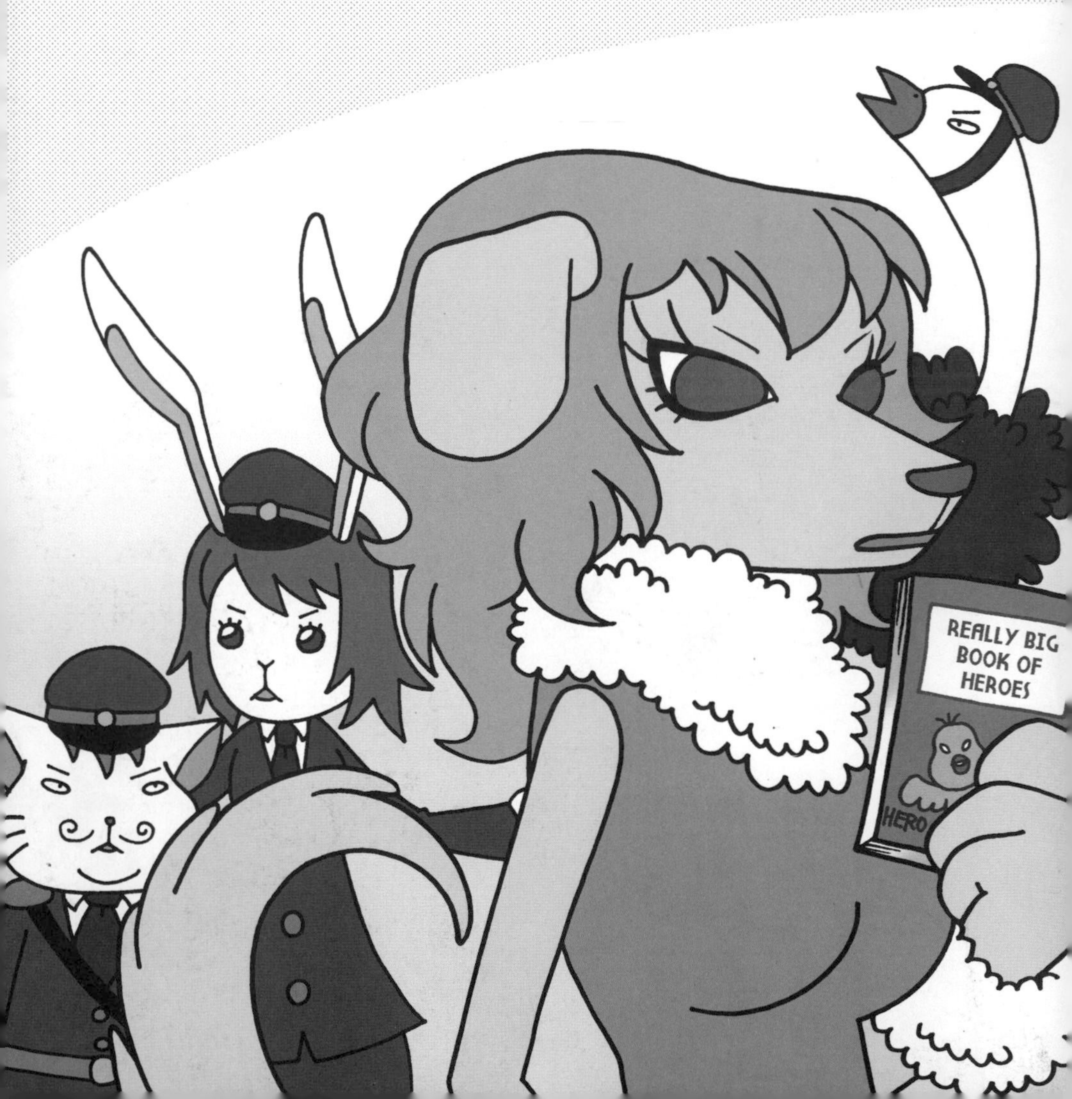
REALLY BIG BOOK OF HEROES
HERO

"Th-that's me,"
Panda Man replied.

"Then I have a request,"
the woman said.

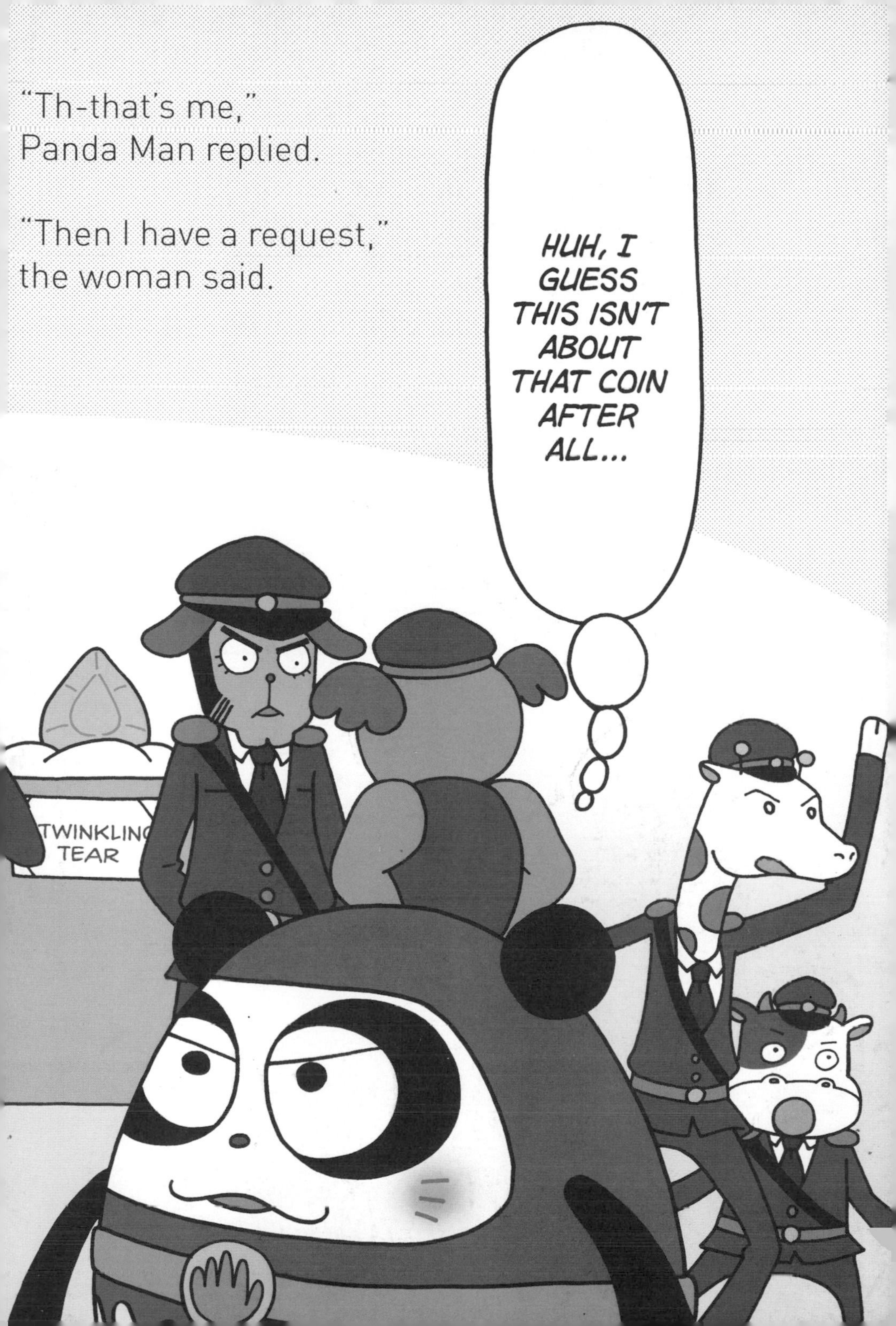
HUH, I GUESS THIS ISN'T ABOUT THAT COIN AFTER ALL...
TWINKLING TEAR

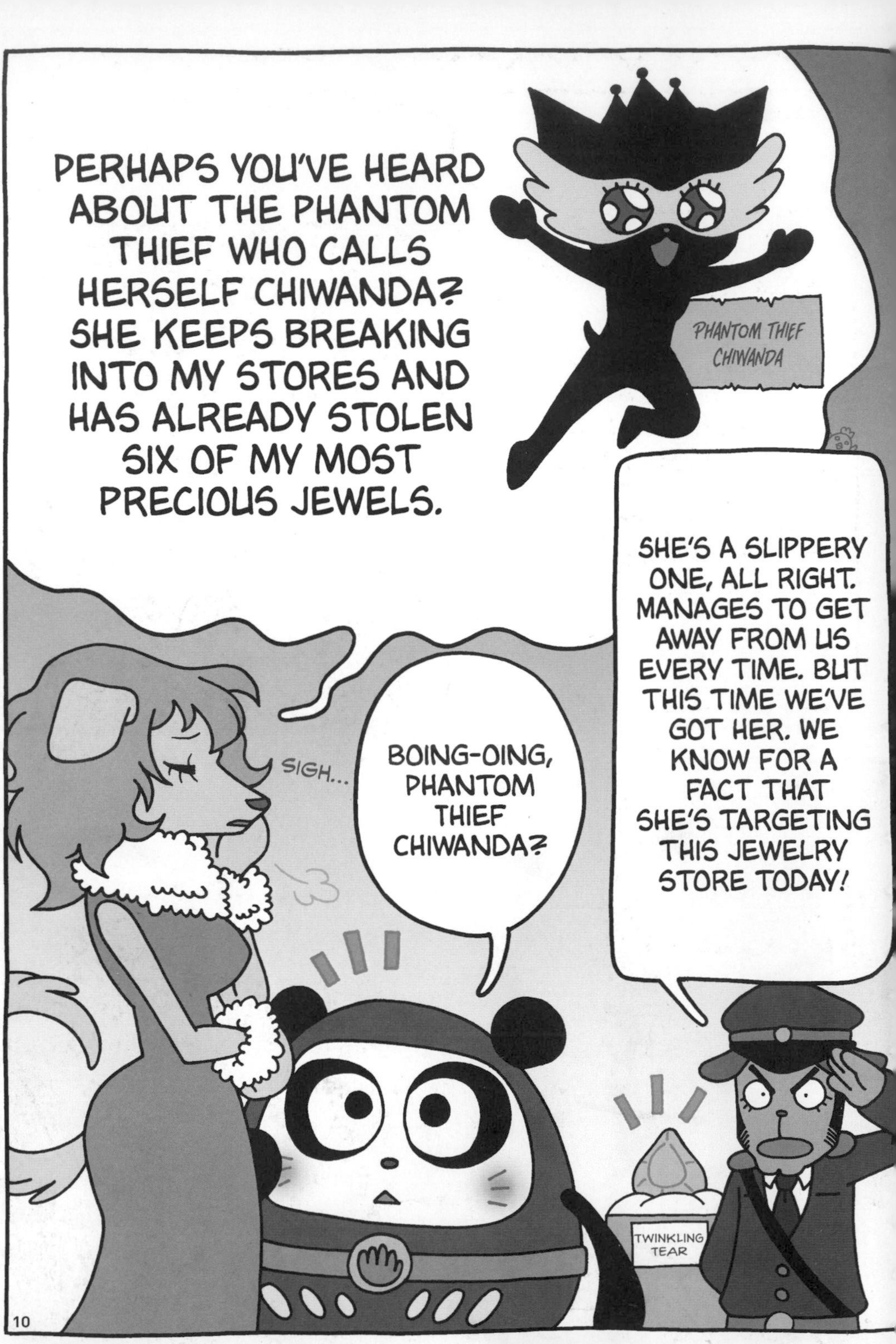
PERHAPS YOU'VE HEARD ABOUT THE PHANTOM THIEF WHO CALLS HERSELF CHIWANDA? SHE KEEPS BREAKING INTO MY STORES AND HAS ALREADY STOLEN SIX OF MY MOST PRECIOUS JEWELS.
PHANTOM THIEF CHIWANDA
SHE'S A SLIPPERY ONE, ALL RIGHT. MANAGES TO GET AWAY FROM US EVERY TIME. BUT THIS TIME WE'VE GOT HER. WE KNOW FOR A FACT THAT SHE'S TARGETING THIS JEWELRY STORE TODAY!
BOING-OING, PHANTOM THIEF CHIWANDA?
SIGH...
TWINKLING TEAR

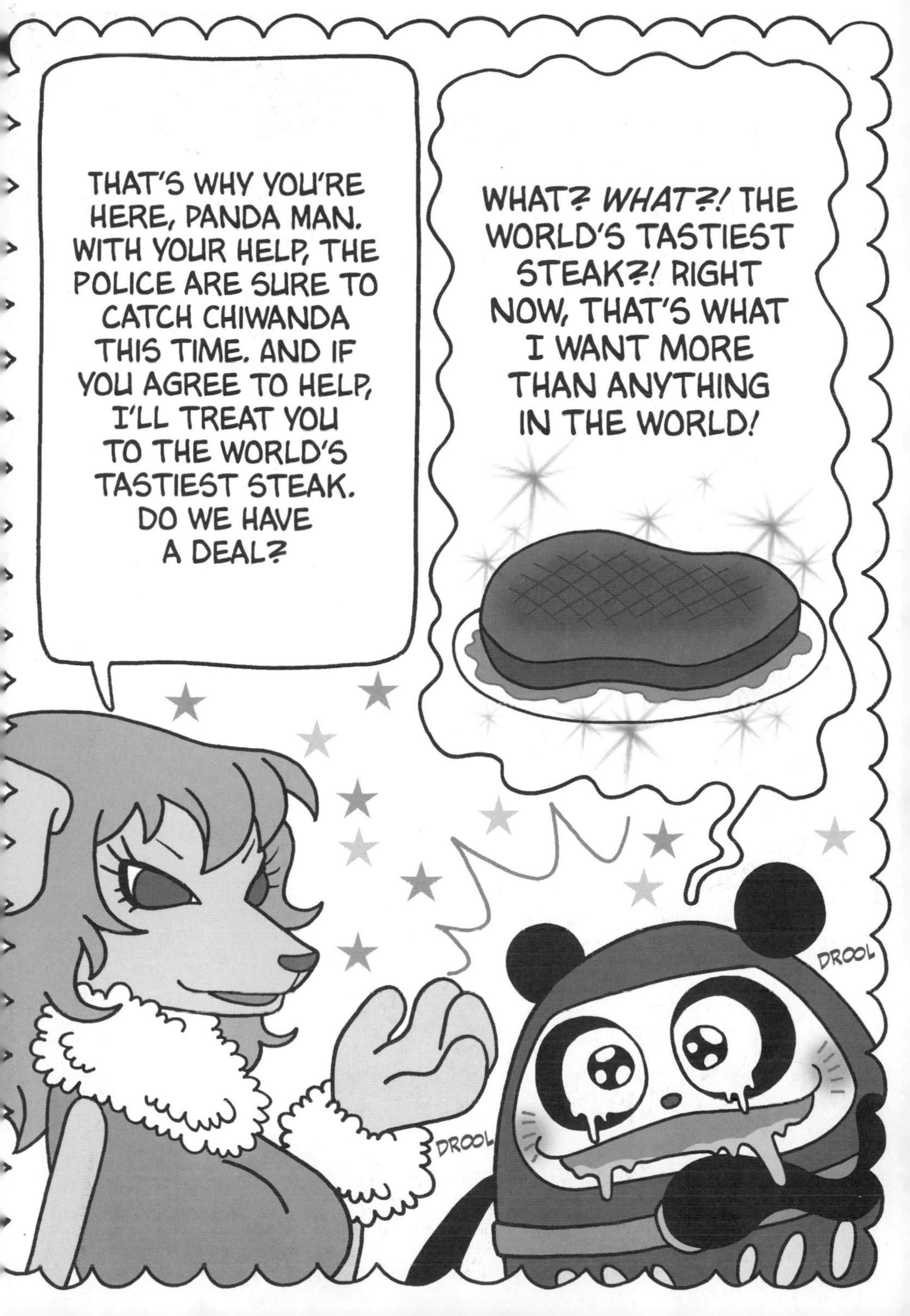
WHAT? WHAT?! THE WORLD'S TASTIEST STEAK?! RIGHT NOW, THAT'S WHAT I WANT MORE THAN ANYTHING IN THE WORLD!
THAT'S WHY YOU'RE HERE, PANDA MAN. WITH YOUR HELP, THE POLICE ARE SURE TO CATCH CHIWANDA THIS TIME. AND IF YOU AGREE TO HELP, I'LL TREAT YOU TO THE WORLD'S TASTIEST STEAK. DO WE HAVE A DEAL?
DROOL
DROOL

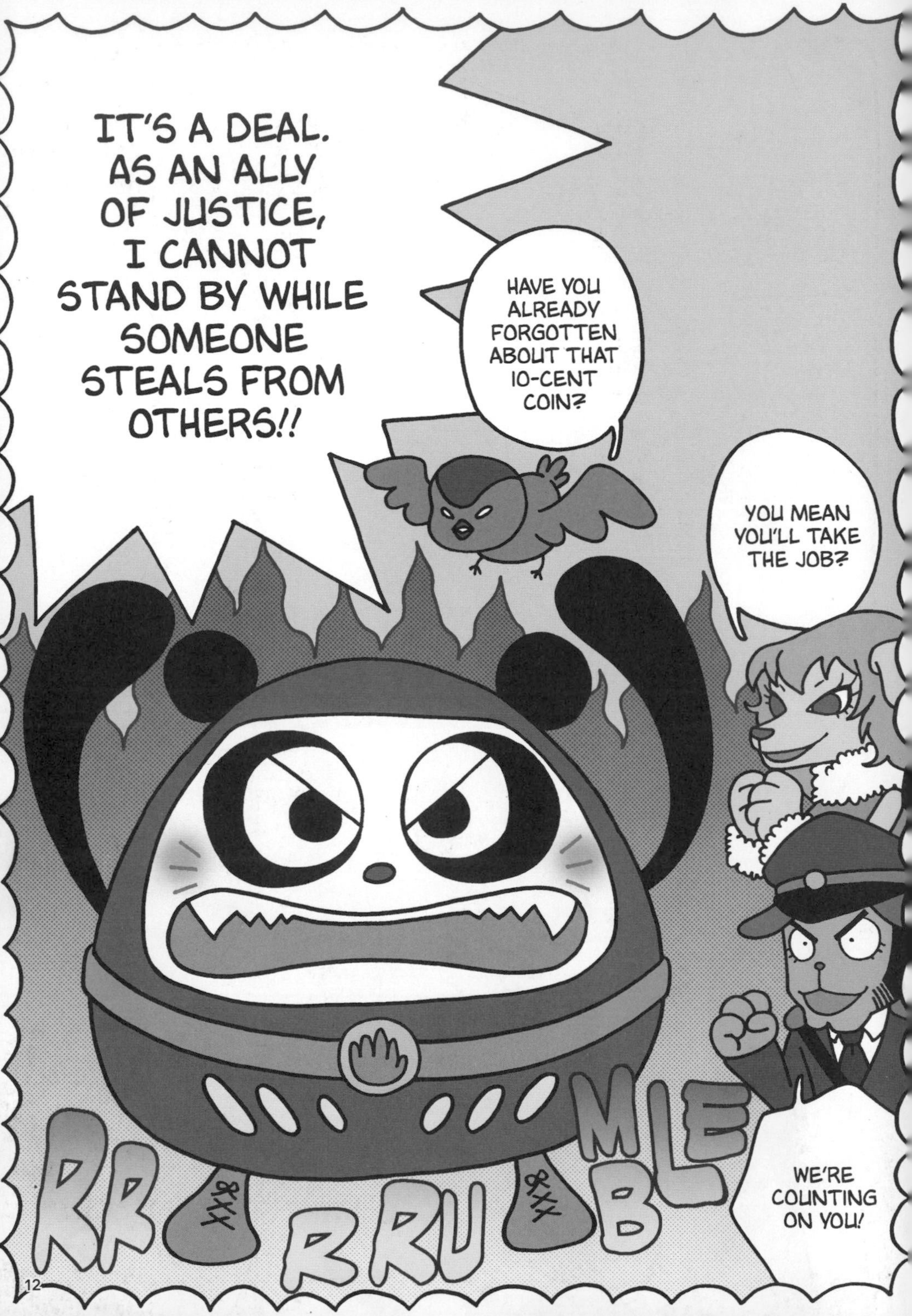
IT'S A DEAL. AS AN ALLY OF JUSTICE, I CANNOT STAND BY WHILE SOMEONE STEALS FROM OTHERS!!
HAVE YOU ALREADY FORGOTTEN ABOUT THAT 10-CENT COIN?
YOU MEAN YOU'LL TAKE THE JOB?
WE'RE COUNTING ON YOU!
RRRRUMBLE

Help Panda Man decipher Chiwanda's message!

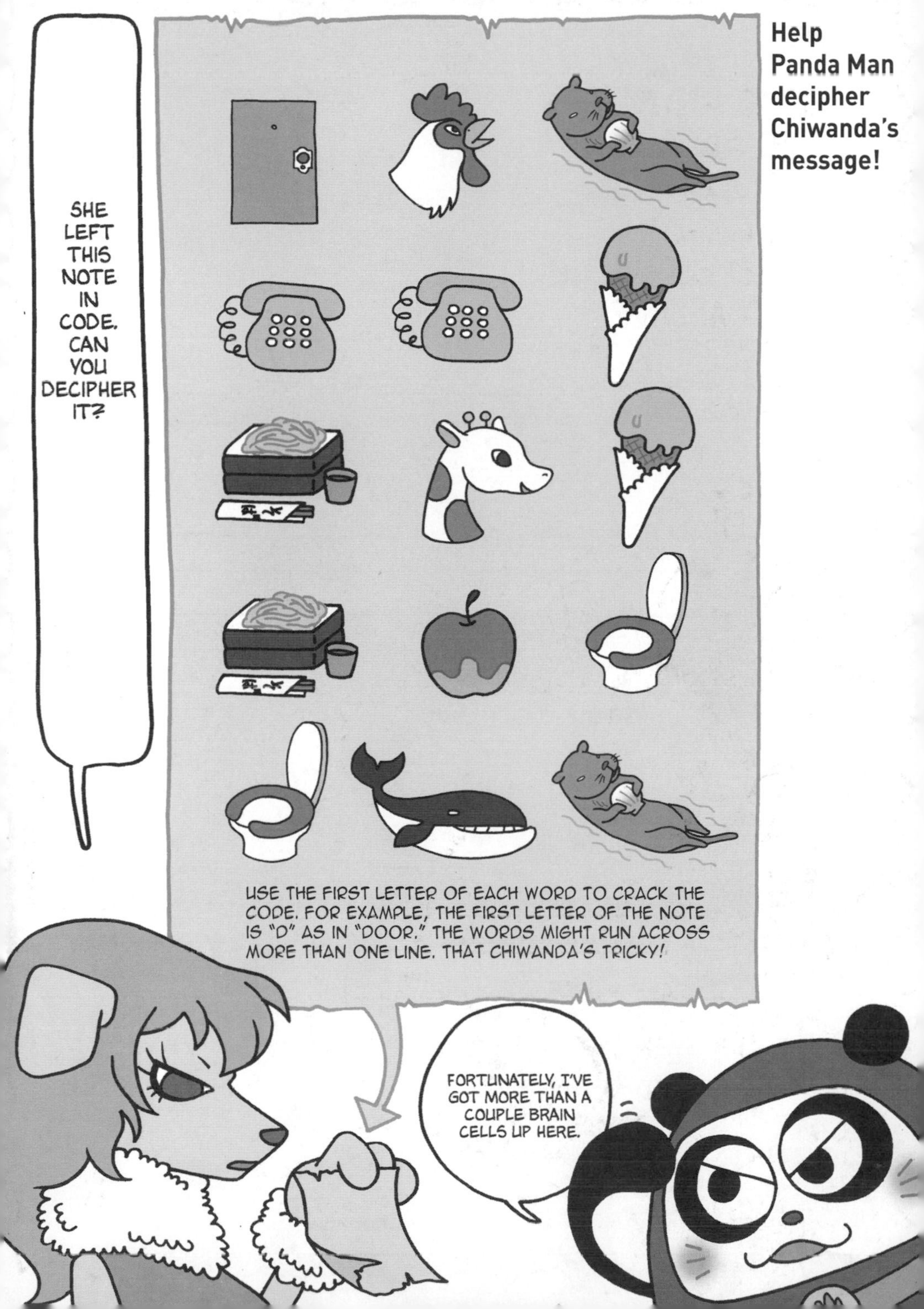
SHE LEFT THIS NOTE IN CODE. CAN YOU DECIPHER IT?
USE THE FIRST LETTER OF EACH WORD TO CRACK THE CODE. FOR EXAMPLE, THE FIRST LETTER OF THE NOTE IS "D" AS IN "DOOR." THE WORDS MIGHT RUN ACROSS MORE THAN ONE LINE. THAT CHIWANDA'S TRICKY!
FORTUNATELY, I'VE GOT MORE THAN A COUPLE BRAIN CELLS UP HERE.

Thanks to you Panda Man
cracked the code!

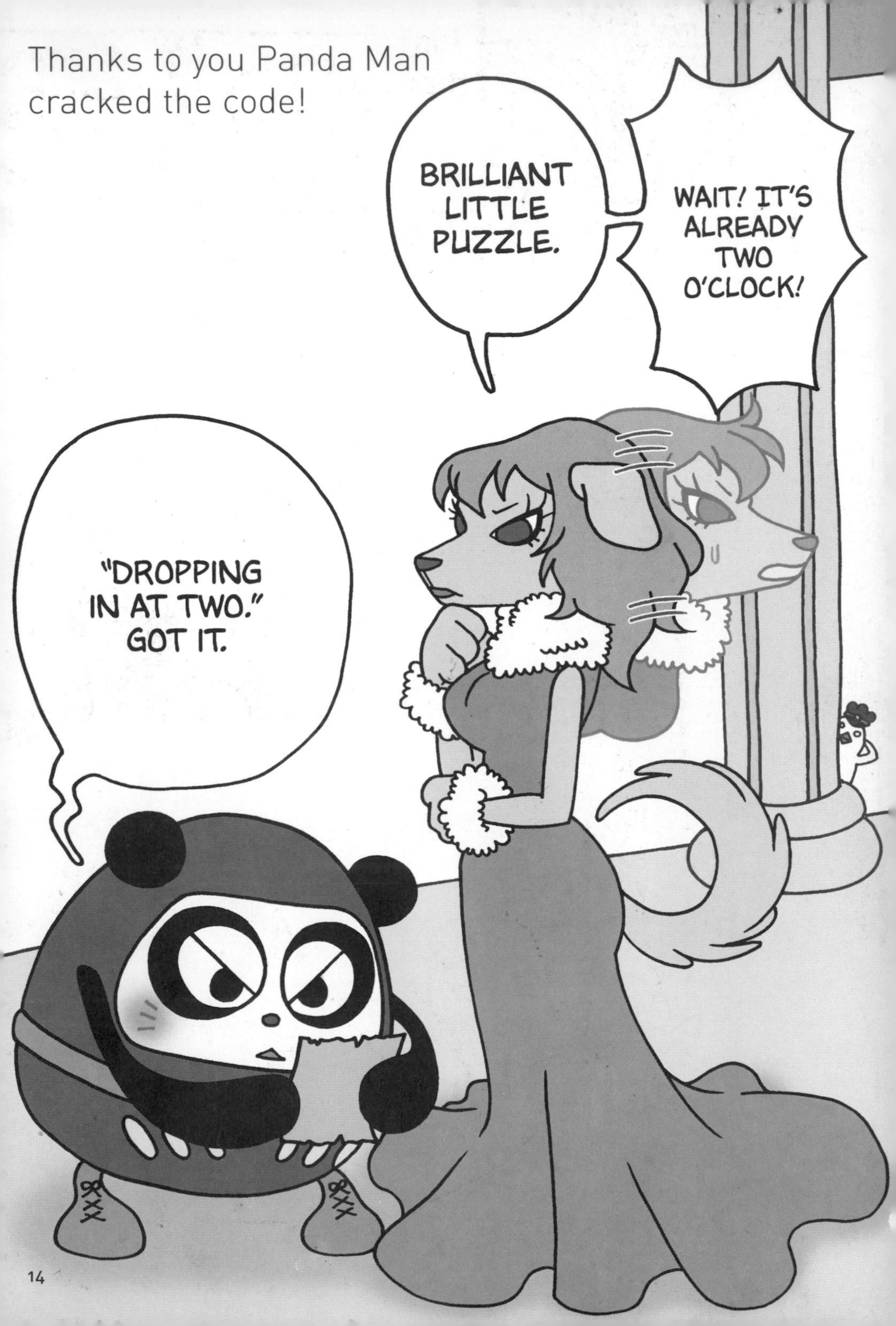
WAIT! IT'S ALREADY TWO O'CLOCK!
BRILLIANT LITTLE PUZZLE.
"DROPPING IN AT TWO." GOT IT.

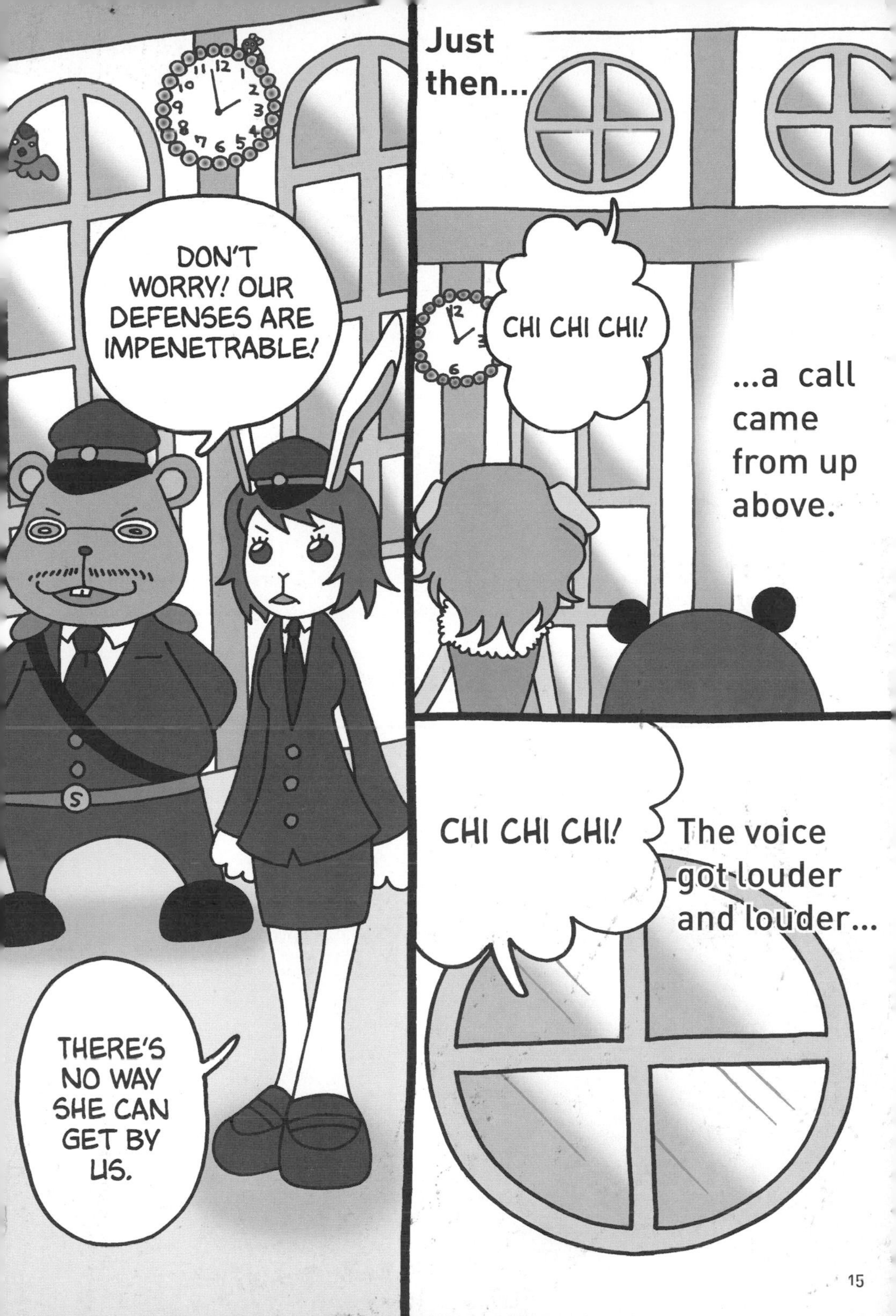
DON'T WORRY! OUR DEFENSES ARE IMPENETRABLE!
THERE'S NO WAY SHE CAN GET BY US.
Just then...
CHI CHI CHI!
...a call came from up above.
CHI CHI CHI!
The voice got louder and louder...

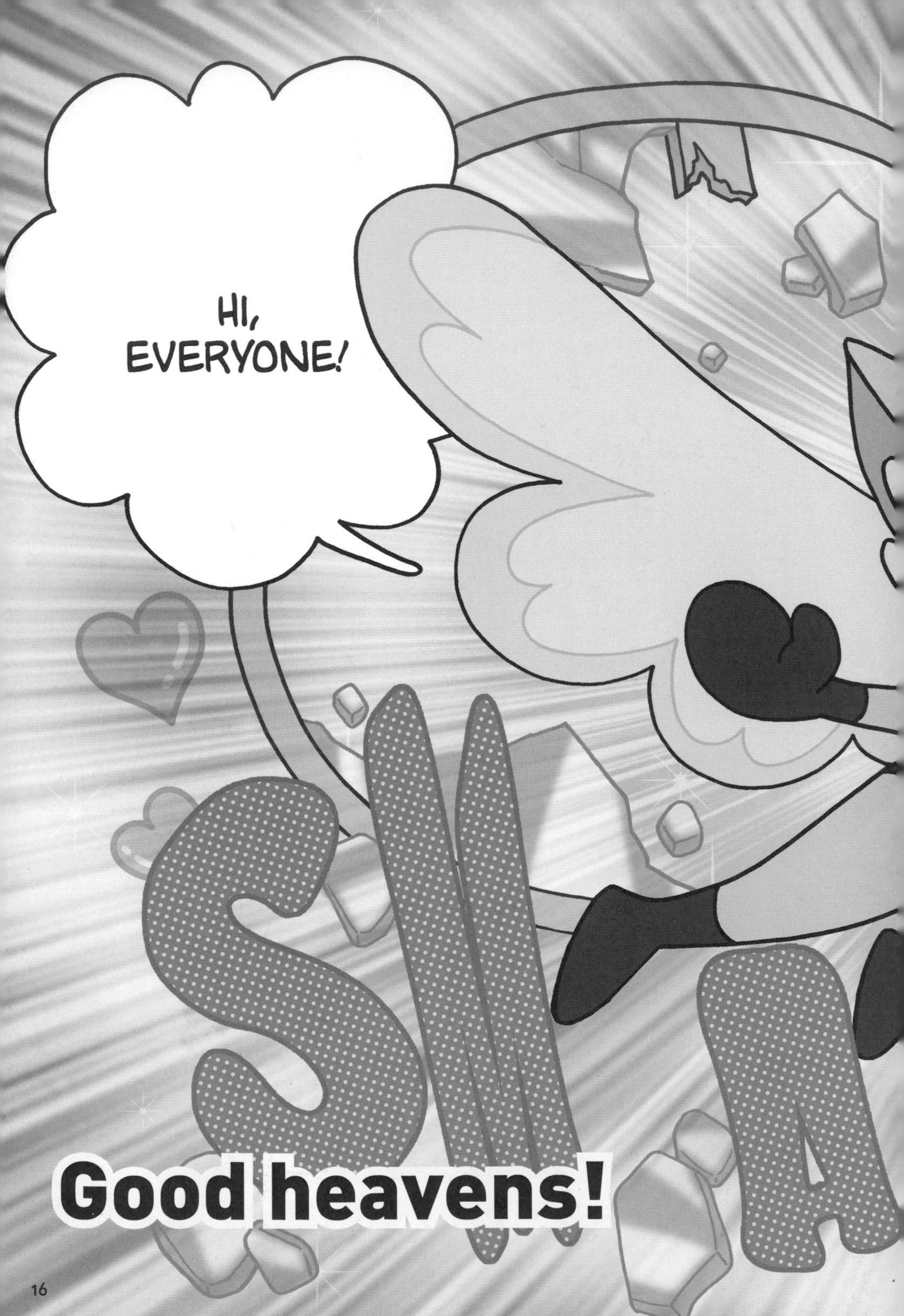
HI, EVERYONE!
Good heavens!

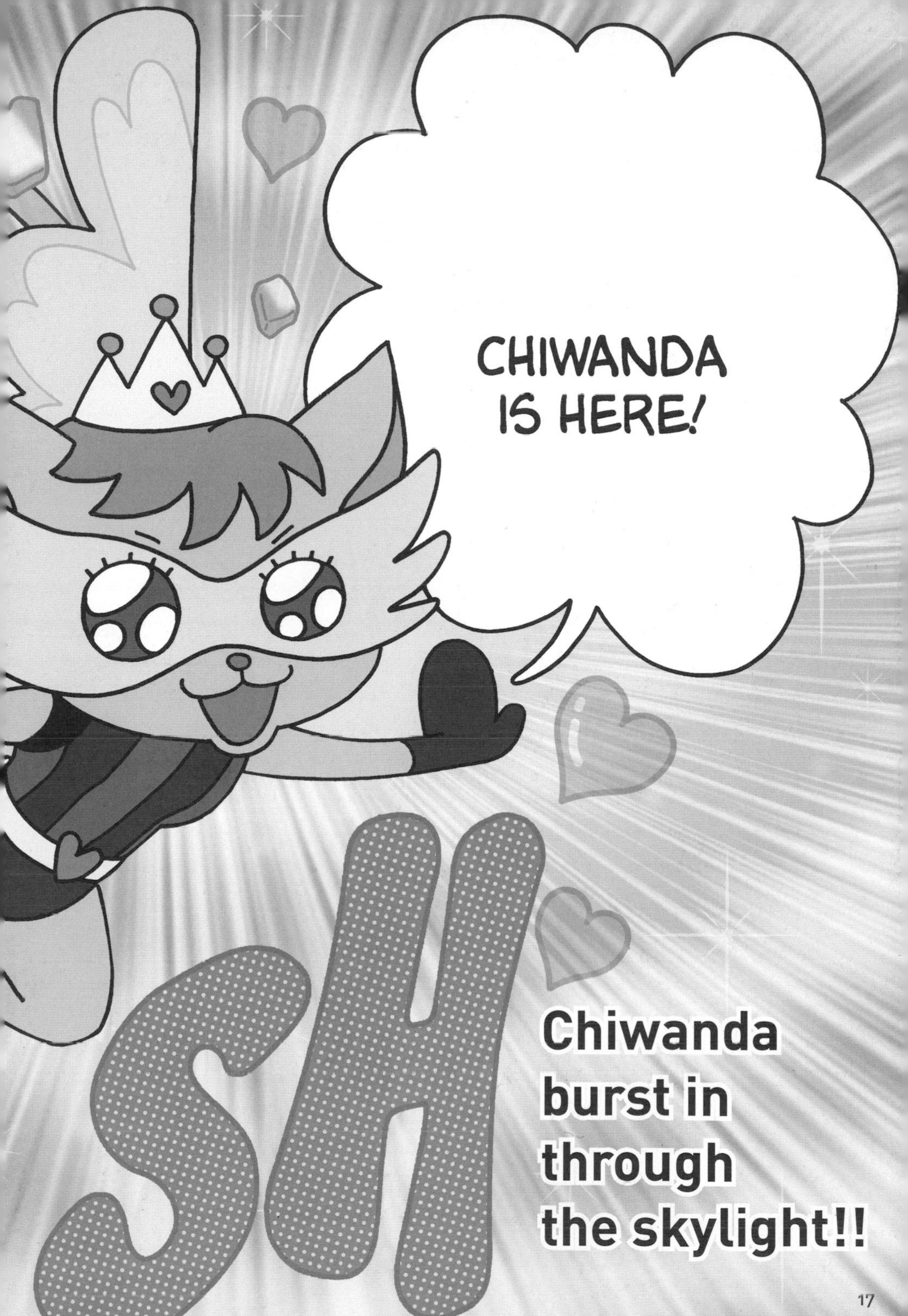
CHIWANDA IS HERE!
SH
Chiwanda burst in through the skylight!!

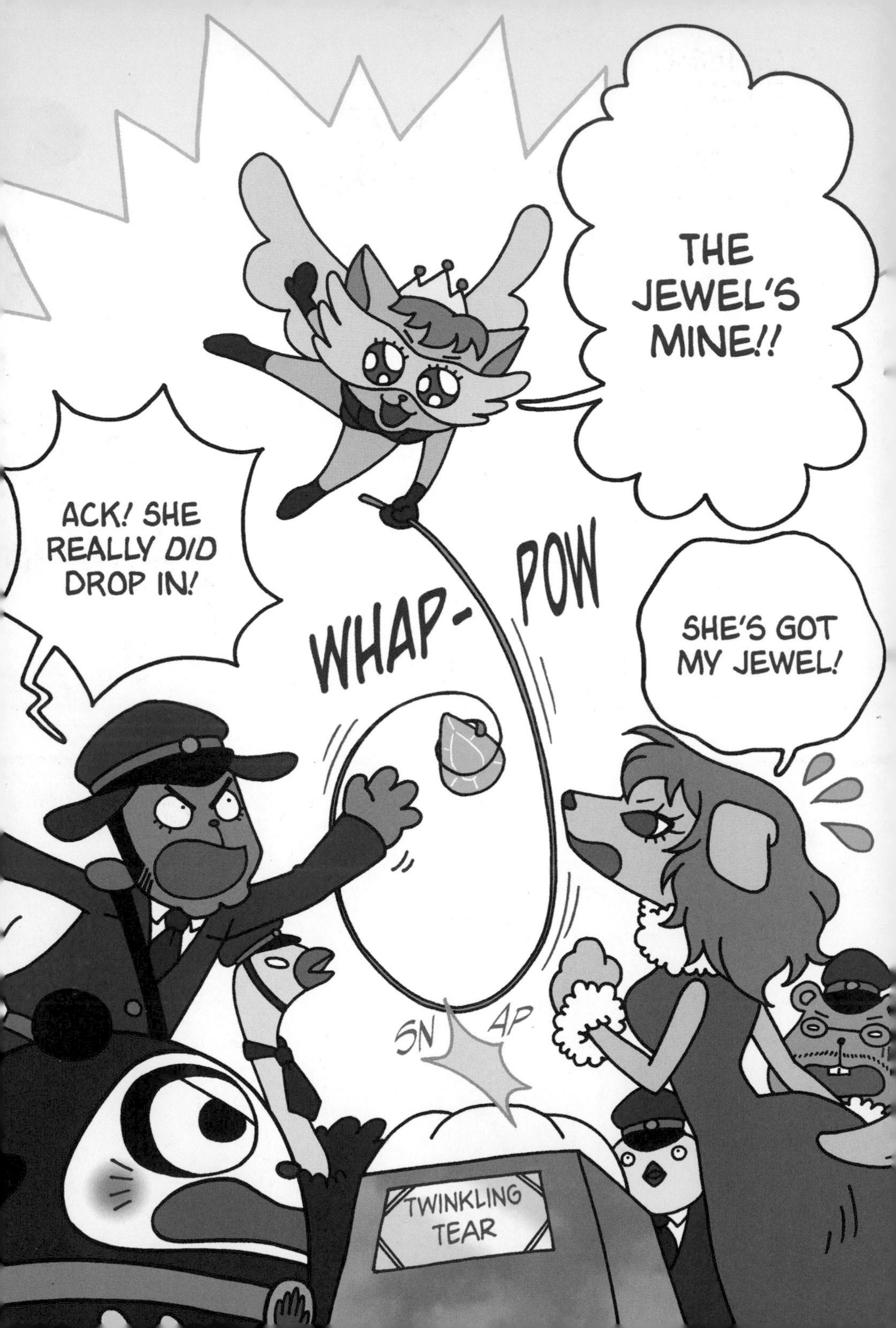
THE JEWEL'S MINE!!
ACK! SHE REALLY *DID* DROP IN!
WHAP-POW
SHE'S GOT MY JEWEL!
SNAP
TWINKLING TEAR

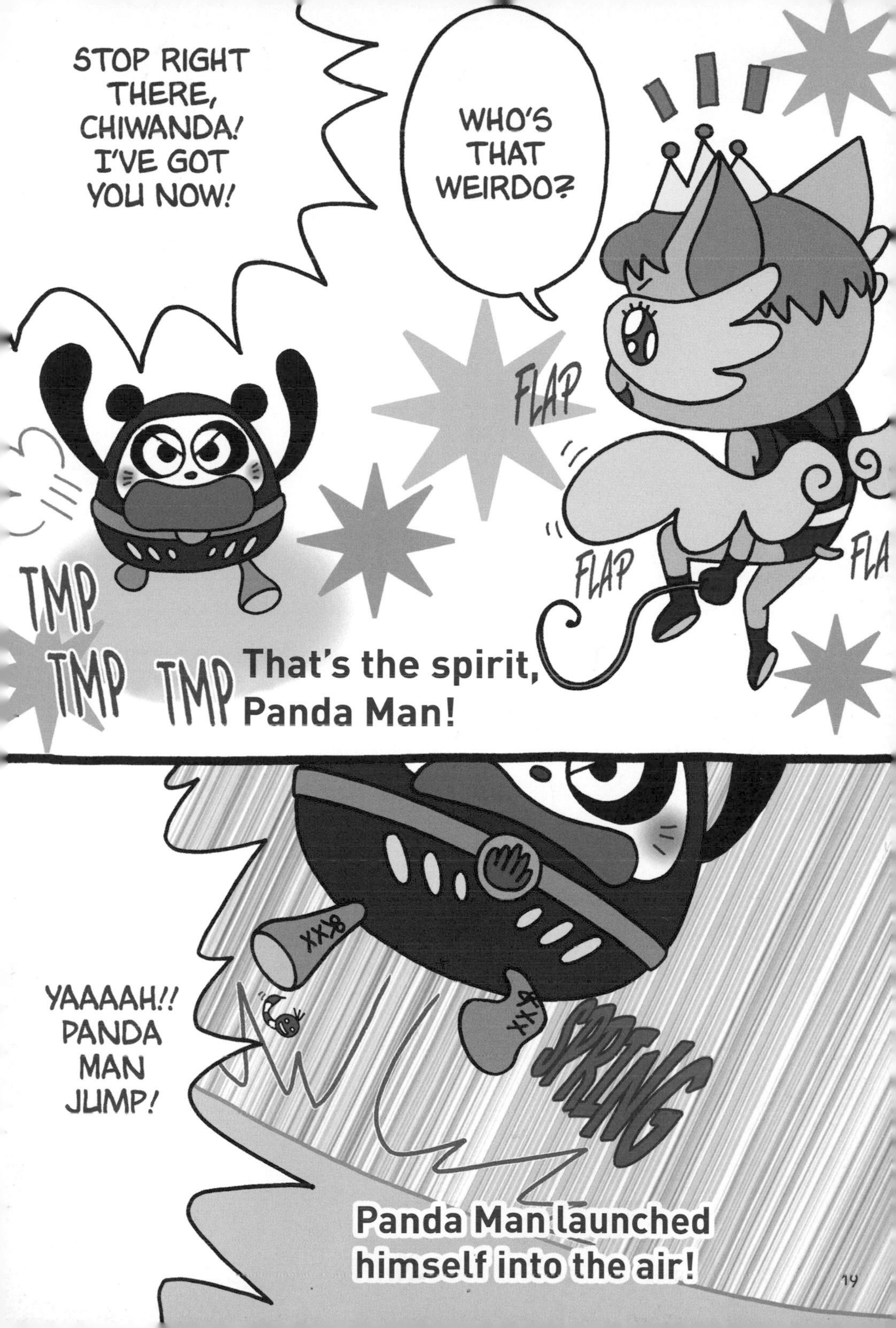
STOP RIGHT THERE, CHIWANDA! I'VE GOT YOU NOW!
WHO'S THAT WEIRDO?
FLAP
FLAP
FLA
TMP
TMP
TMP
That's the spirit, Panda Man!
YAAAAH!! PANDA MAN JUMP!
SPRING
Panda Man launched himself into the air!

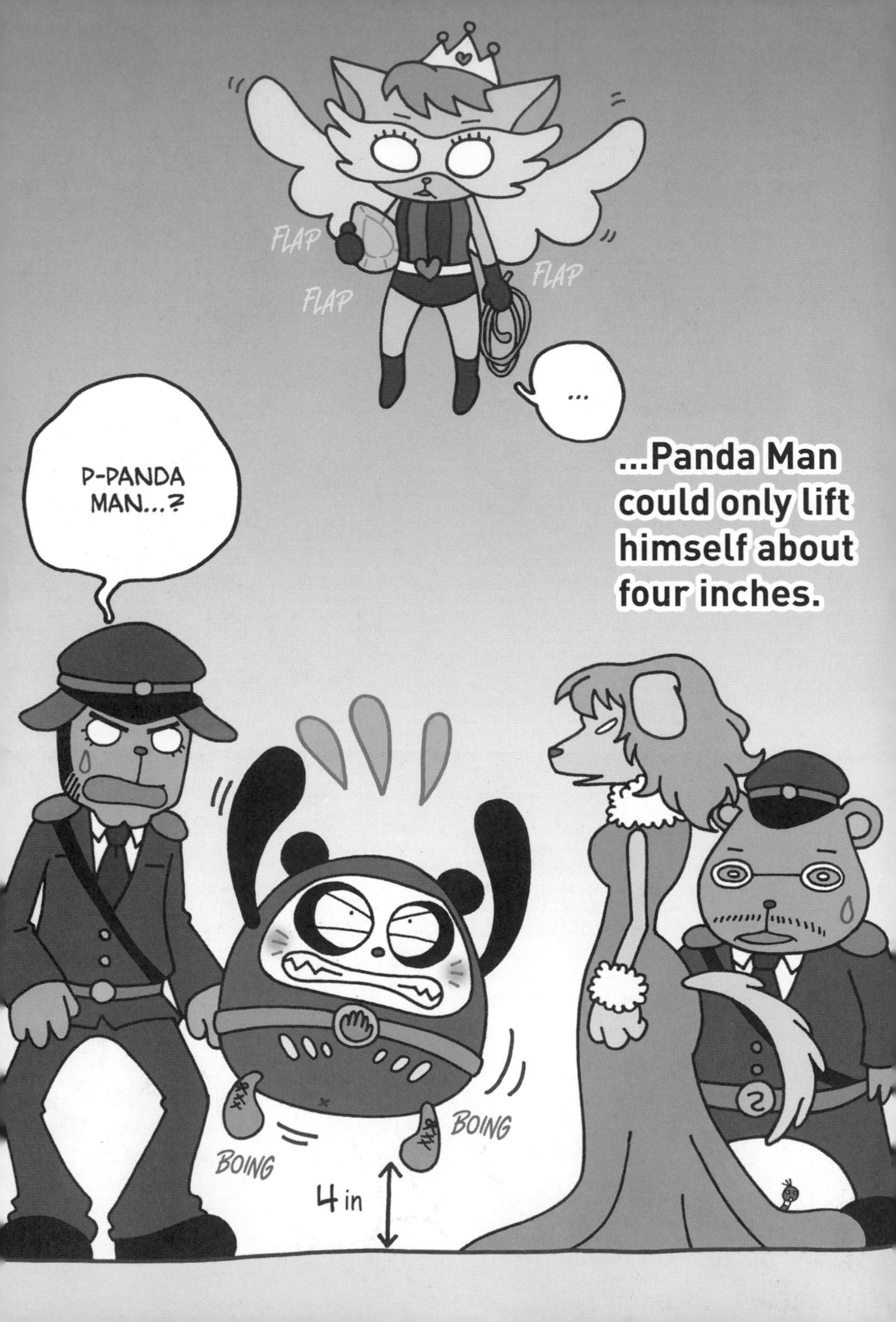
FLAP
FLAP
FLAP
...
P-PANDA MAN...?
...Panda Man could only lift himself about four inches.
BOING
BOING
4 in

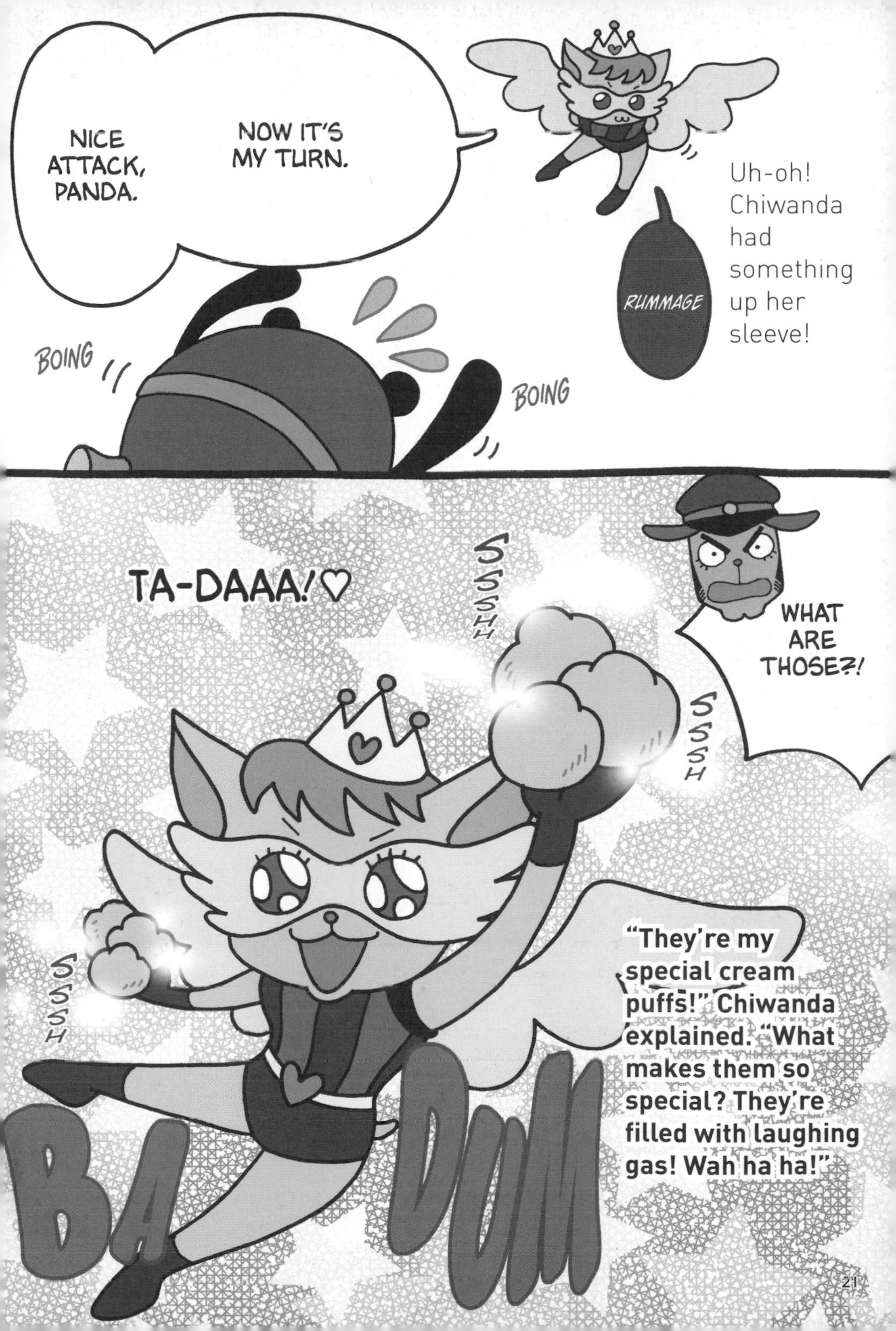
NICE ATTACK, PANDA.
NOW IT'S MY TURN.
Uh-oh! Chiwanda had something up her sleeve!
RUMMAGE
BOING
BOING
TA-DAAA!♡
SSSHH
WHAT ARE THOSE?!
SSSH
SSSH
"They're my special cream puffs!" Chiwanda explained. "What makes them so special? They're filled with laughing gas! Wah ha ha!"
BA DUM

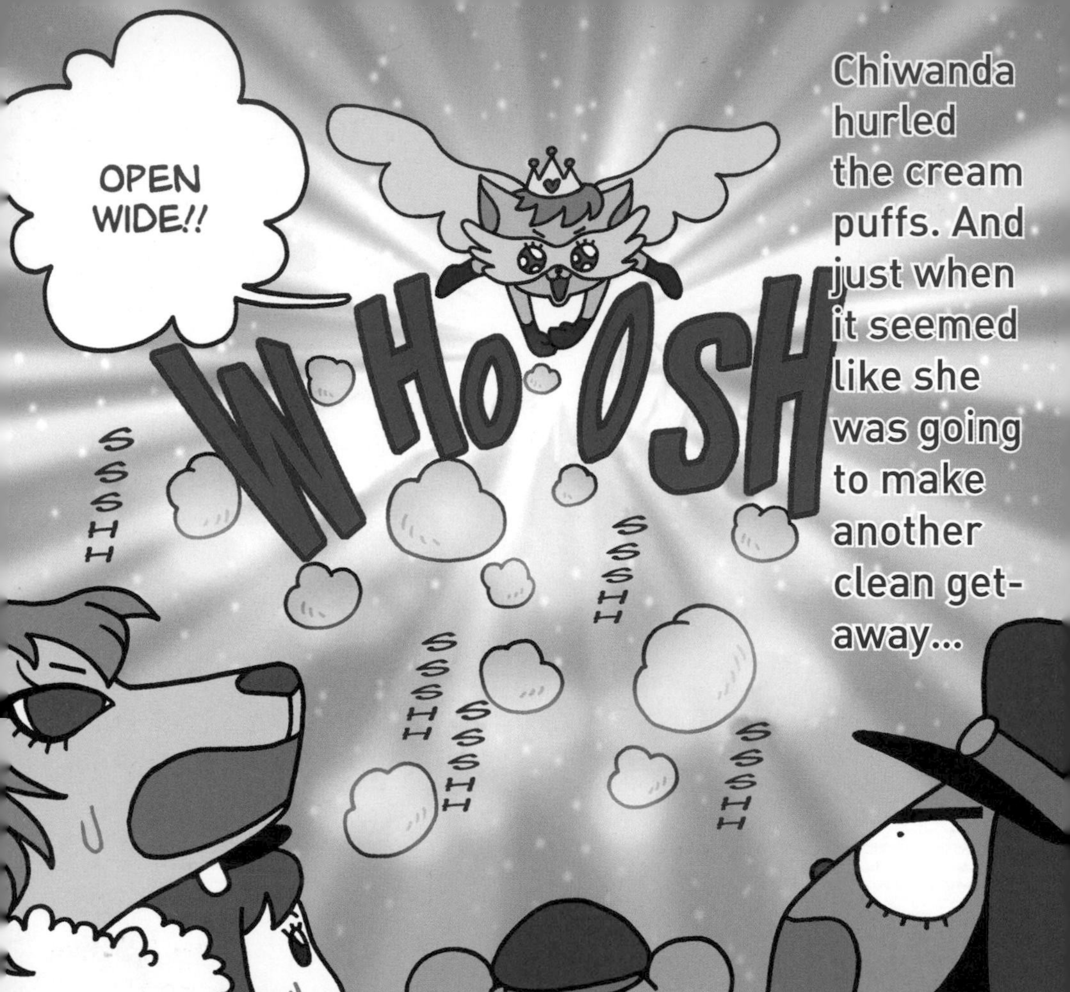
Chiwanda hurled the cream puffs. And just when it seemed like she was going to make another clean get-away...
OPEN WIDE!!
WHOOSH
SSSHH
SSSHH
SSSHH
SSSHH
SSSHH

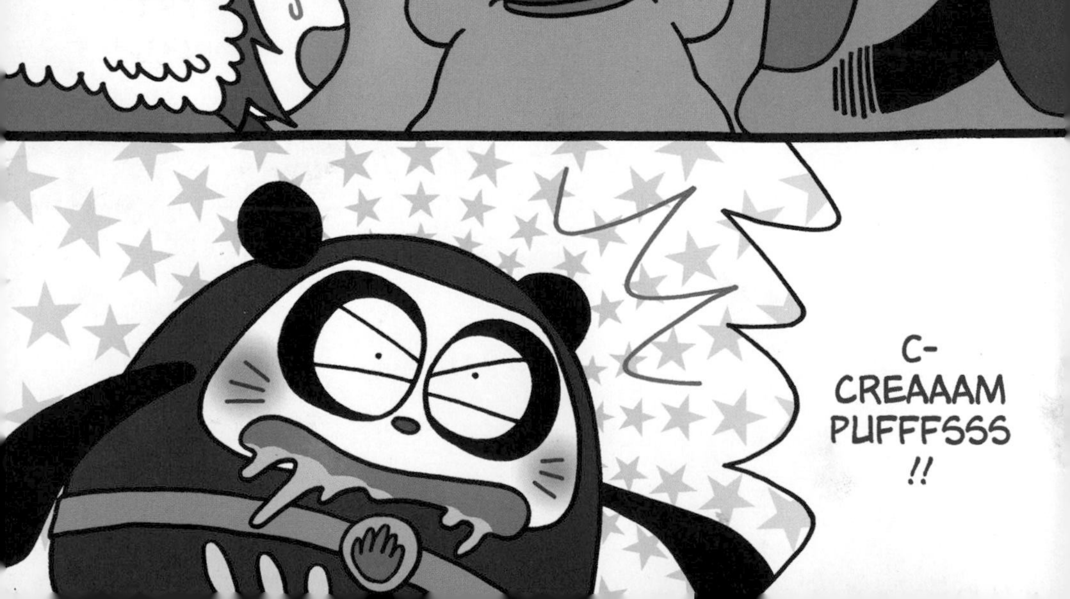
C-CREAAAM PUFFFSSS!!

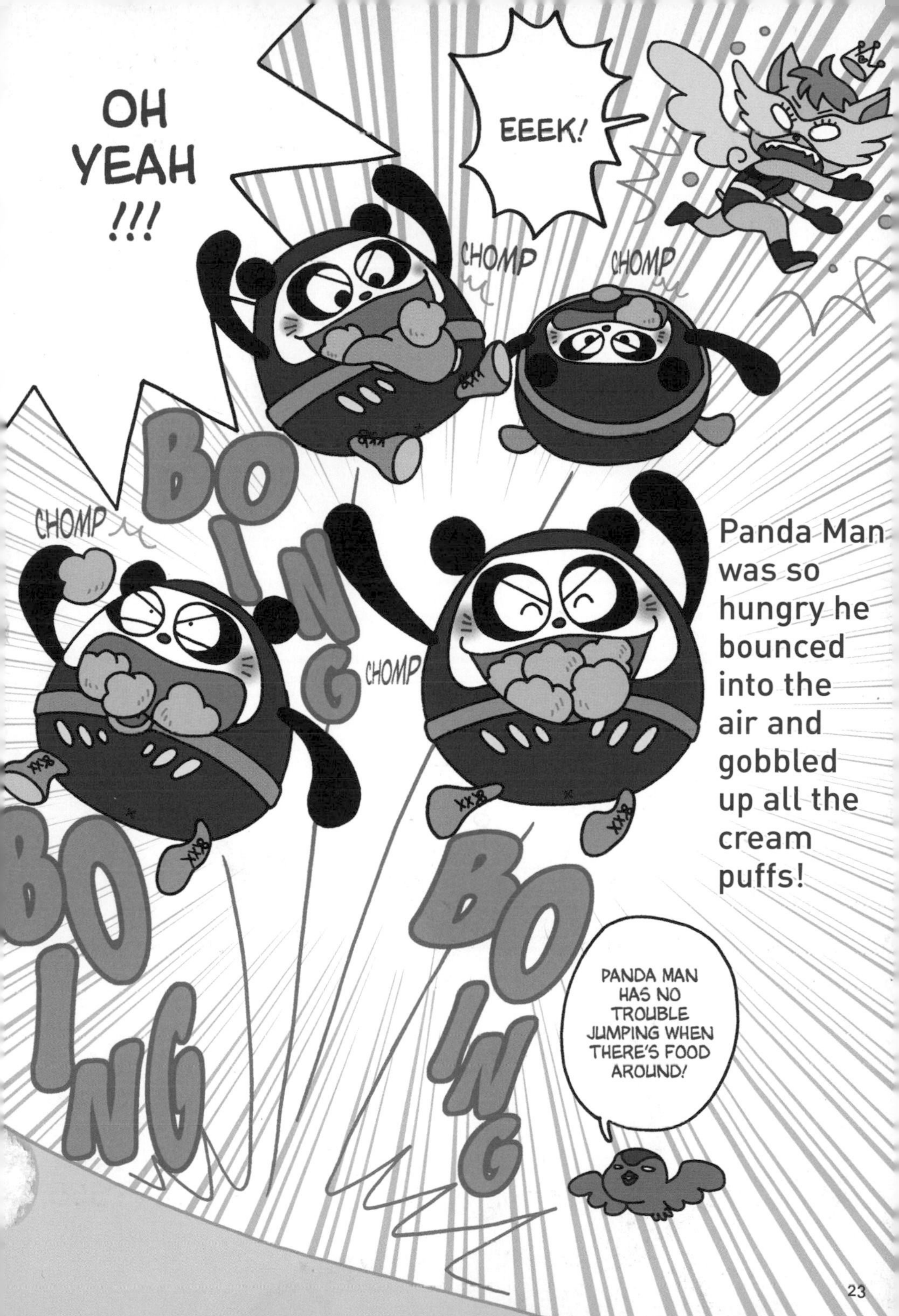
EEEK!
OH YEAH!!!
CHOMP
CHOMP
CHOMP
CHOMP
BOING
BOING
BOING
Panda Man was so hungry he bounced into the air and gobbled up all the cream puffs!
PANDA MAN HAS NO TROUBLE JUMPING WHEN THERE'S FOOD AROUND!

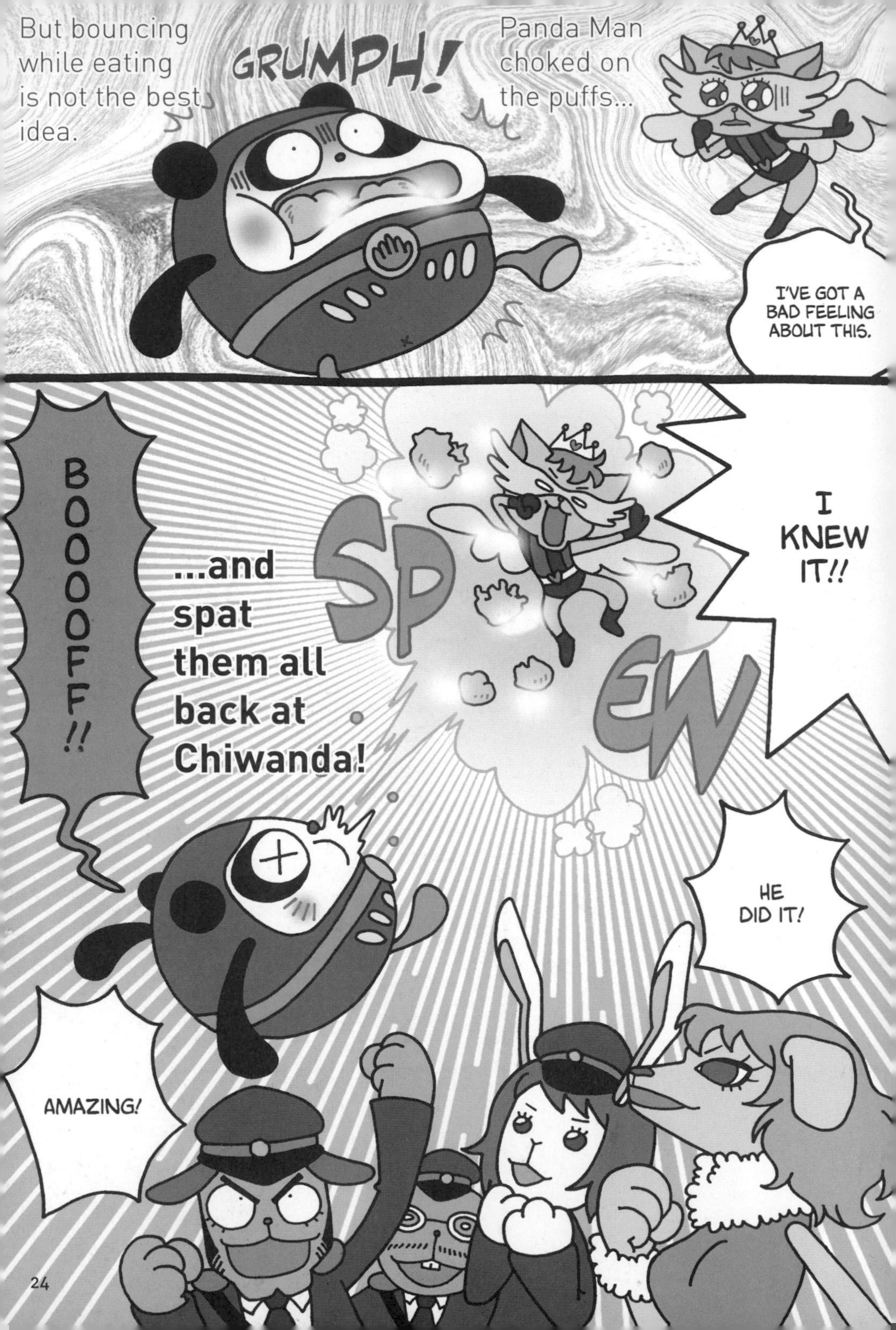
But bouncing while eating is not the best idea.
GRUMPH!
Panda Man choked on the puffs...
I'VE GOT A BAD FEELING ABOUT THIS.
BOOOOOFF!!
...and spat them all back at Chiwanda!
SPEW
I KNEW IT!!
HE DID IT!
AMAZING!

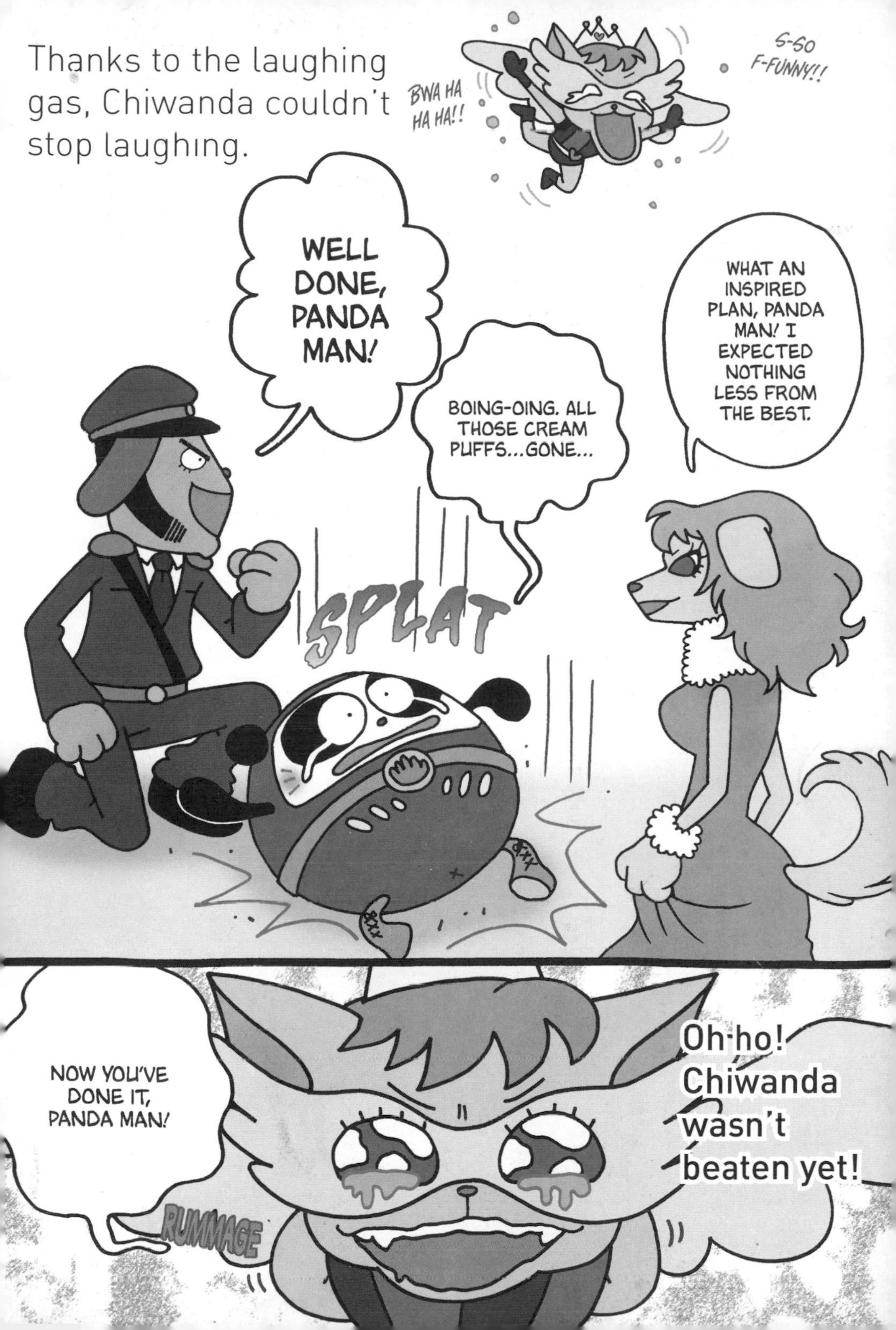
Thanks to the laughing gas, Chiwanda couldn't stop laughing.
BWA HA HA HA!!
S-SO F-FUNNY!!
WELL DONE, PANDA MAN!
BOING-OING. ALL THOSE CREAM PUFFS...GONE...
WHAT AN INSPIRED PLAN, PANDA MAN! I EXPECTED NOTHING LESS FROM THE BEST.
SPLAT
NOW YOU'VE DONE IT, PANDA MAN!
RUMMAGE
Oh-ho! Chiwanda wasn't beaten yet!

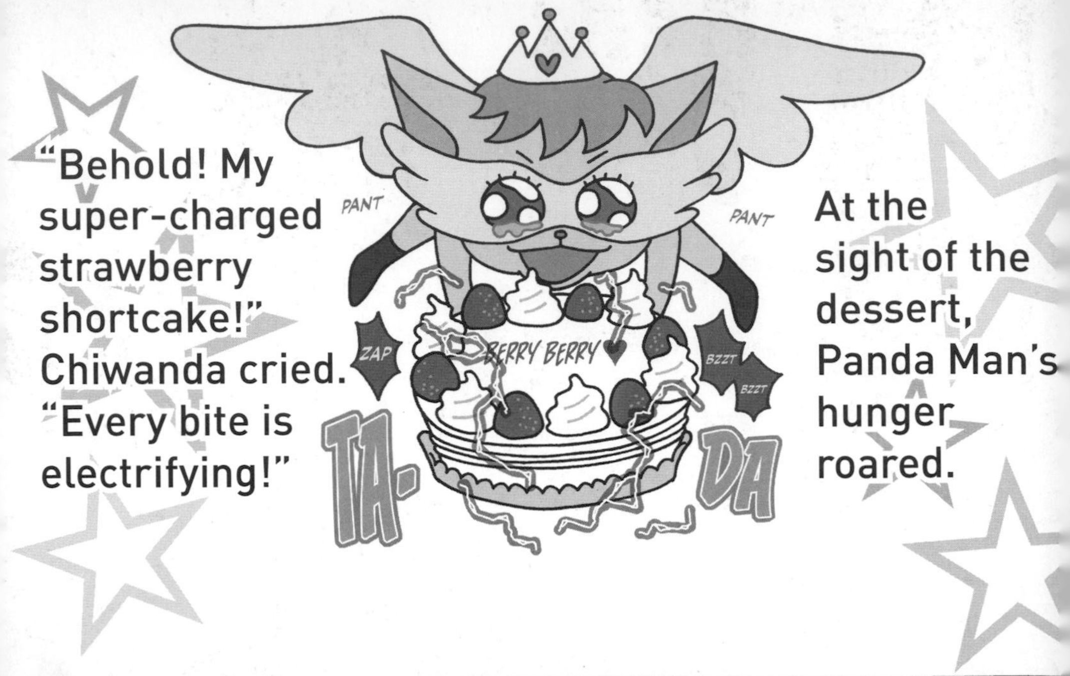
"Behold! My super-charged strawberry shortcake!" Chiwanda cried. "Every bite is electrifying!"
PANT
PANT
ZAP
BERRY BERRY
BZZT
BZZT
TA-
DA
At the sight of the dessert, Panda Man's hunger roared.

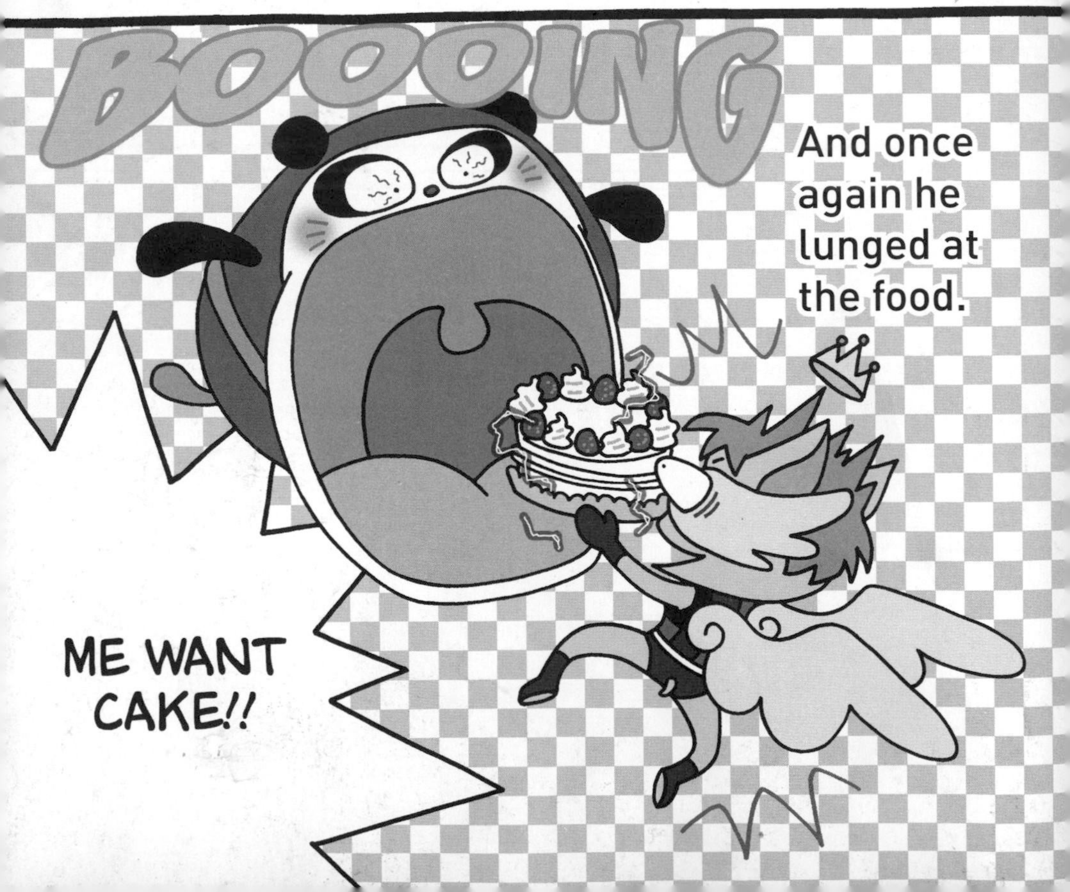
BOOOING
And once again he lunged at the food.
ME WANT CAKE!!

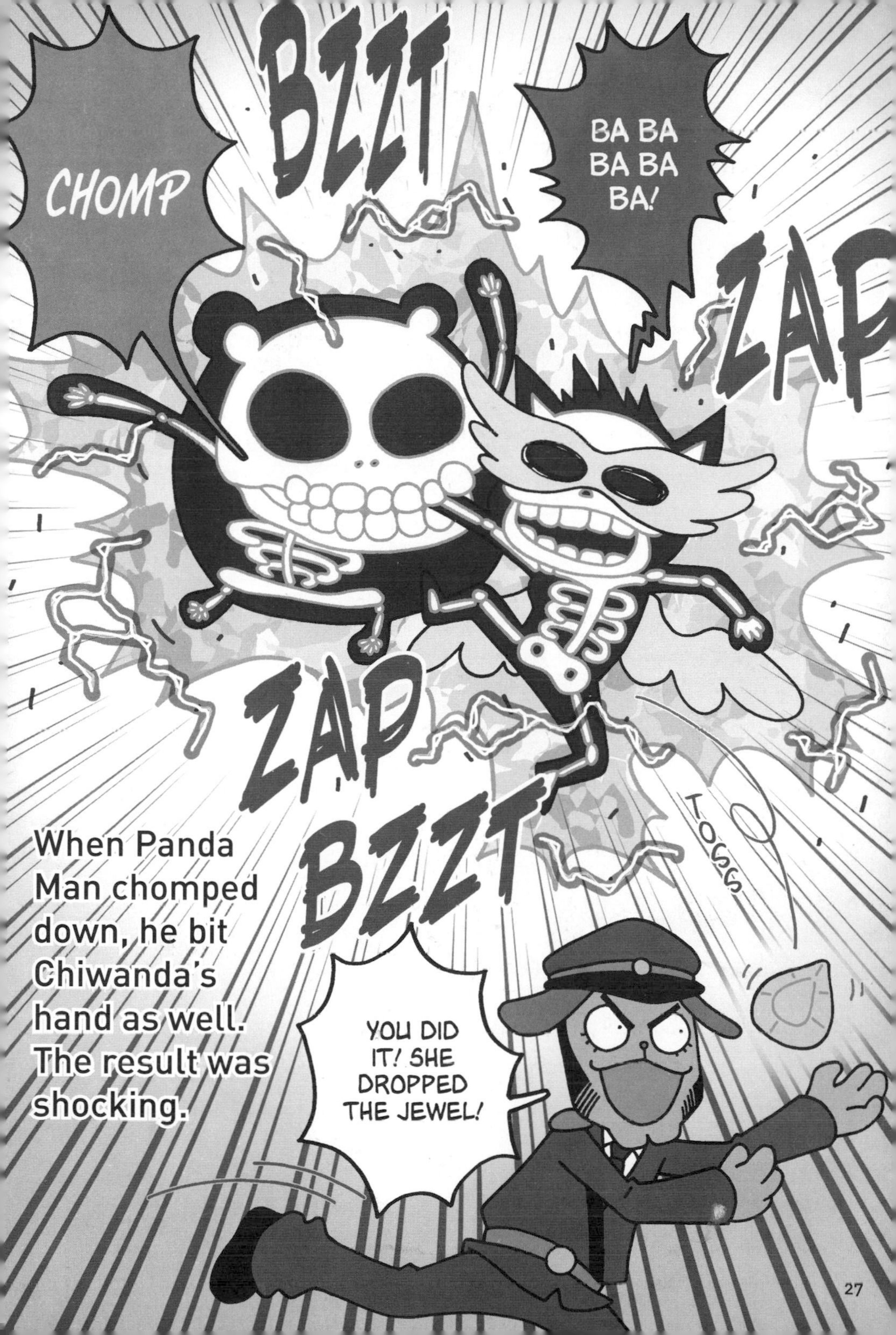
BA BA
BA BA
BA!
ZAP
BZZT
CHOMP
ZAP
TOSS
BZZT
YOU DID IT! SHE DROPPED THE JEWEL!
When Panda Man chomped down, he bit Chiwanda's hand as well. The result was shocking.

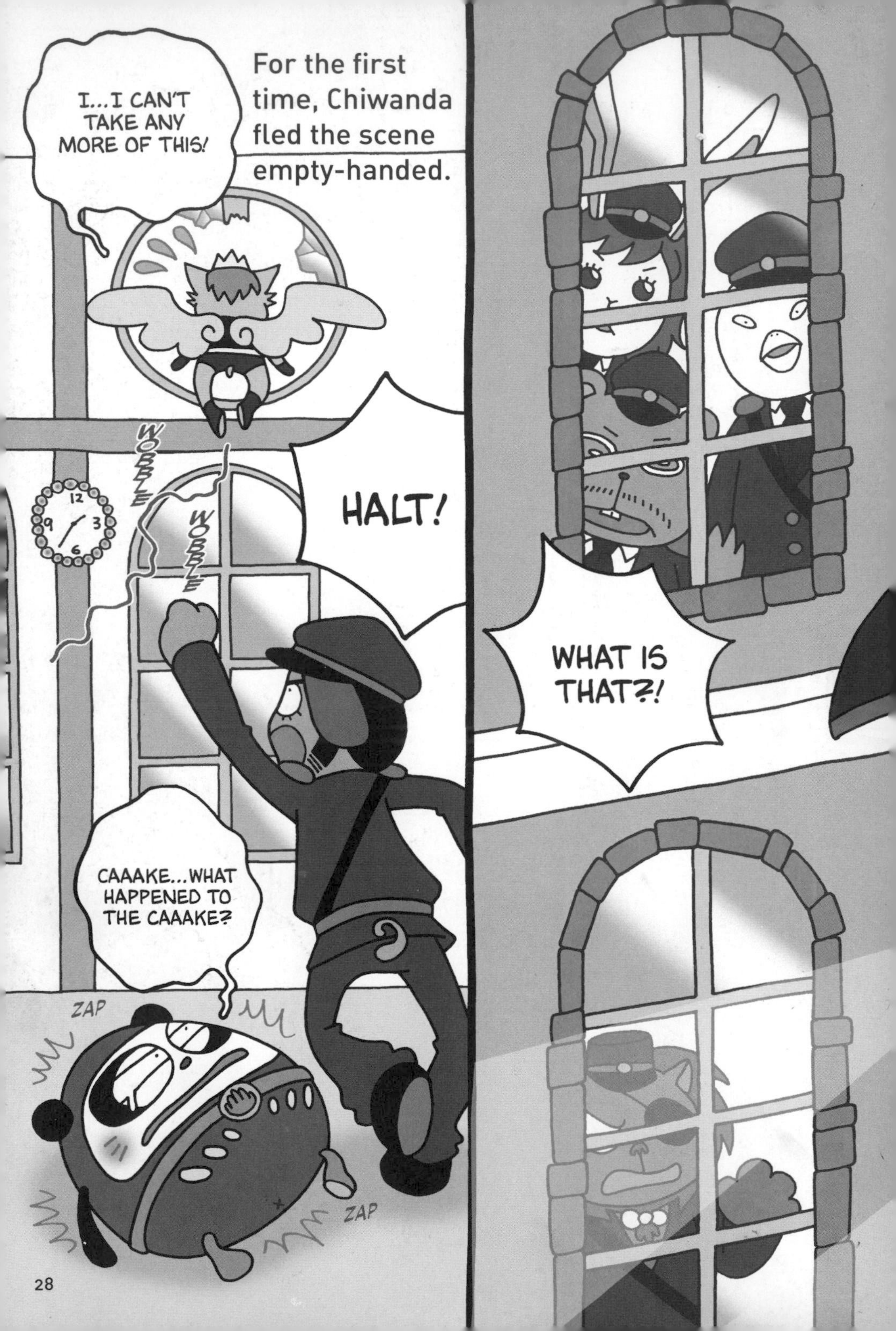
I...I CAN'T TAKE ANY MORE OF THIS!
For the first time, Chiwanda fled the scene empty-handed.
WOBBLE
WOBBLE
HALT!
CAAAKE...WHAT HAPPENED TO THE CAAAKE?
ZAP
ZAP
WHAT IS THAT?!

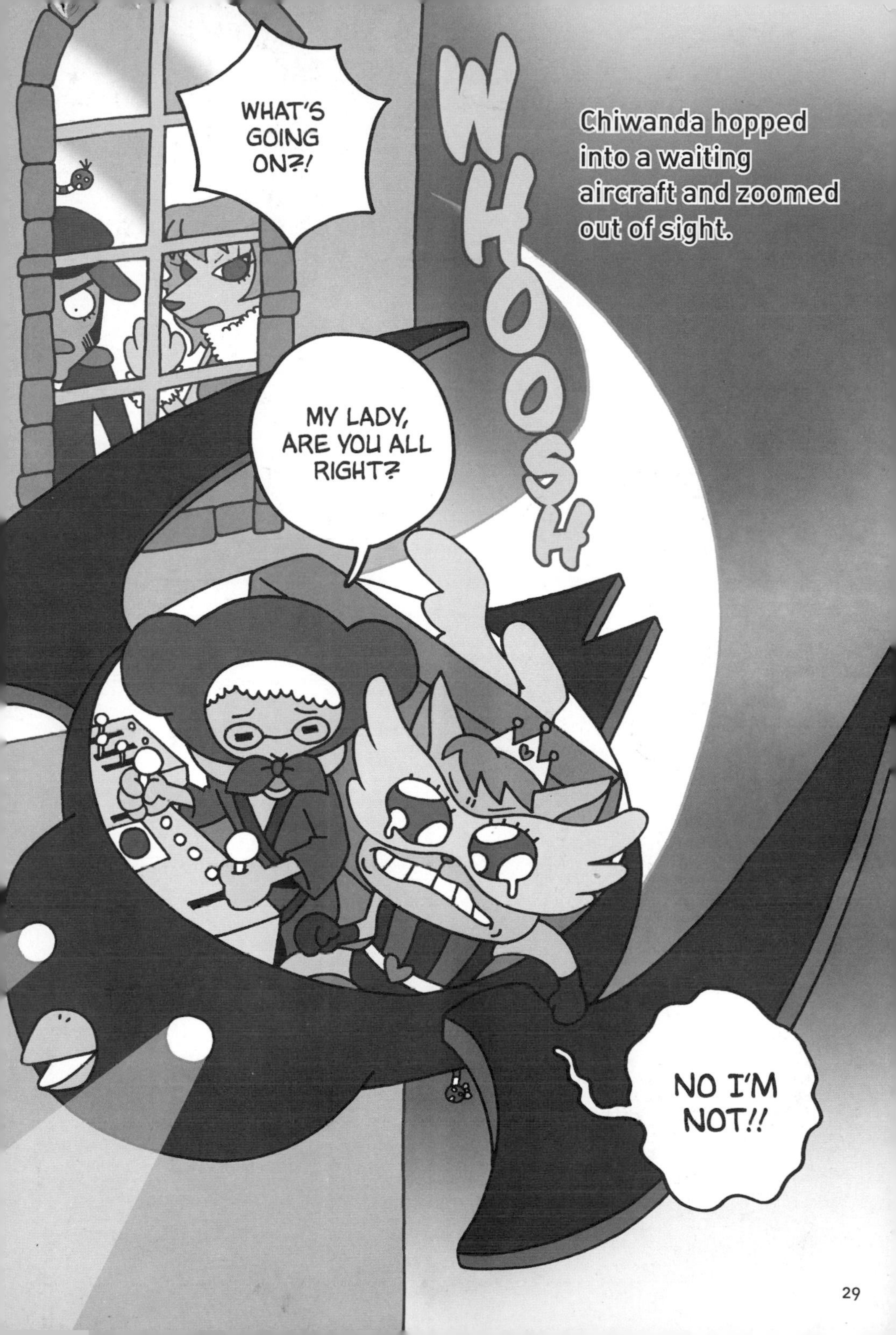
WHAT'S GOING ON?!
WHOOSH
Chiwanda hopped into a waiting aircraft and zoomed out of sight.
MY LADY, ARE YOU ALL RIGHT?
NO I'M NOT!!

"Never mind Chiwanda. The important thing is my jewel is safe!" Madam Stone exclaimed. "All thanks to Panda Man's heroic protection!"

"He really is the world's greatest," the police captain cheered.

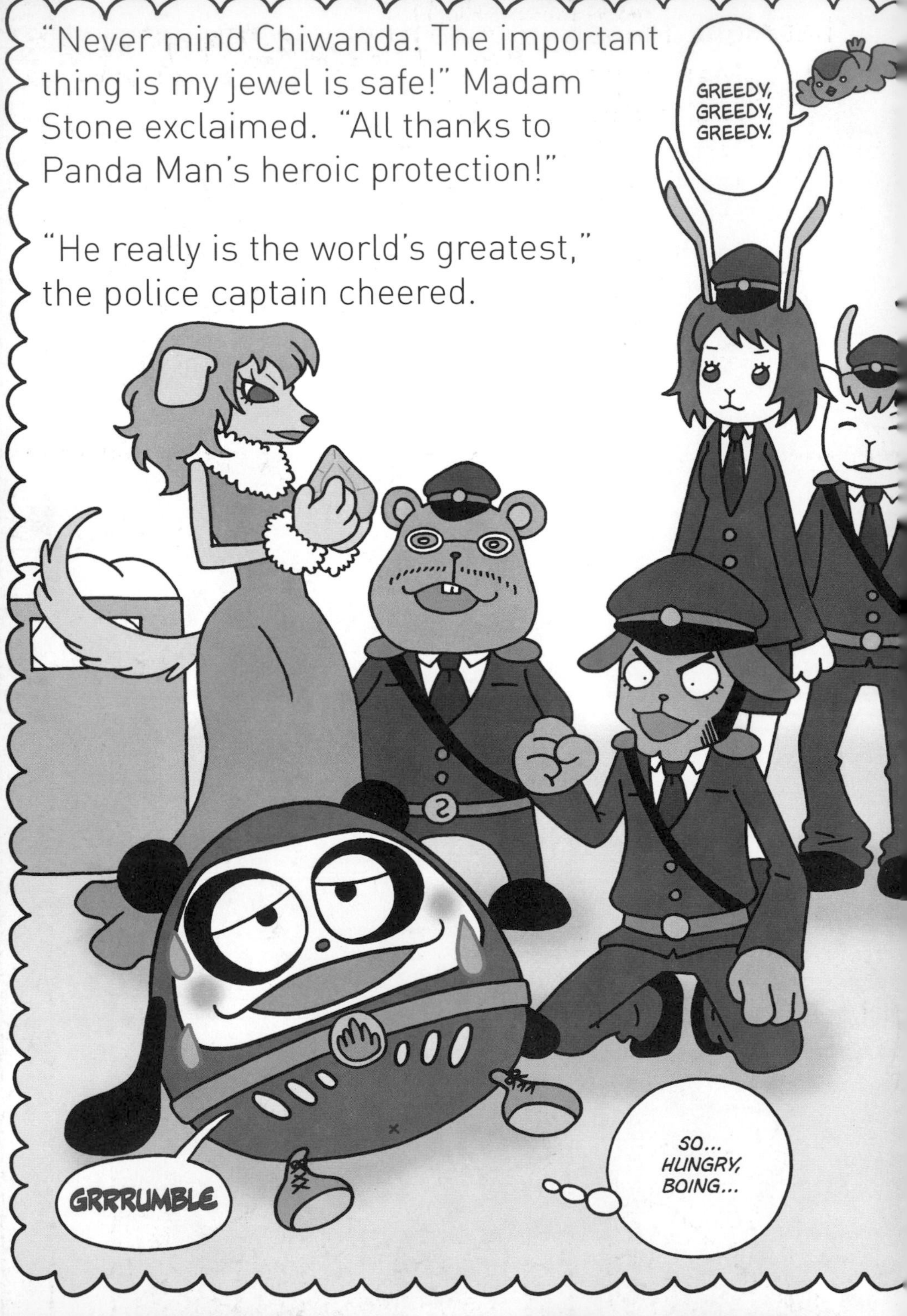
GREEDY, GREEDY, GREEDY.
SO... HUNGRY, BOING...
GRRRUMBLE

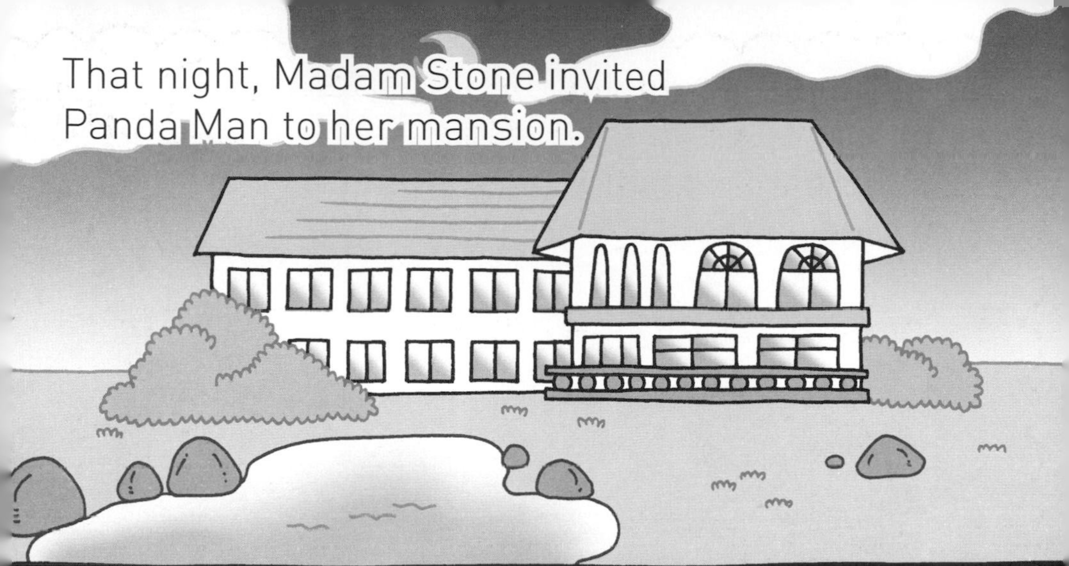
That night, Madam Stone invited Panda Man to her mansion.

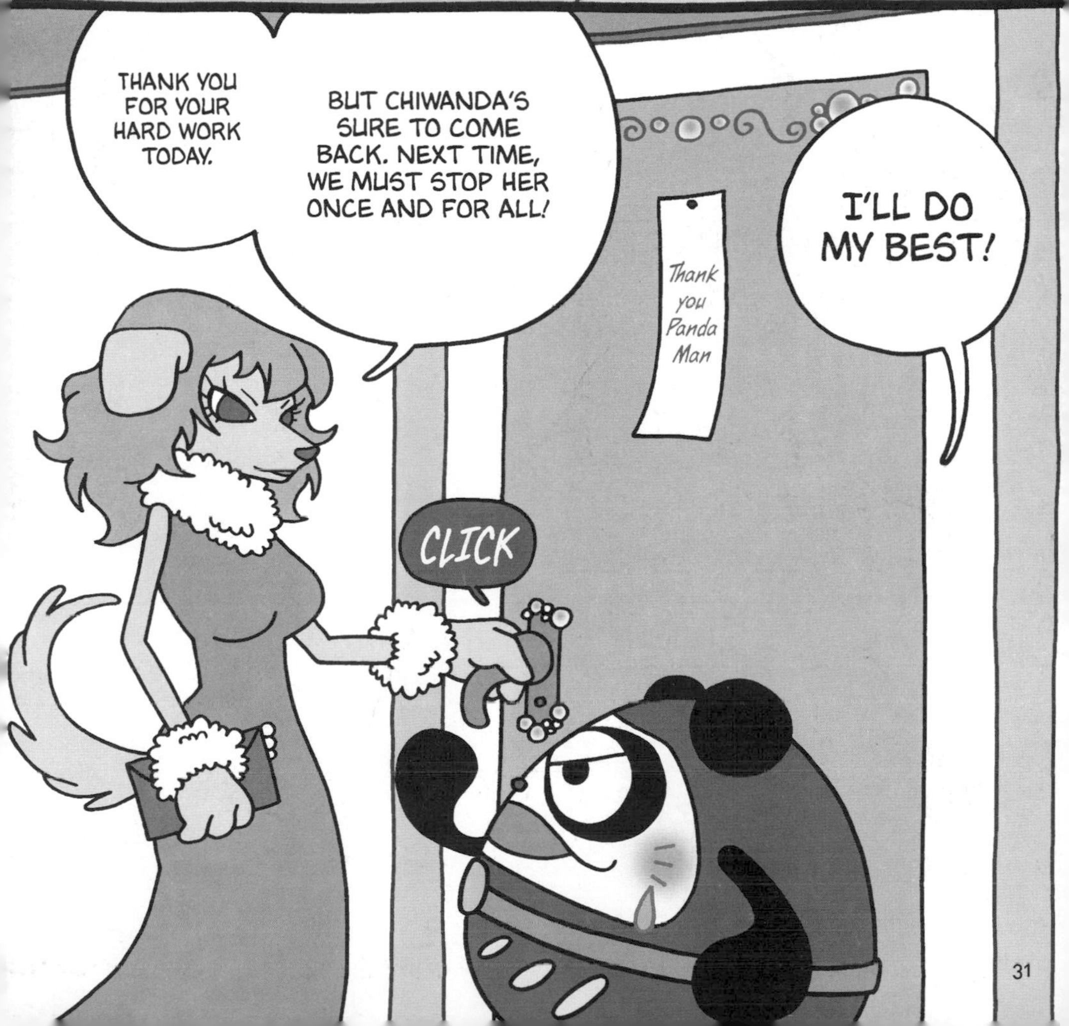
THANK YOU FOR YOUR HARD WORK TODAY.
BUT CHIWANDA'S SURE TO COME BACK. NEXT TIME, WE MUST STOP HER ONCE AND FOR ALL!
I'LL DO MY BEST!
Thank you Panda Man
CLICK

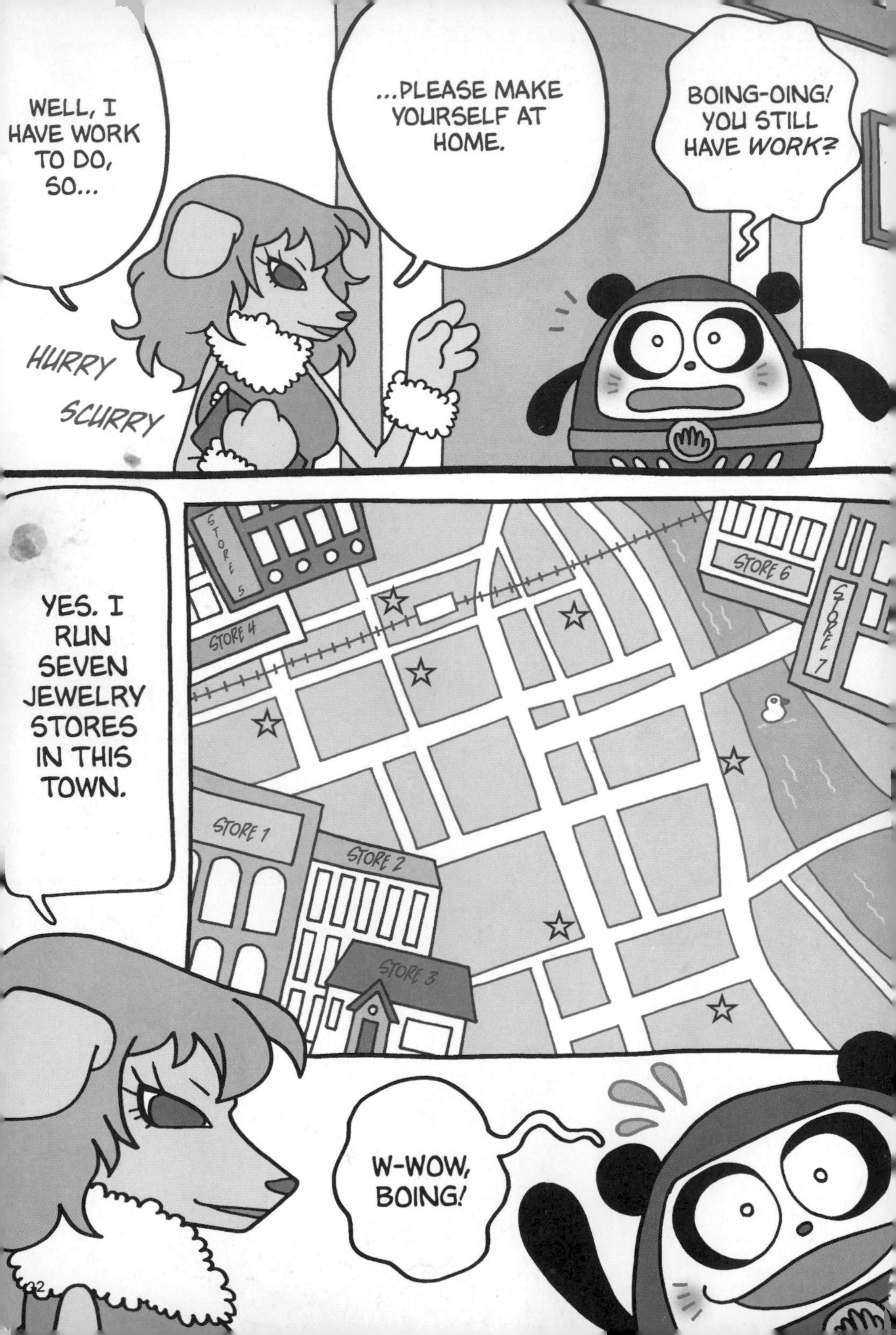
WELL, I HAVE WORK TO DO, SO...
...PLEASE MAKE YOURSELF AT HOME.
BOING-OING! YOU STILL HAVE *WORK*?
HURRY
SCURRY
YES. I RUN SEVEN JEWELRY STORES IN THIS TOWN.
STORE 5
STORE 4
STORE 6
STORE 7
STORE 1
STORE 2
STORE 3
W-WOW, BOING!

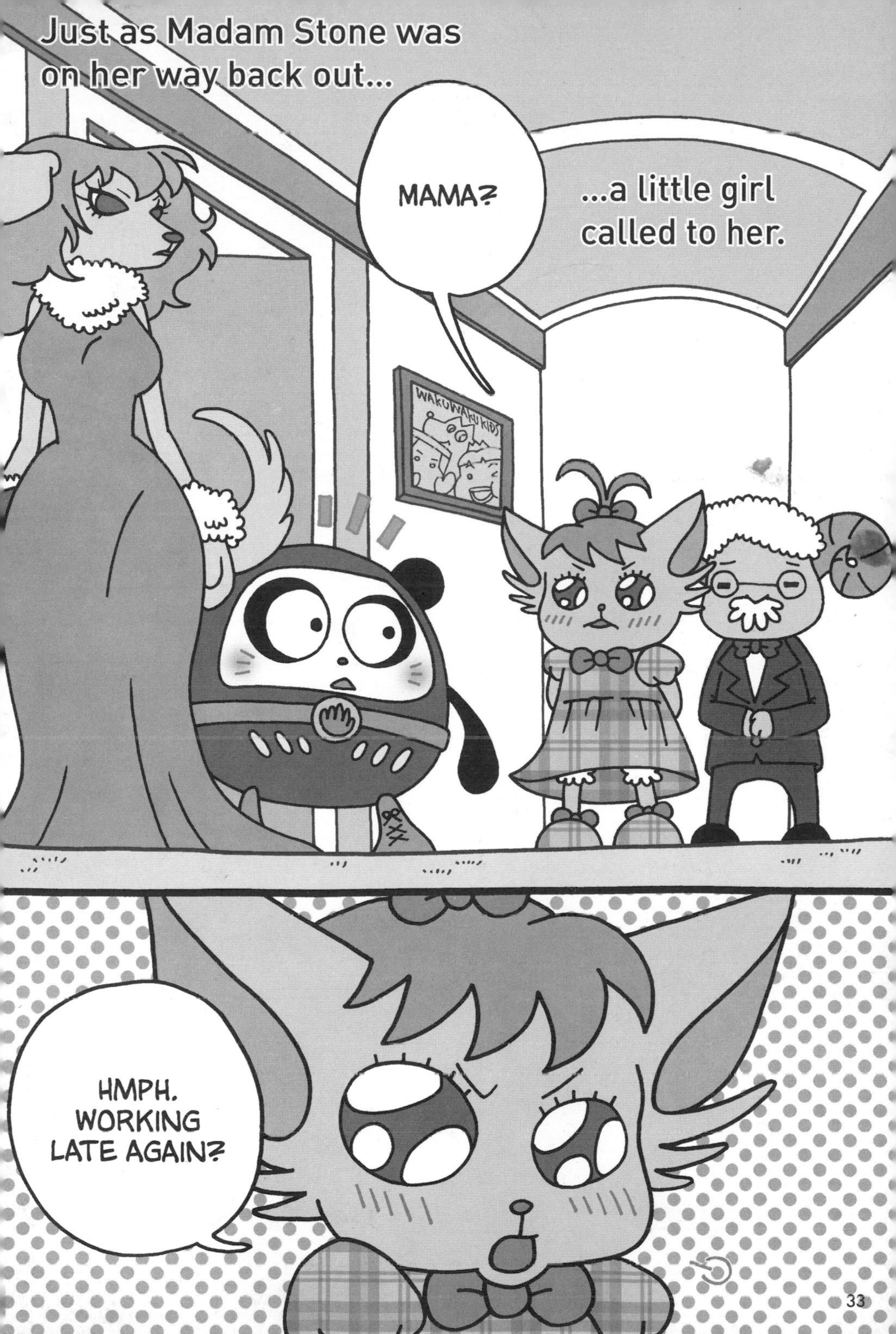
Just as Madam Stone was on her way back out...
MAMA?
...a little girl called to her.
WAKUWAKU KIDS
HMPH. WORKING LATE AGAIN?

"Yes, little one," Madam Stone sighed. "Mommy's busy, so you'll have to take care of yourself tonight."

"Hmph! Just like every night!" the girl snapped angrily. "Go ahead and do your stupid work!"

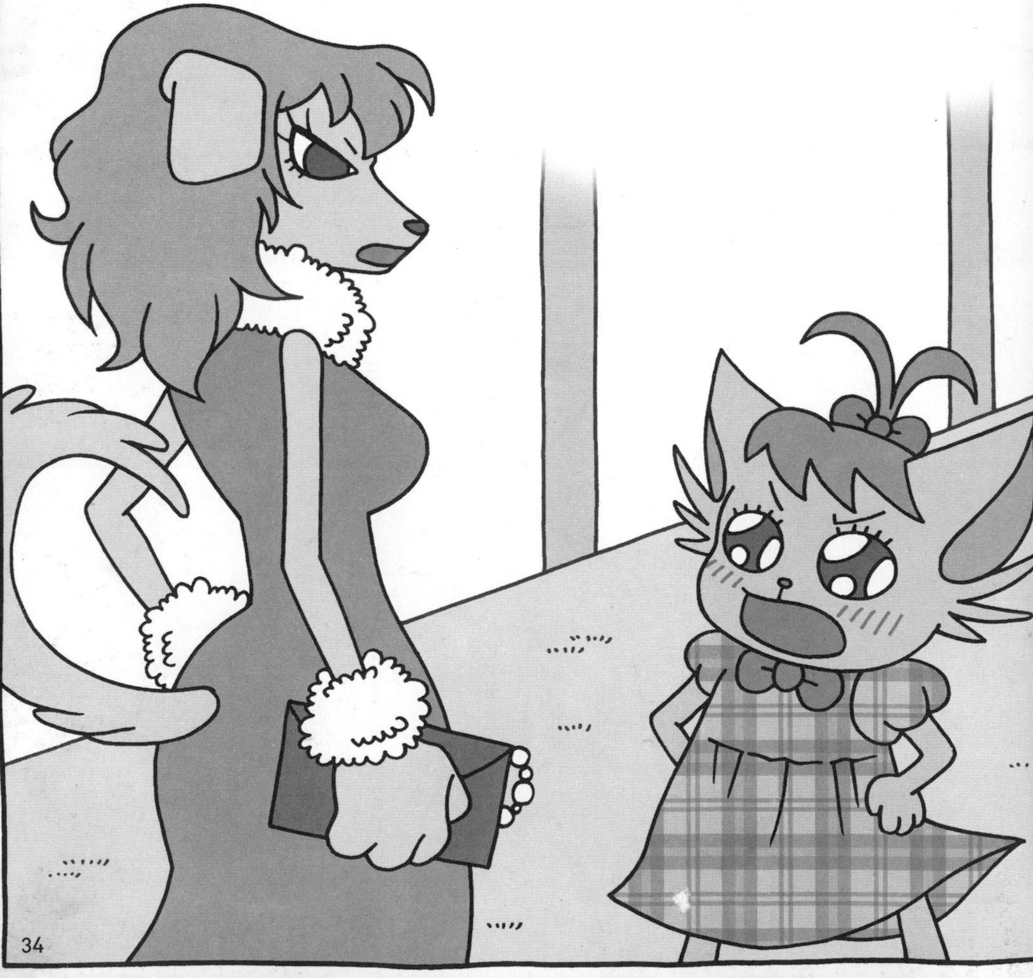

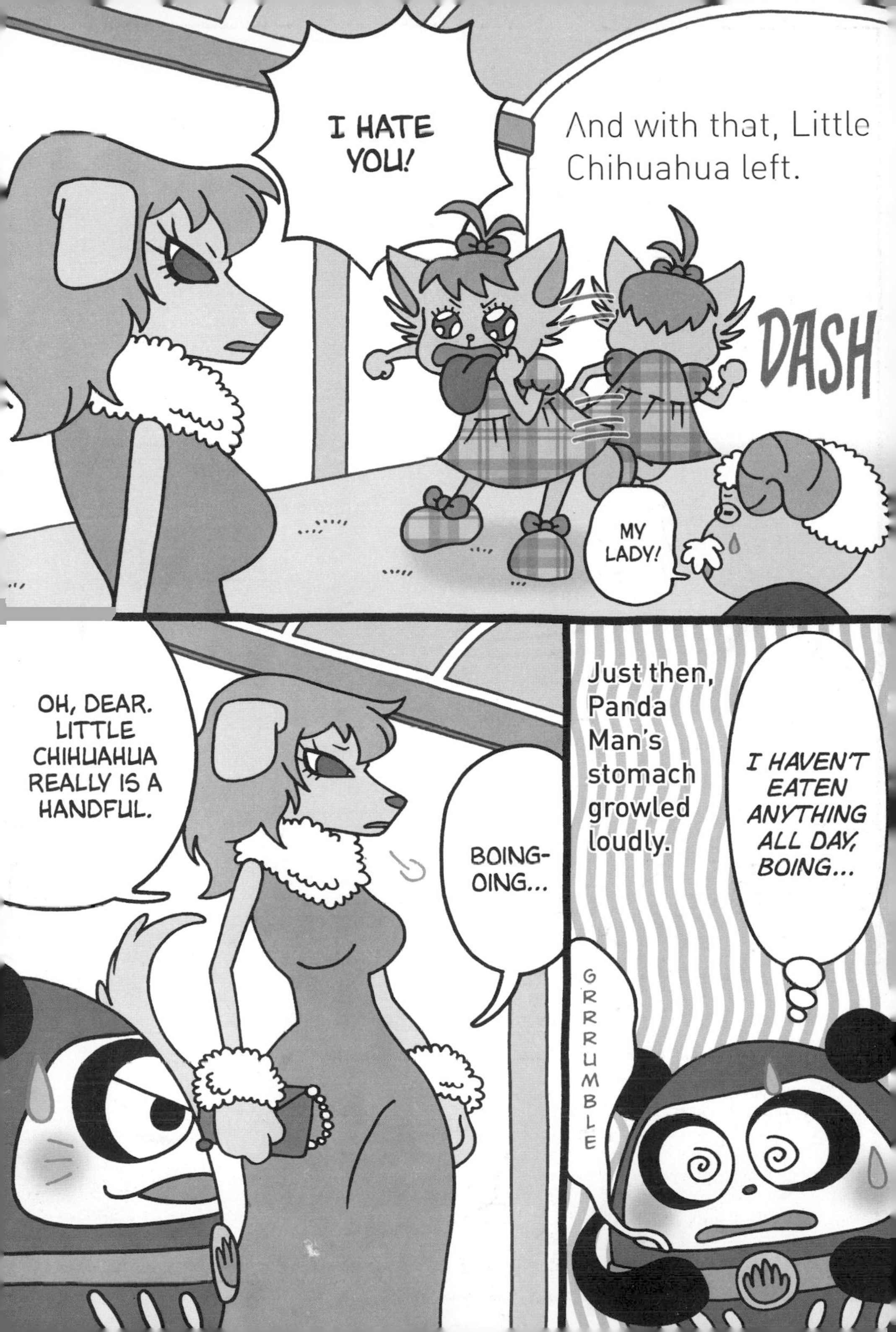
I HATE YOU!
And with that, Little Chihuahua left.
DASH
MY LADY!
OH, DEAR. LITTLE CHIHUAHUA REALLY IS A HANDFUL.
BOING-OING...
Just then, Panda Man's stomach growled loudly.
I HAVEN'T EATEN ANYTHING ALL DAY, BOING...
GRRRUMBLE

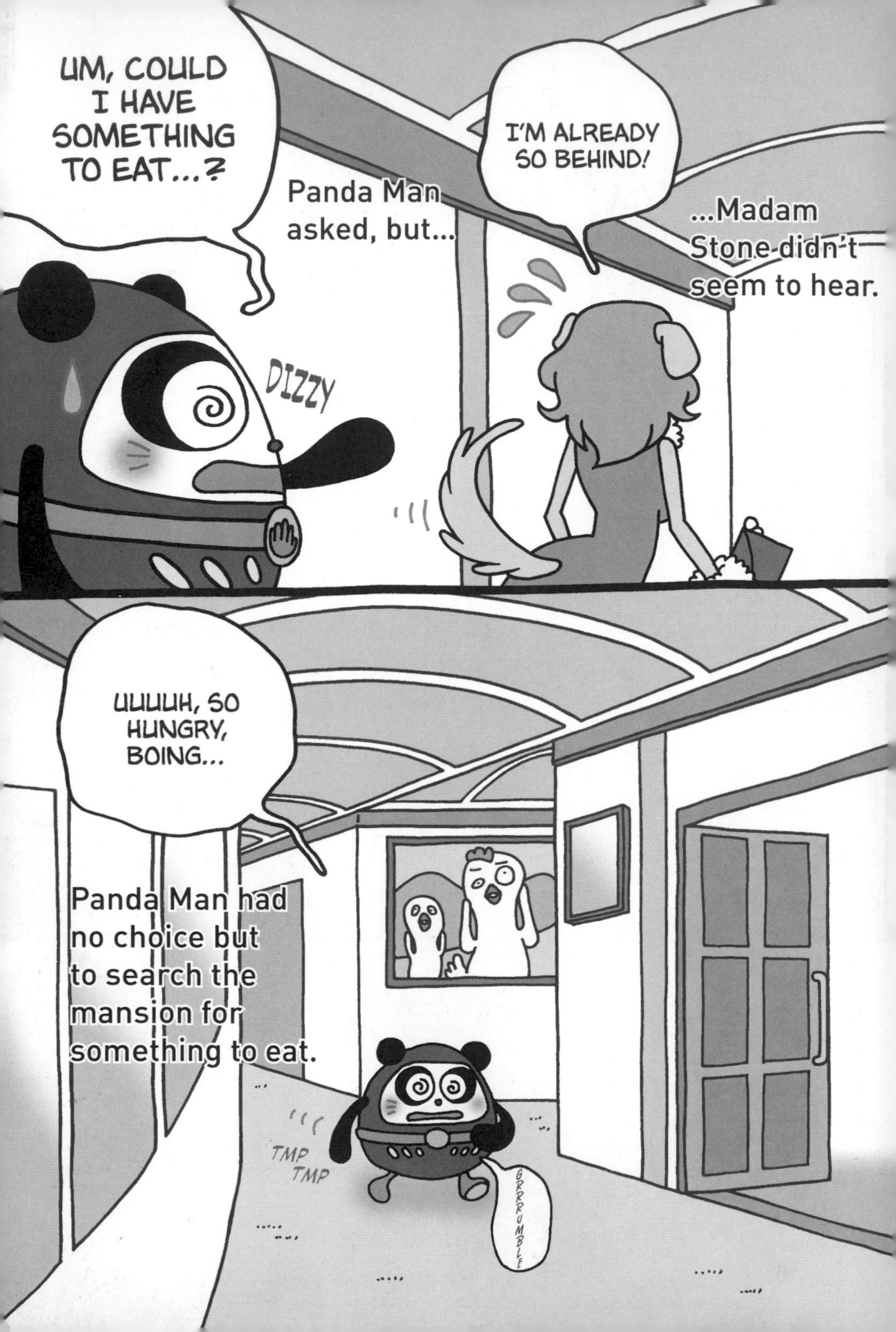
UM, COULD I HAVE SOMETHING TO EAT...?
DIZZY
Panda Man asked, but...
I'M ALREADY SO BEHIND!
...Madam Stone didn't seem to hear.
UUUUH, SO HUNGRY, BOING...
Panda Man had no choice but to search the mansion for something to eat.
TMP TMP
GRRRUMBLE

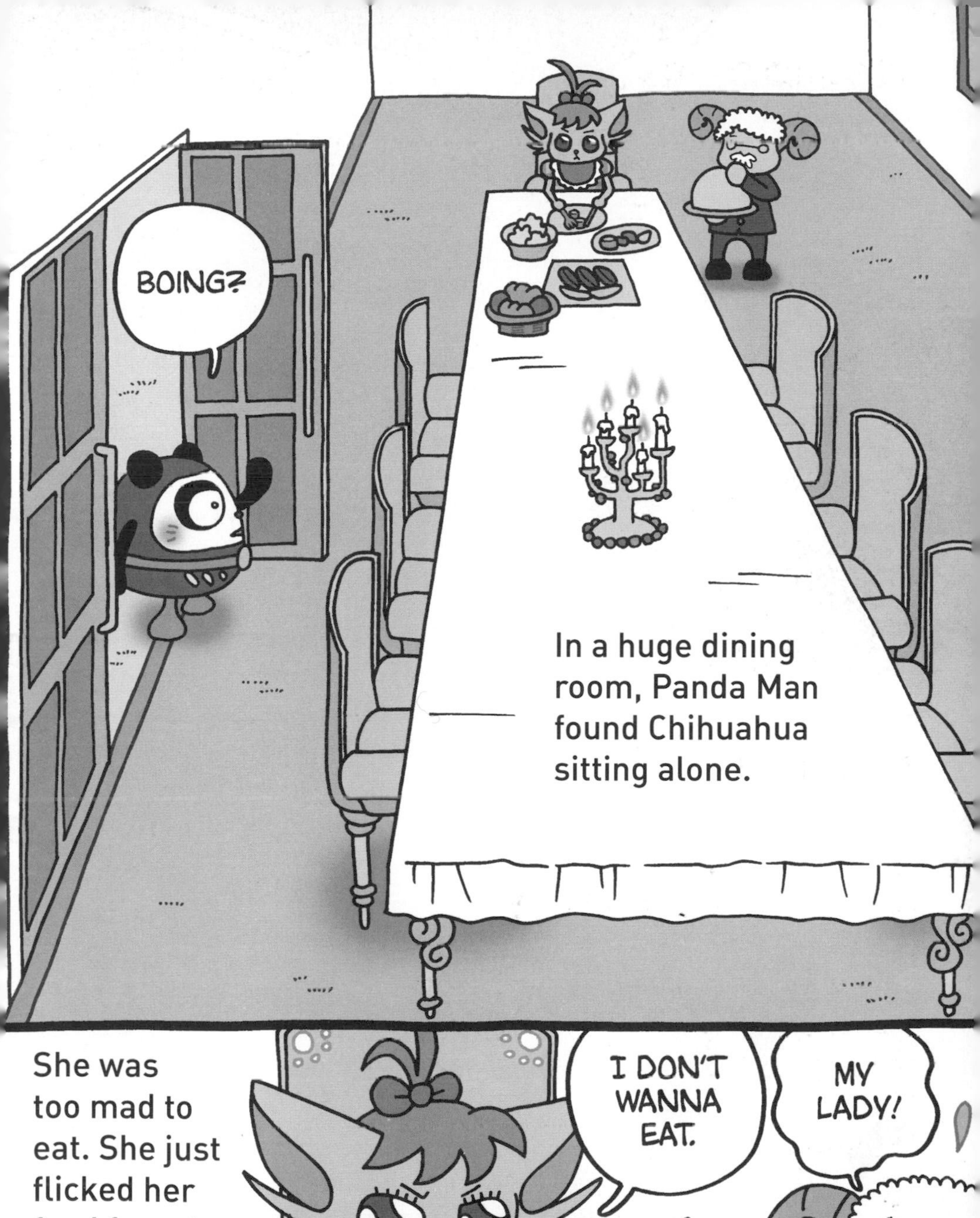
BOING?
In a huge dining room, Panda Man found Chihuahua sitting alone.

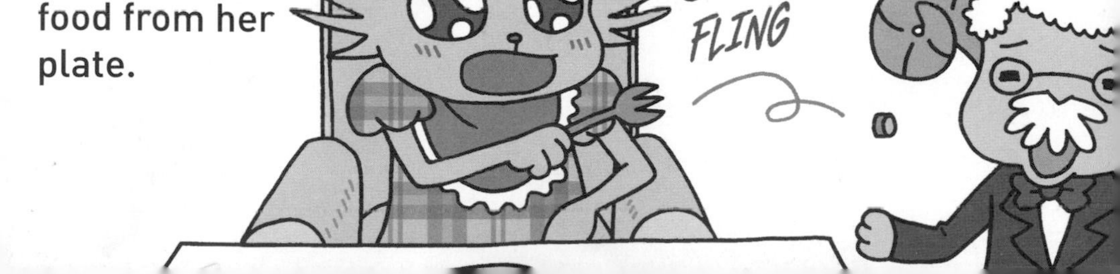
She was too mad to eat. She just flicked her food from her plate.
I DON'T WANNA EAT.
FLING
MY LADY!

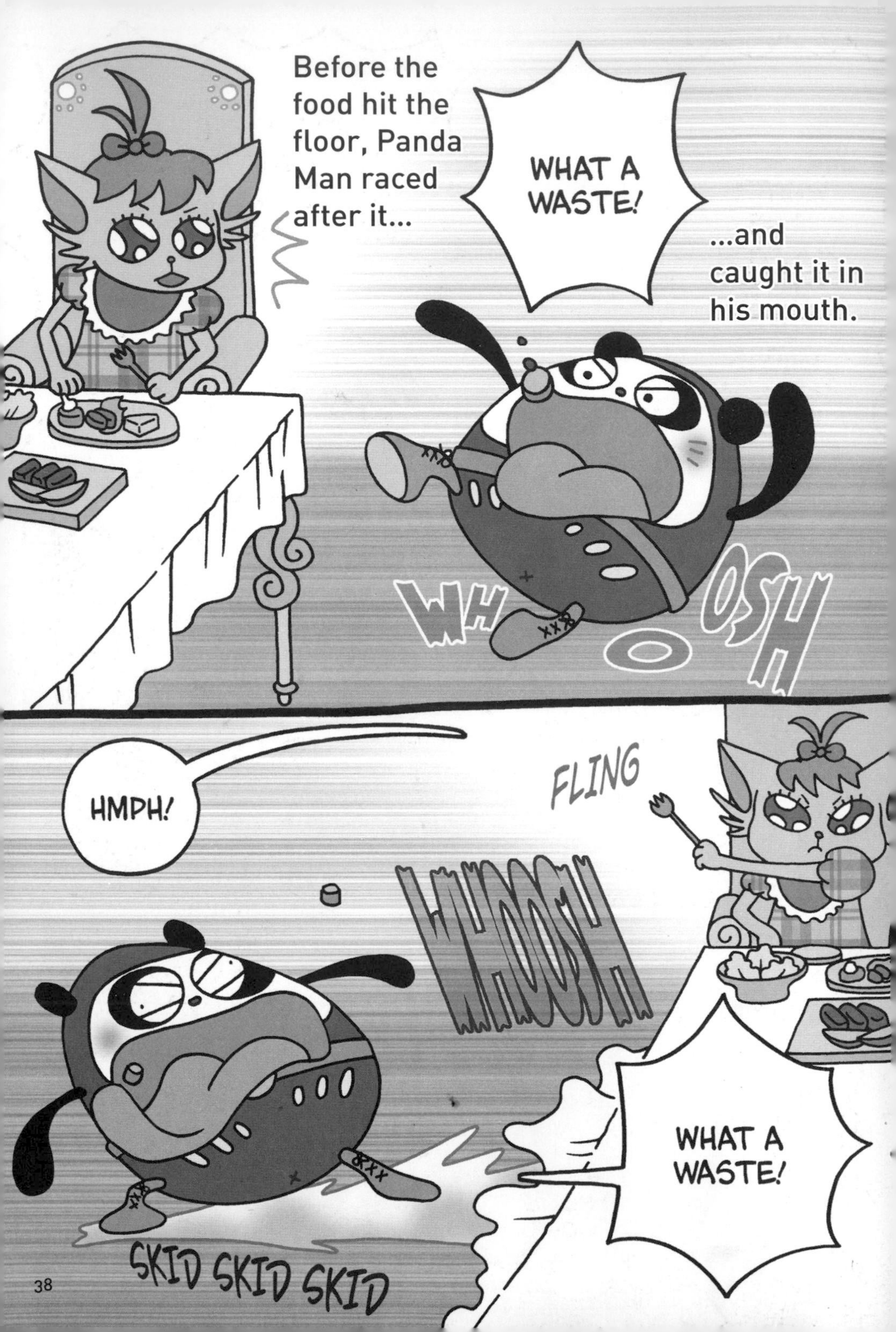
Before the food hit the floor, Panda Man raced after it...
WHAT A WASTE!
...and caught it in his mouth.
WHOOSH
HMPH!
FLING
WHOOSH
WHAT A WASTE!
SKID SKID SKID

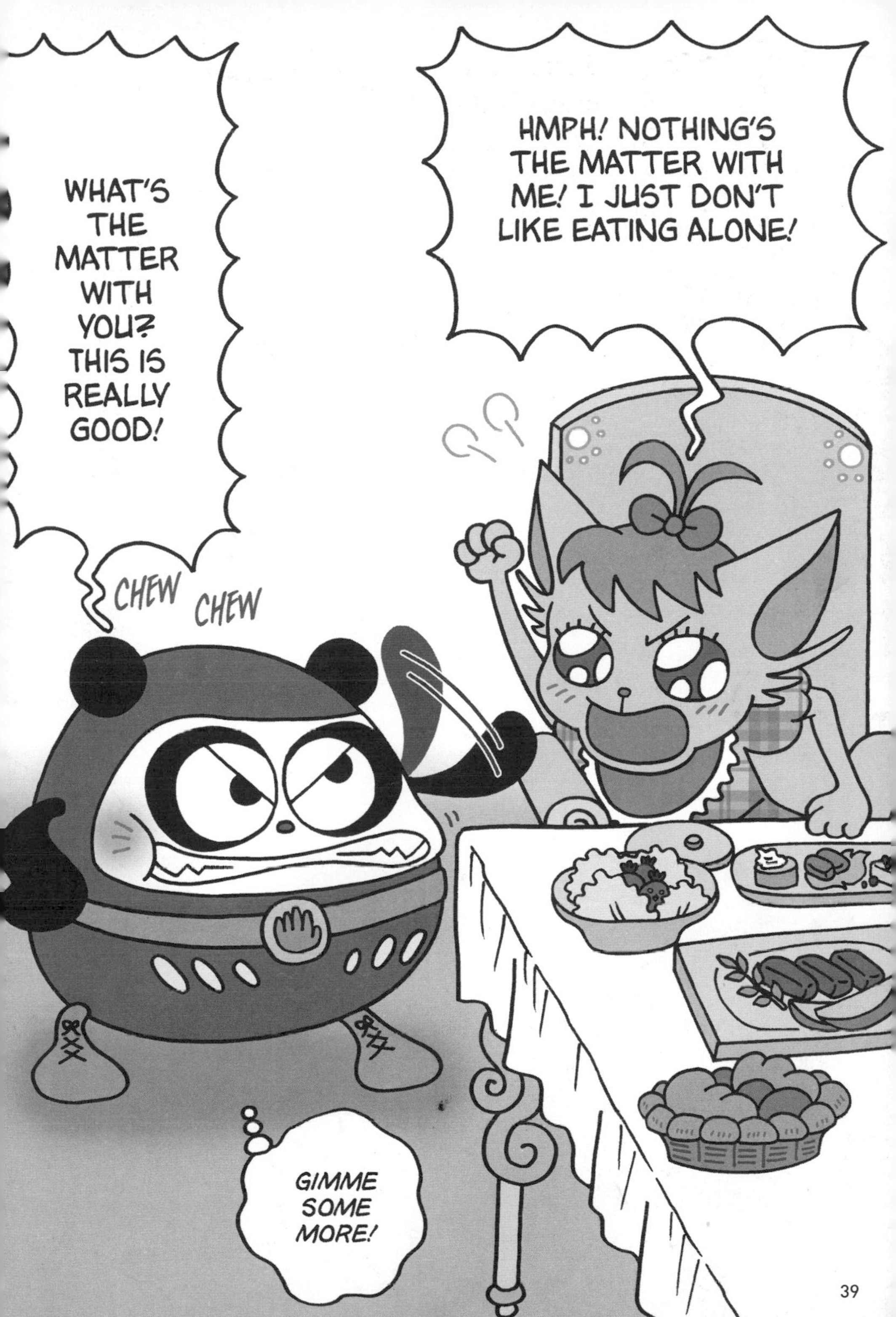
HMPH! NOTHING'S THE MATTER WITH ME! I JUST DON'T LIKE EATING ALONE!
WHAT'S THE MATTER WITH YOU? THIS IS REALLY GOOD!
CHEW CHEW
GIMME SOME MORE!

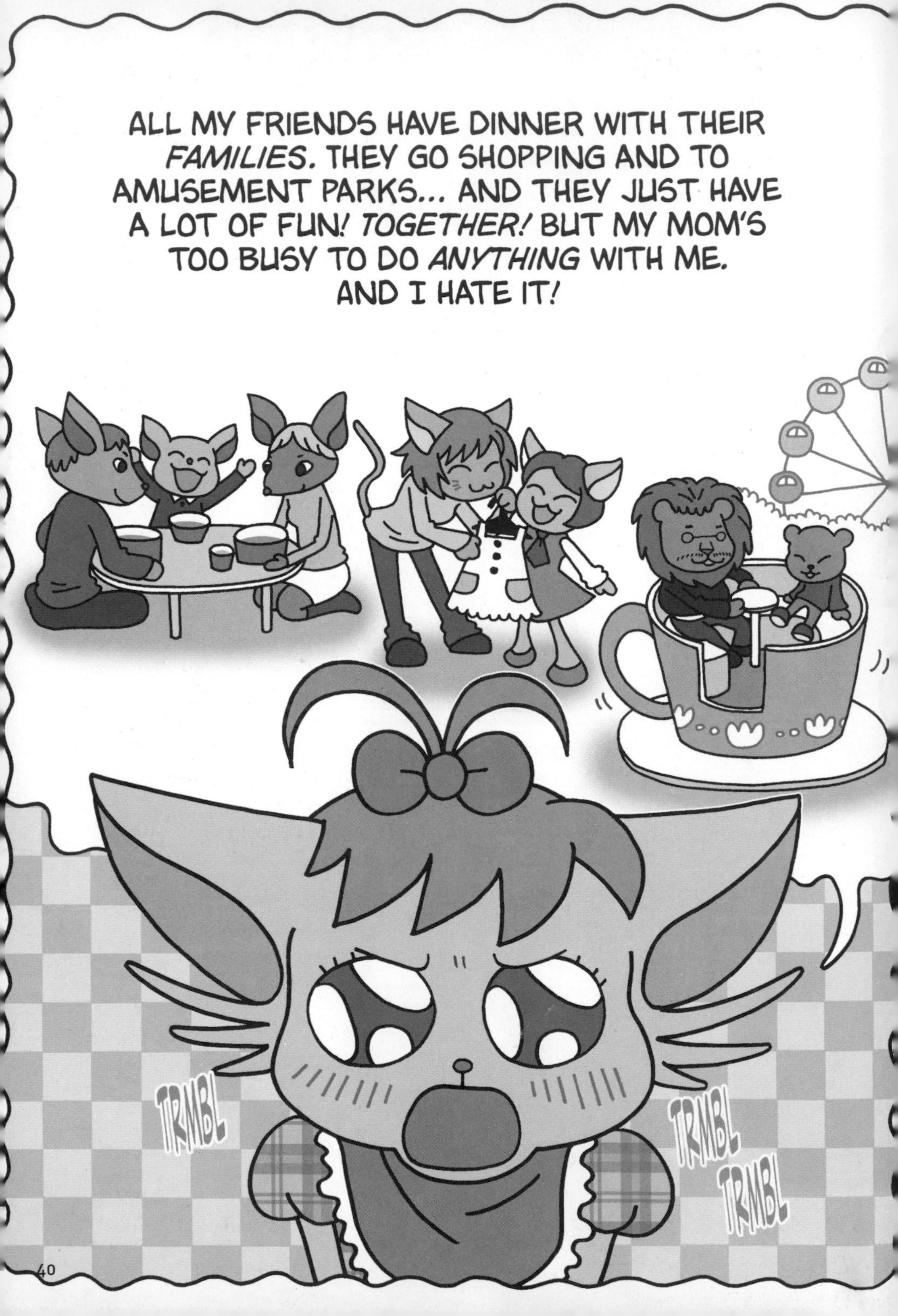
ALL MY FRIENDS HAVE DINNER WITH THEIR *FAMILIES*. THEY GO SHOPPING AND TO AMUSEMENT PARKS... AND THEY JUST HAVE A LOT OF FUN! *TOGETHER!* BUT MY MOM'S TOO BUSY TO DO *ANYTHING* WITH ME. AND I HATE IT!
TRMBL
TRMBL
TRMBL

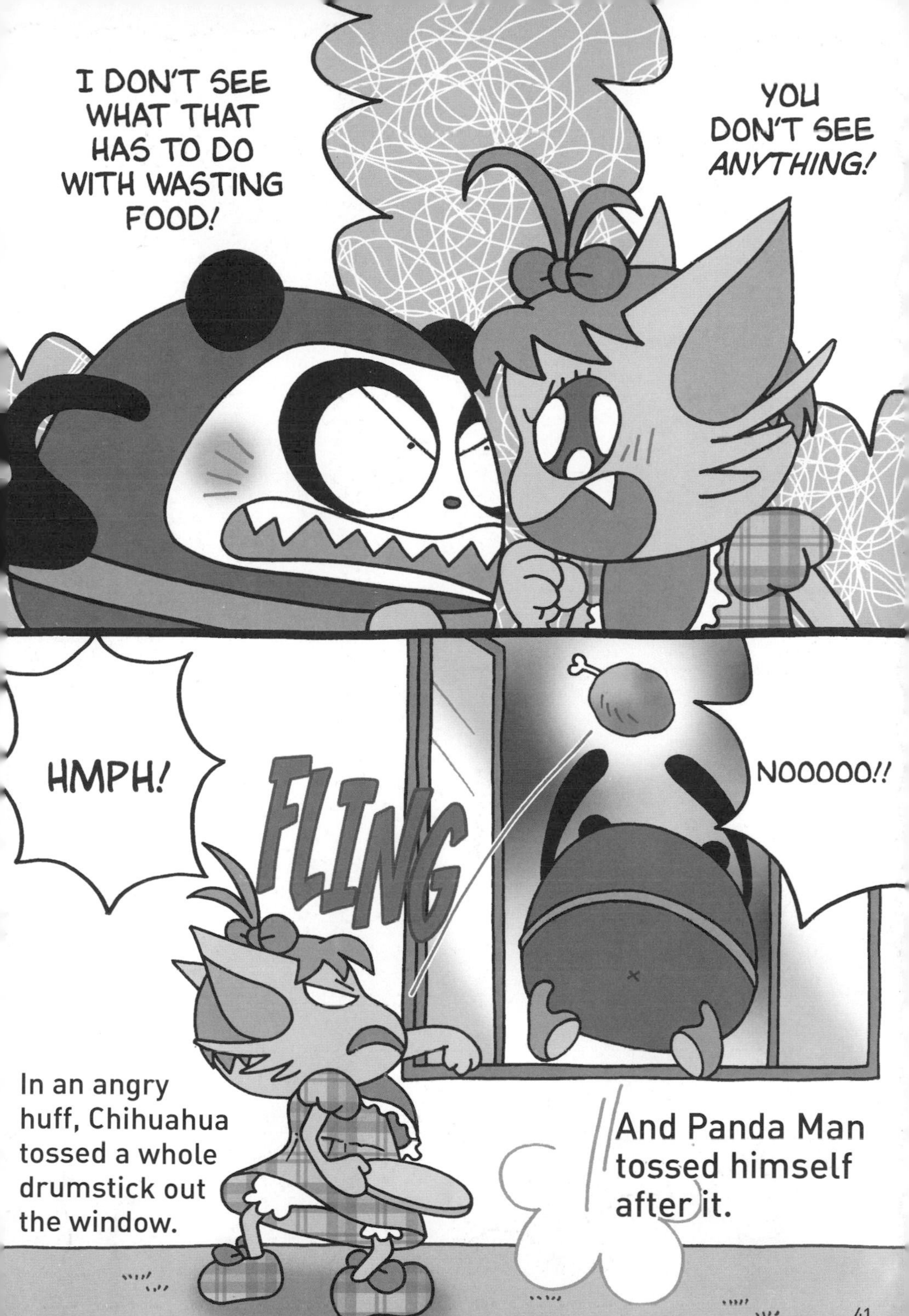
I DON'T SEE WHAT THAT HAS TO DO WITH WASTING FOOD!
YOU DON'T SEE *ANYTHING!*
HMPH!
FLING
NOOOOO!!
In an angry huff, Chihuahua tossed a whole drumstick out the window.
And Panda Man tossed himself after it.

Panda Man hit his head on a rock and was out for the rest of the night.

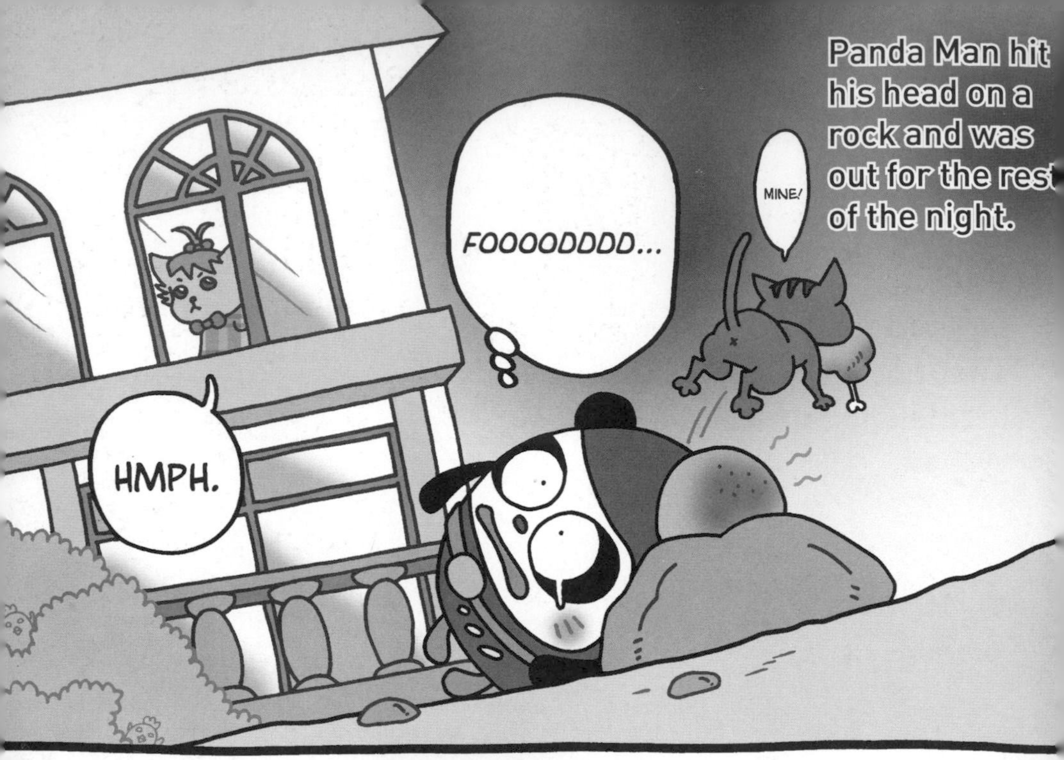
MINE!
FOOOODDDD...
HMPH.

When she was once again alone, Chihuahua pulled a box from her drawer.

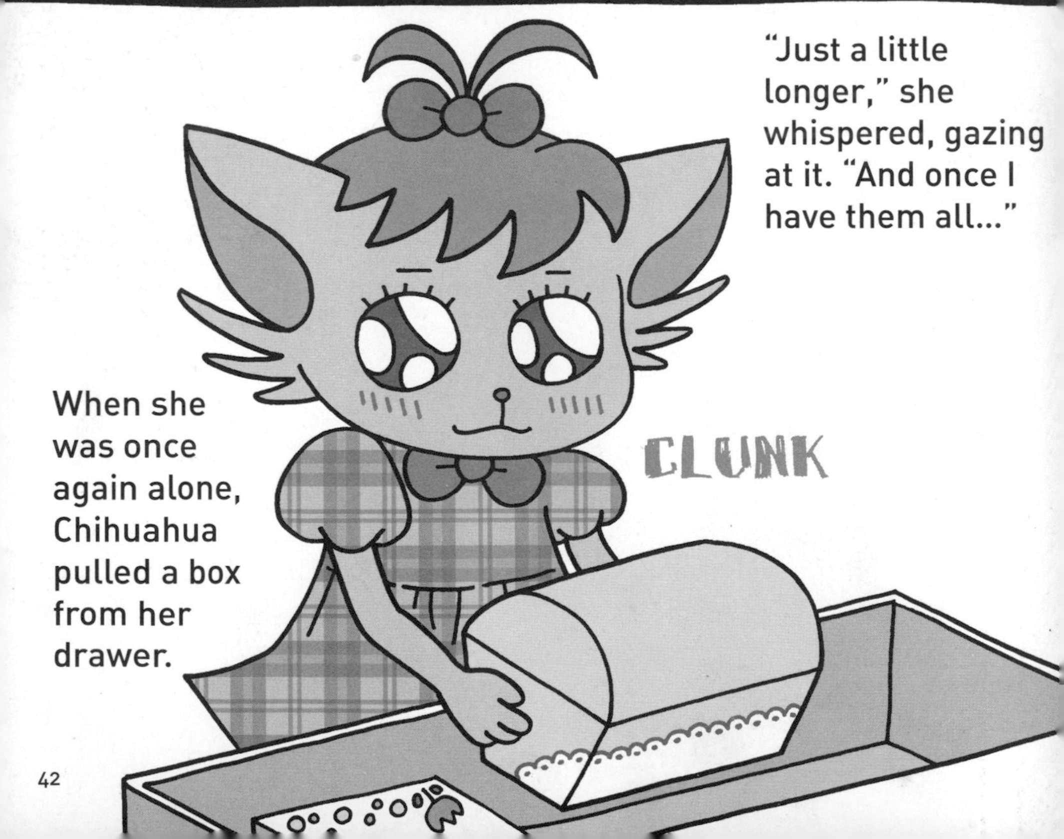
CLUNK

"Just a little longer," she whispered, gazing at it. "And once I have them all..."

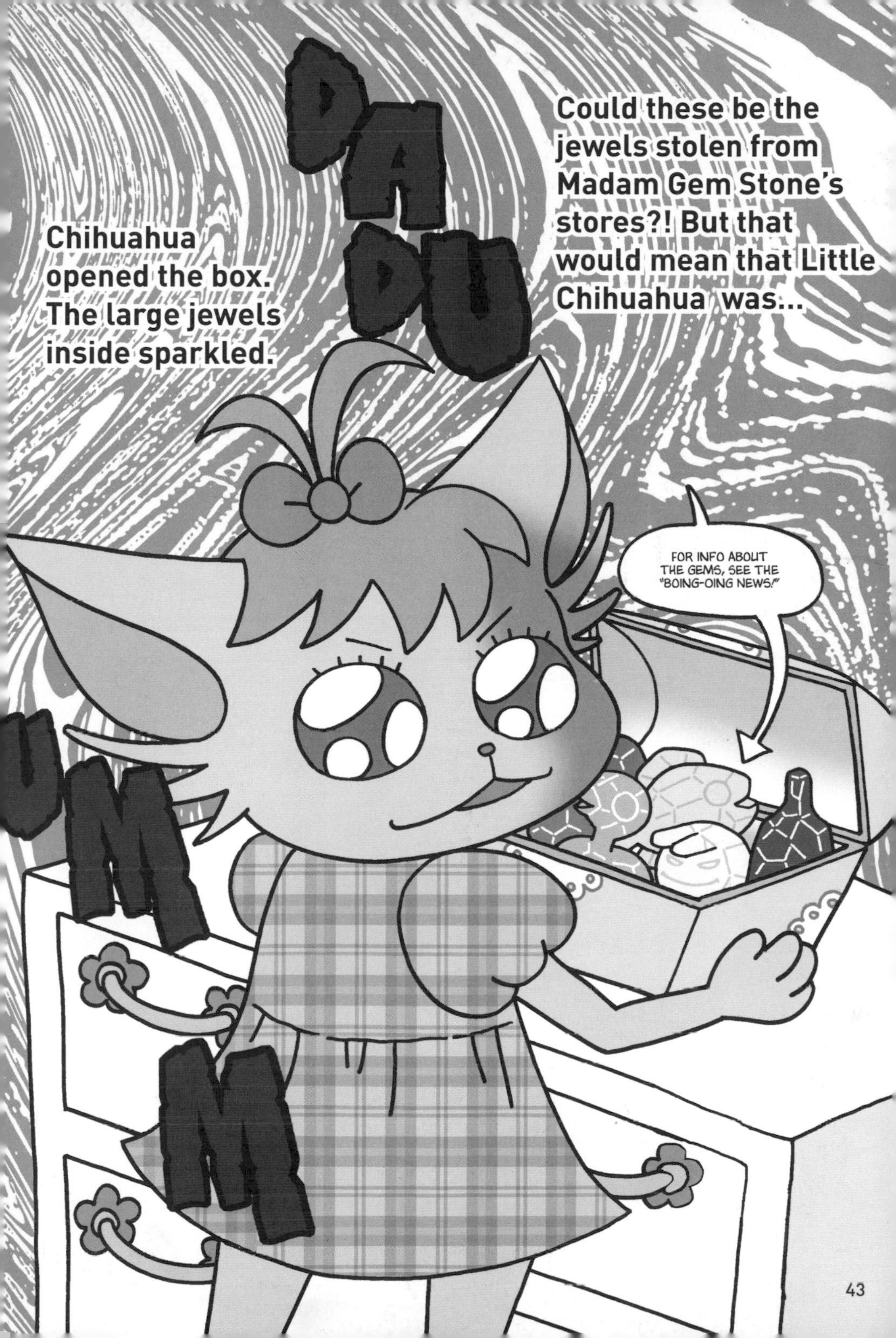
Chihuahua opened the box. The large jewels inside sparkled.
DA DU
Could these be the jewels stolen from Madam Gem Stone's stores?! But that would mean that Little Chihuahua was...
FOR INFO ABOUT THE GEMS, SEE THE "BOING-OING NEWS!"
UMM
M

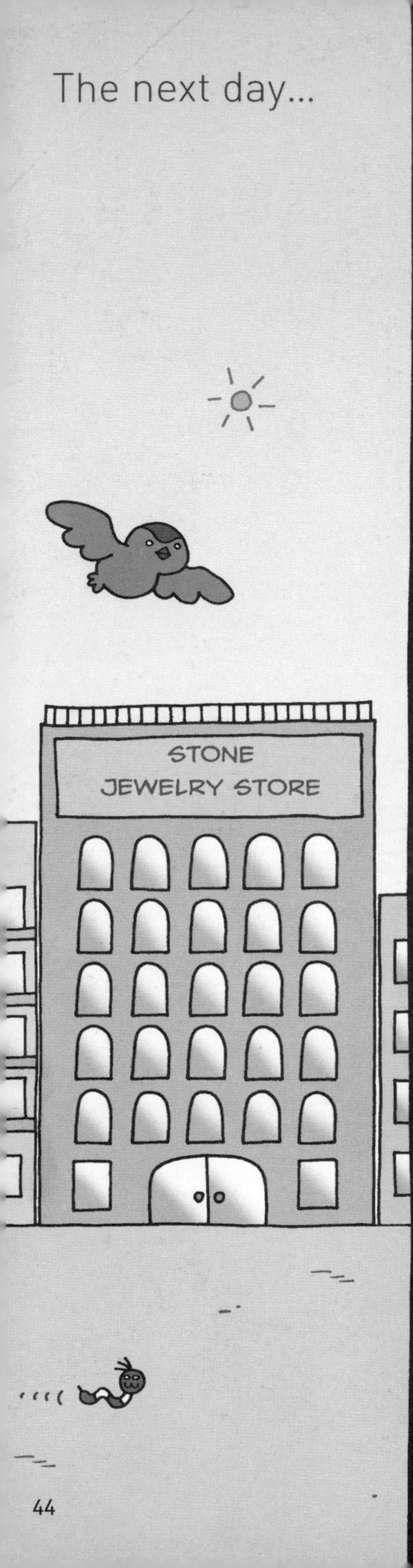
The next day...
STONE
JEWELRY STORE

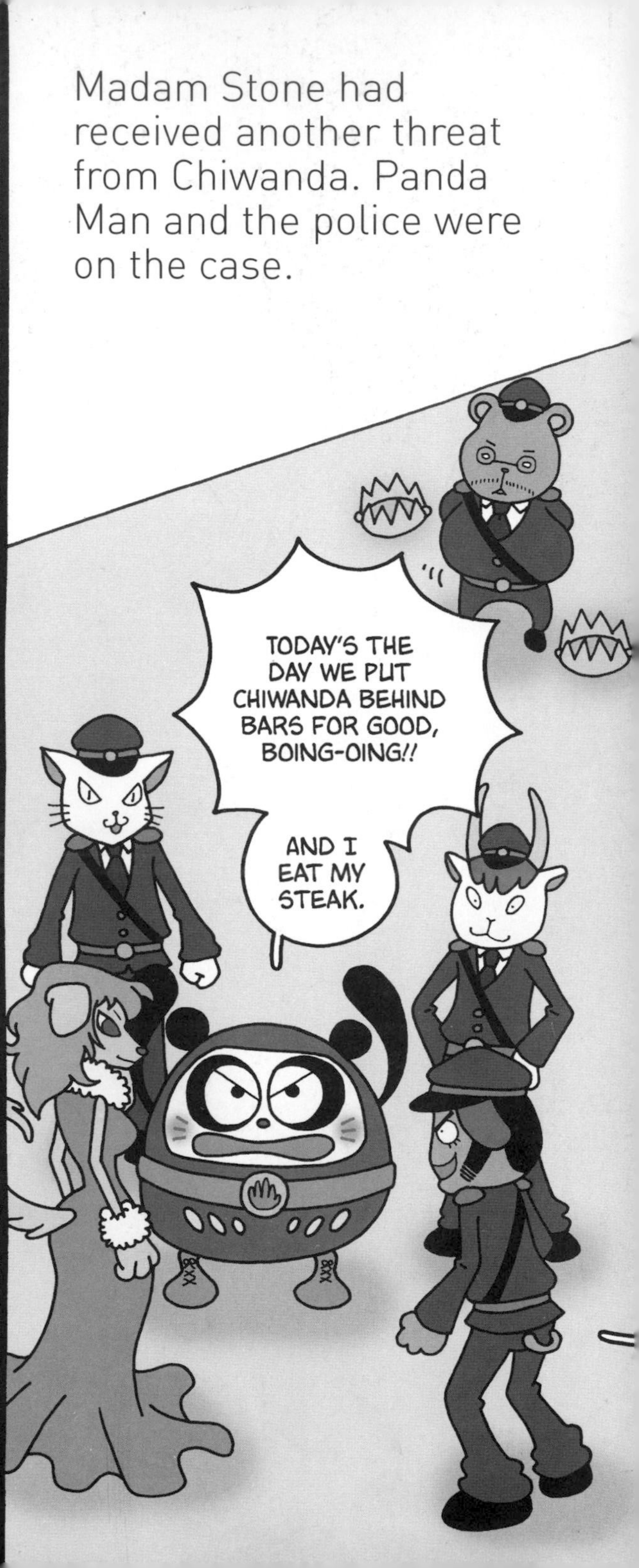
Madam Stone had received another threat from Chiwanda. Panda Man and the police were on the case.
TODAY'S THE DAY WE PUT CHIWANDA BEHIND BARS FOR GOOD, BOING-OING!!
AND I EAT MY STEAK.

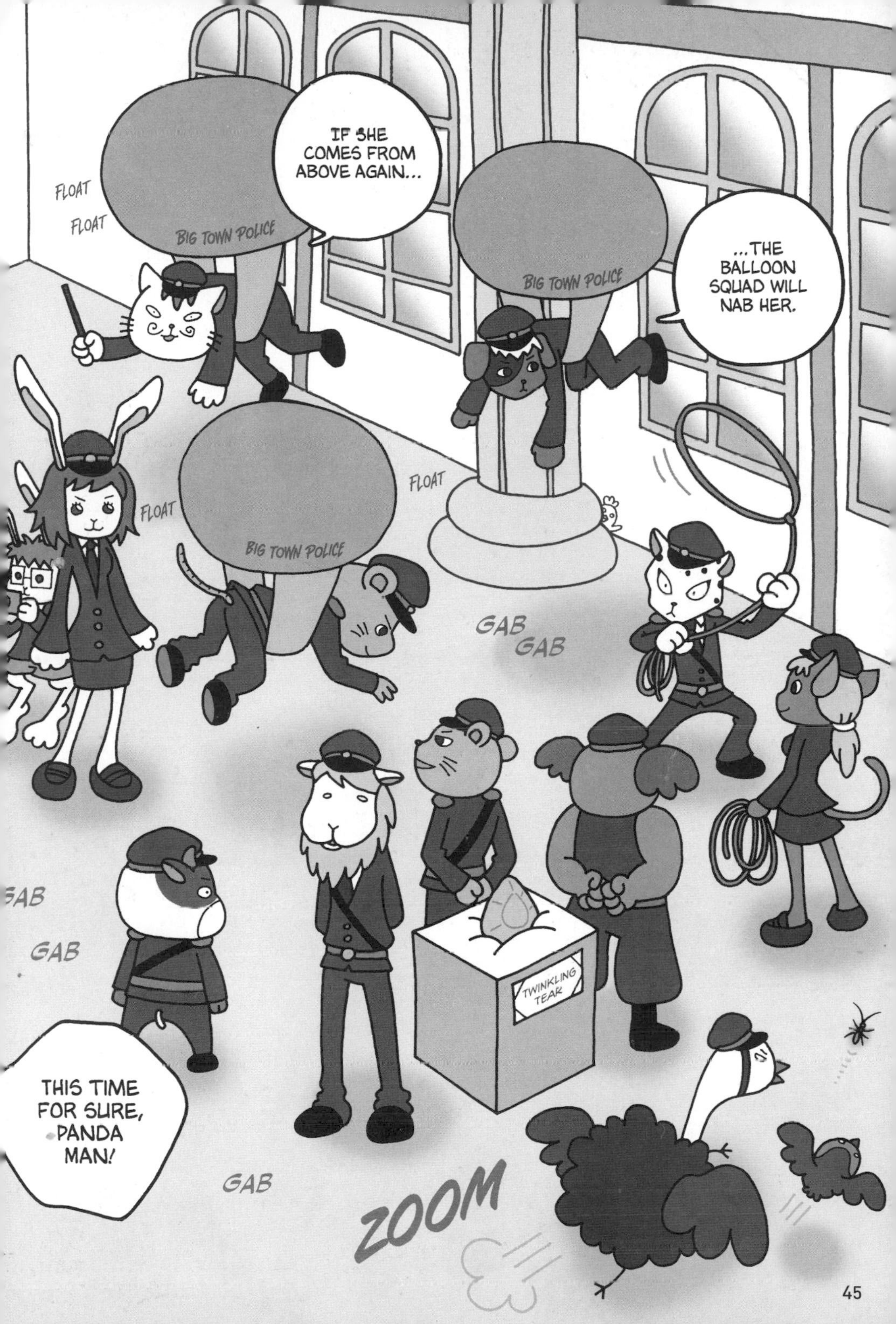
IF SHE COMES FROM ABOVE AGAIN...
...THE BALLOON SQUAD WILL NAB HER.
FLOAT
FLOAT
FLOAT
FLOAT
BIG TOWN POLICE
BIG TOWN POLICE
BIG TOWN POLICE
GAB GAB
TWINKLING TEAR
GAB
GAB
GAB
THIS TIME FOR SURE, PANDA MAN!
ZOOM

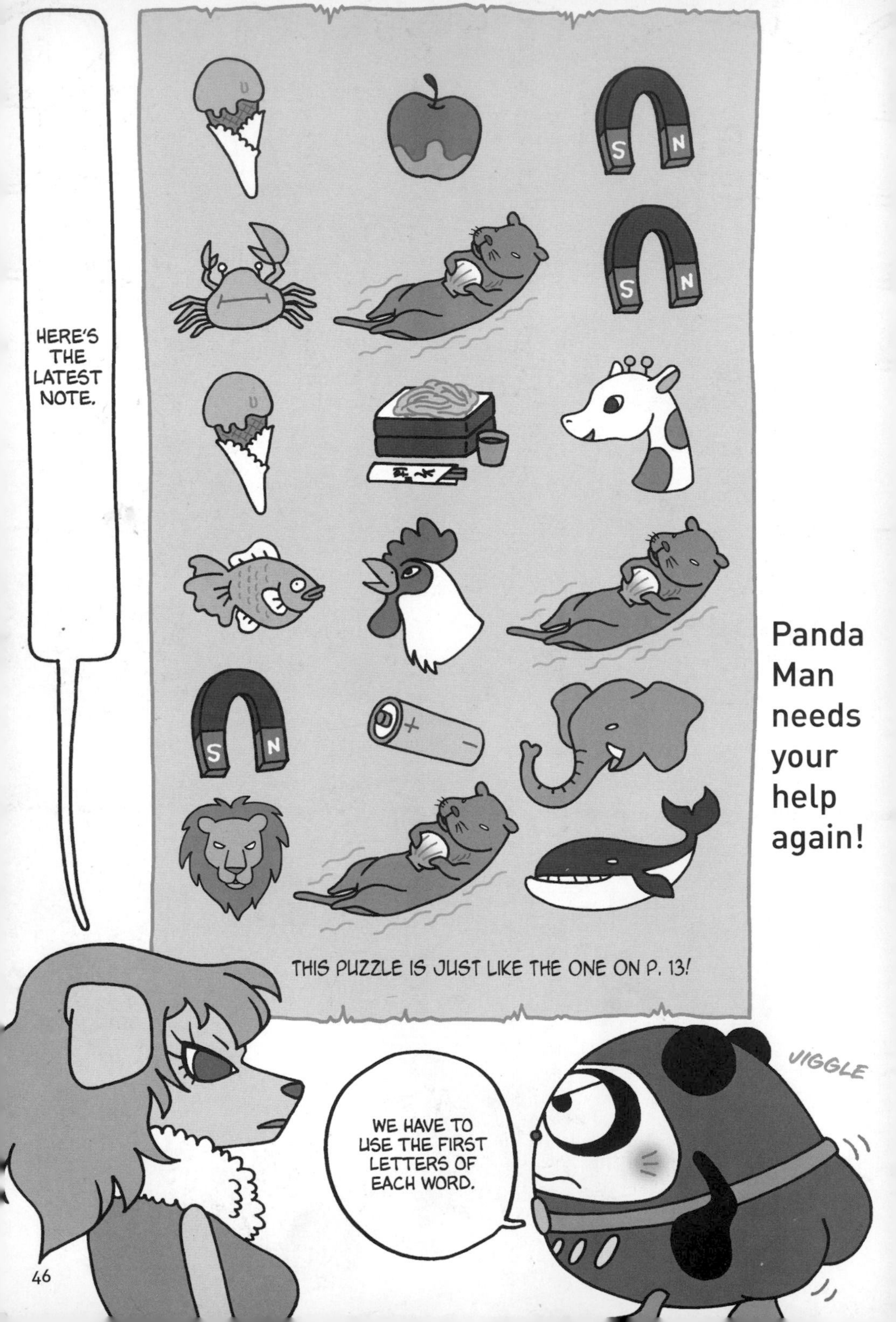
HERE'S THE LATEST NOTE.
S N
S N
S N
THIS PUZZLE IS JUST LIKE THE ONE ON P. 13!
VIGGLE
WE HAVE TO USE THE FIRST LETTERS OF EACH WORD.

Panda Man needs your help again!

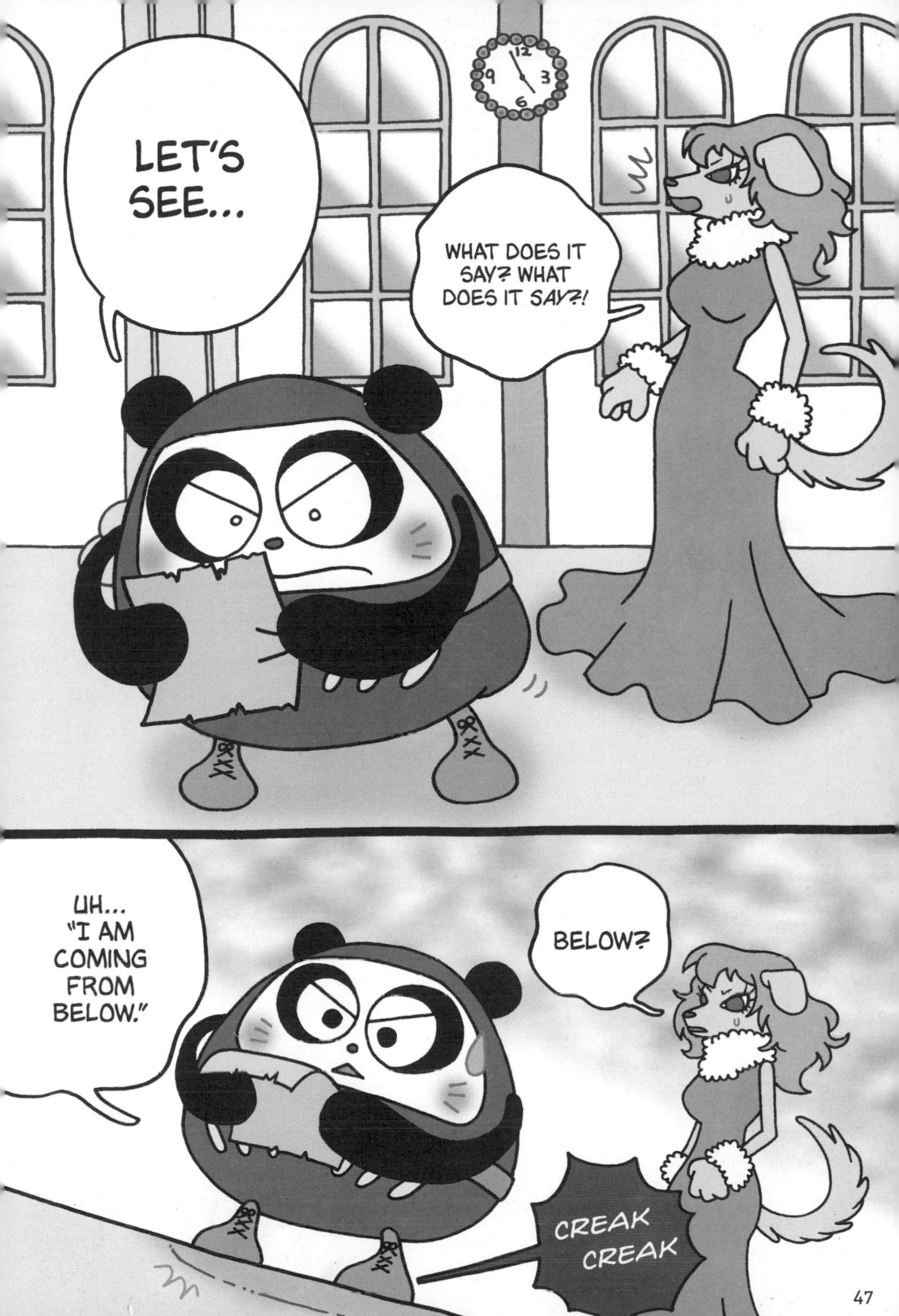
LET'S SEE...
WHAT DOES IT SAY? WHAT DOES IT SAY?!
UH... "I AM COMING FROM BELOW."
BELOW?
CREAK CREAK

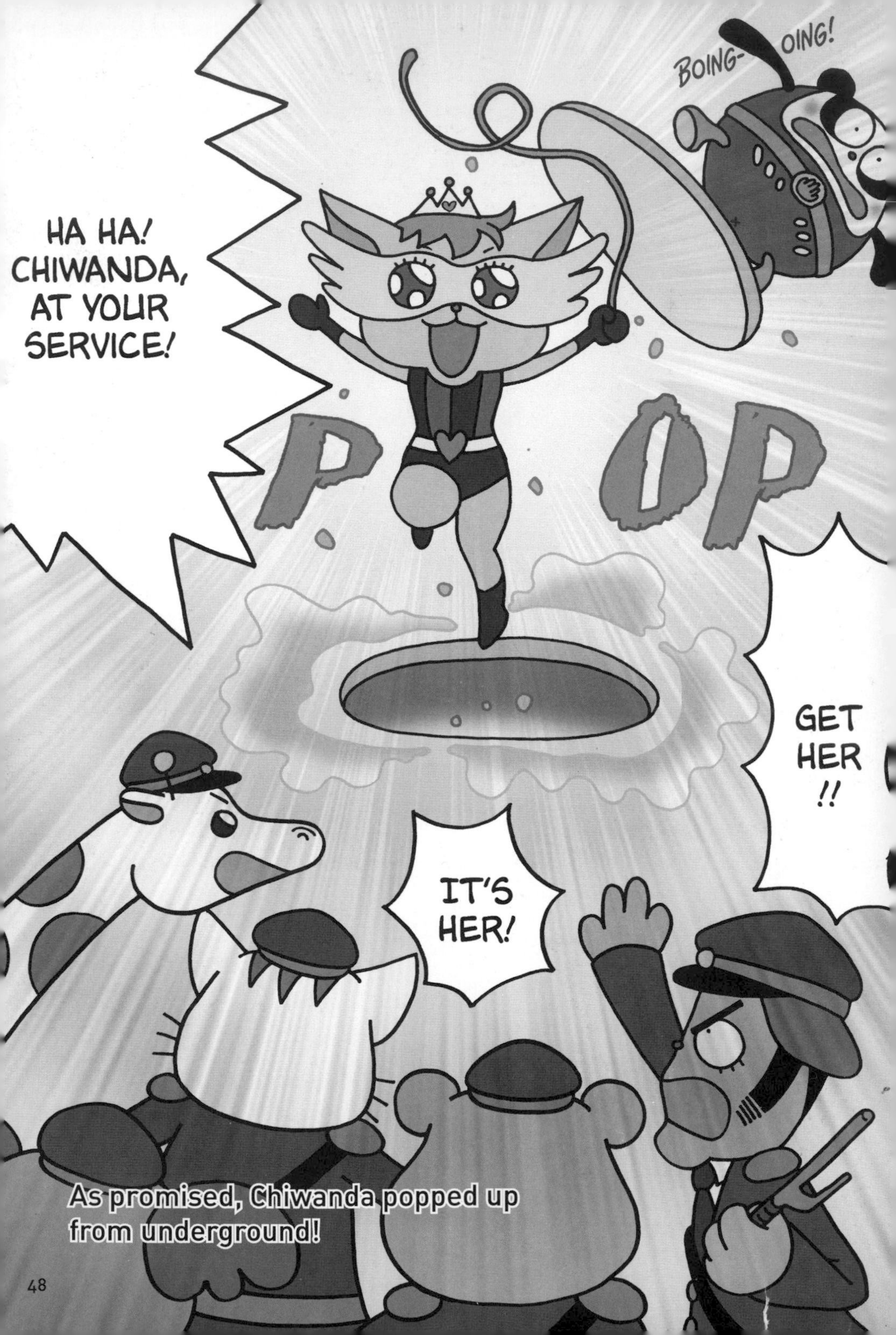
BOING-OING!
HA HA! CHIWANDA, AT YOUR SERVICE!
POP
GET HER !!
IT'S HER!
As promised, Chiwanda popped up from underground!

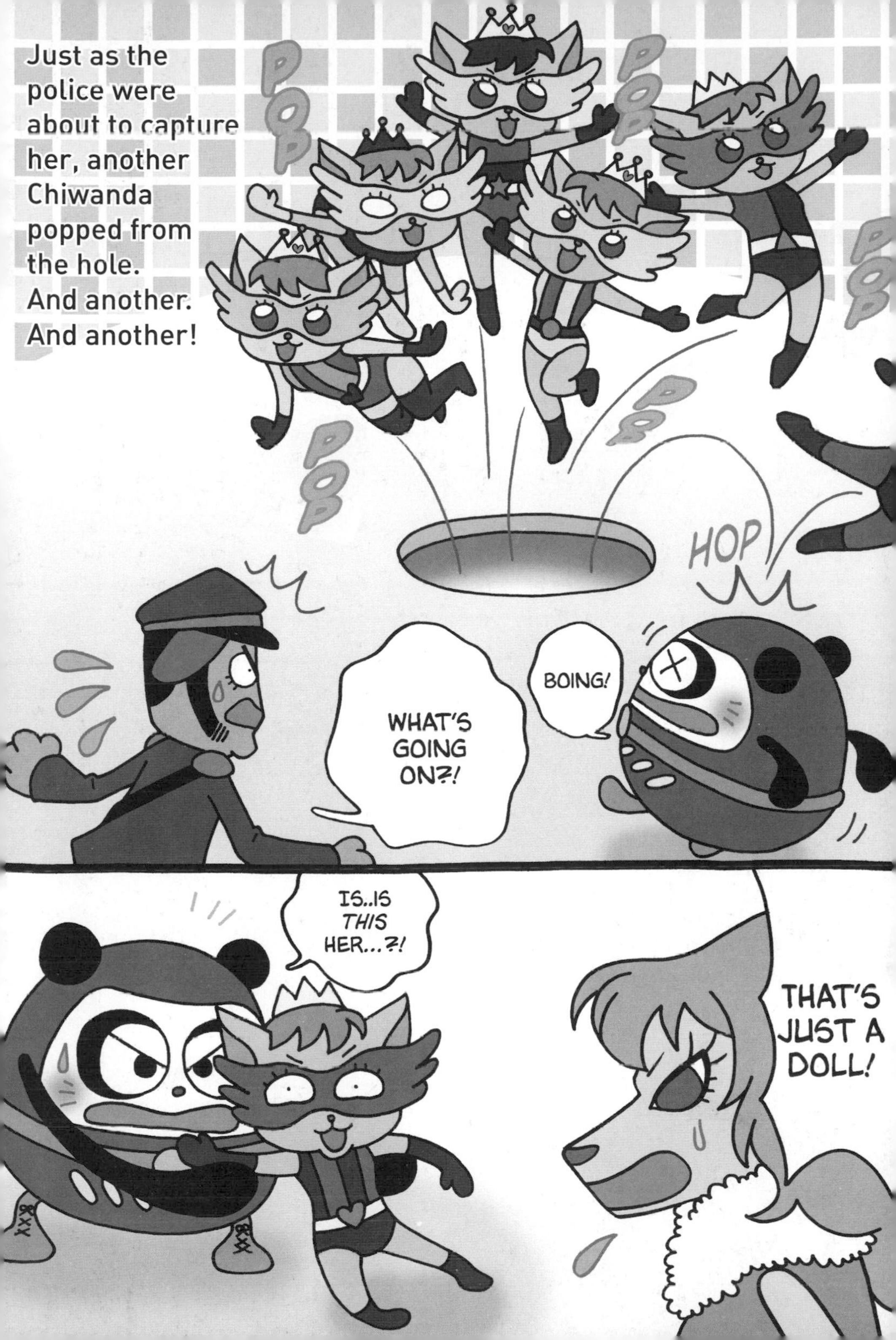
Just as the police were about to capture her, another Chiwanda popped from the hole. And another. And another!
POP
POP
POP
POP
POP
HOP
WHAT'S GOING ON?!
BOING!
IS..IS THIS HER...?!
THAT'S JUST A DOLL!

Help Panda Man find the real Chiwanda!

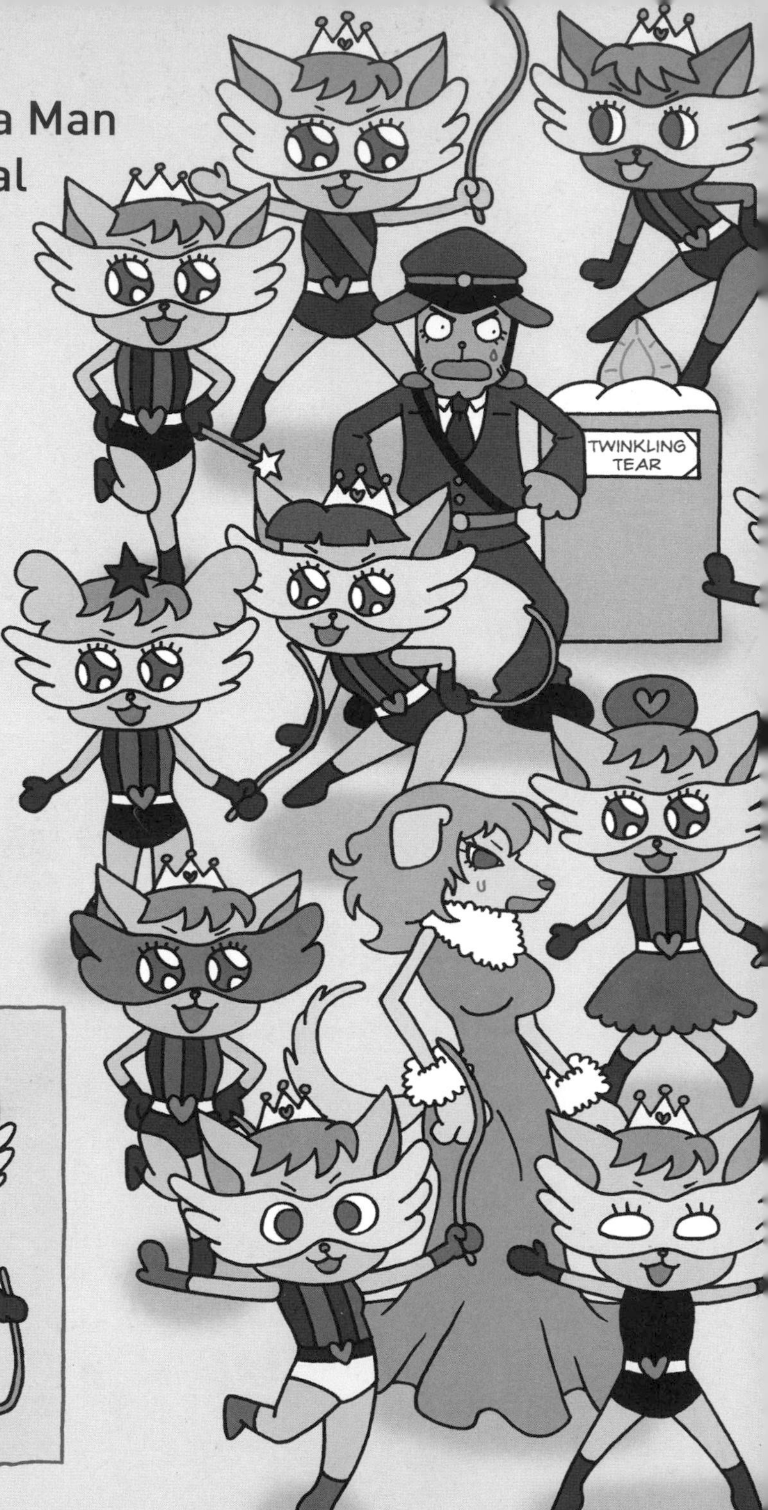
TWINKLING TEAR

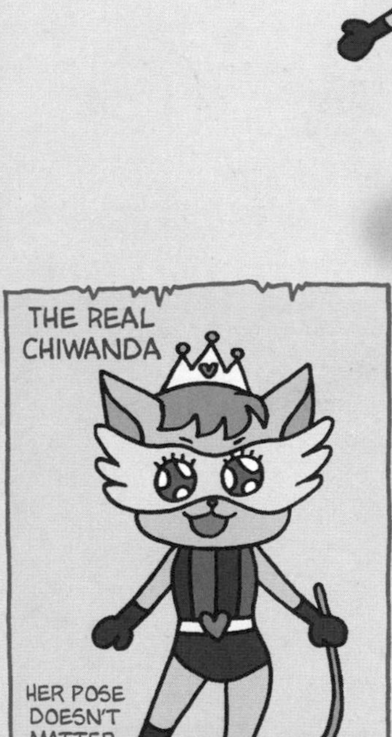
THE REAL CHIWANDA
HER POSE DOESN'T MATTER.

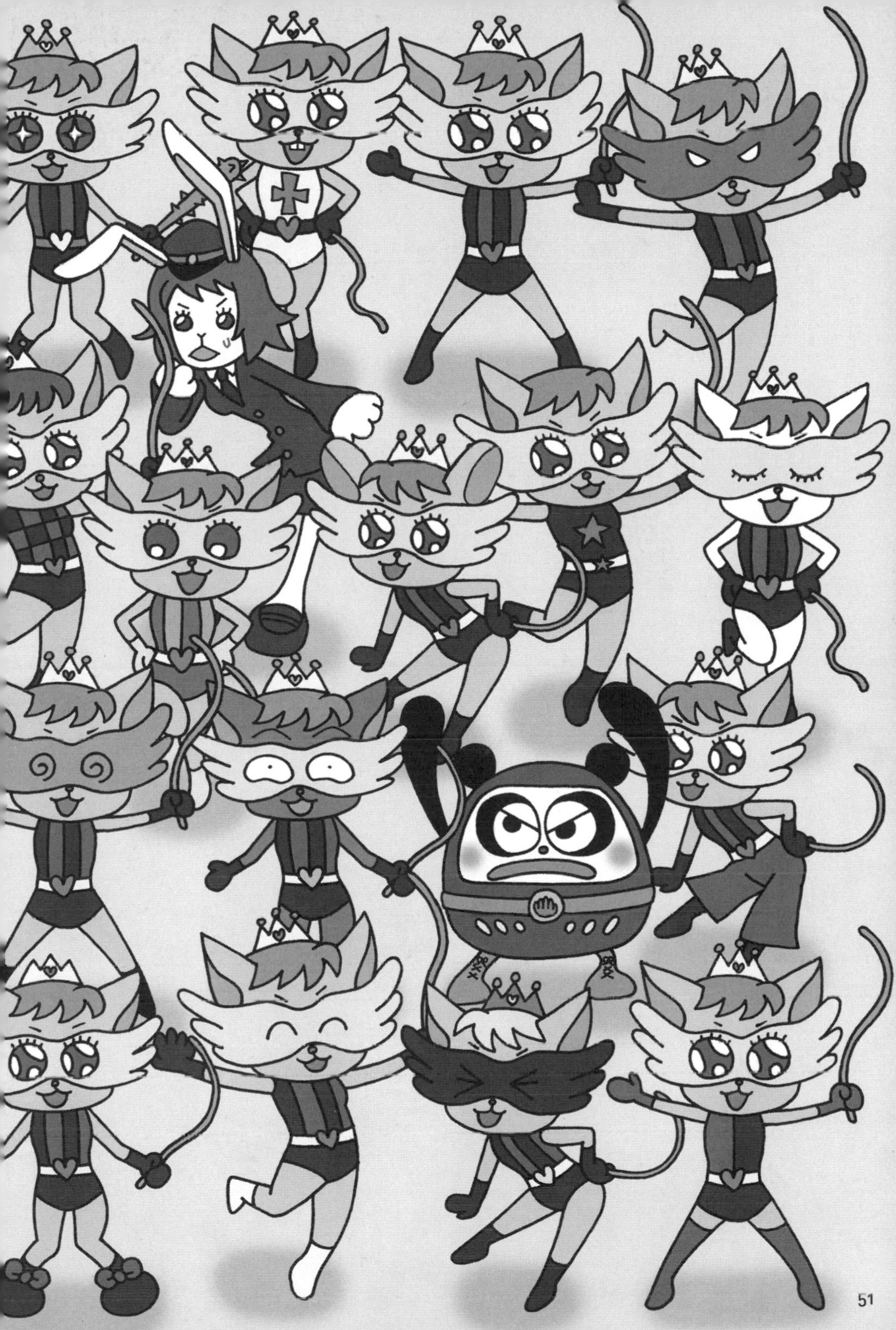

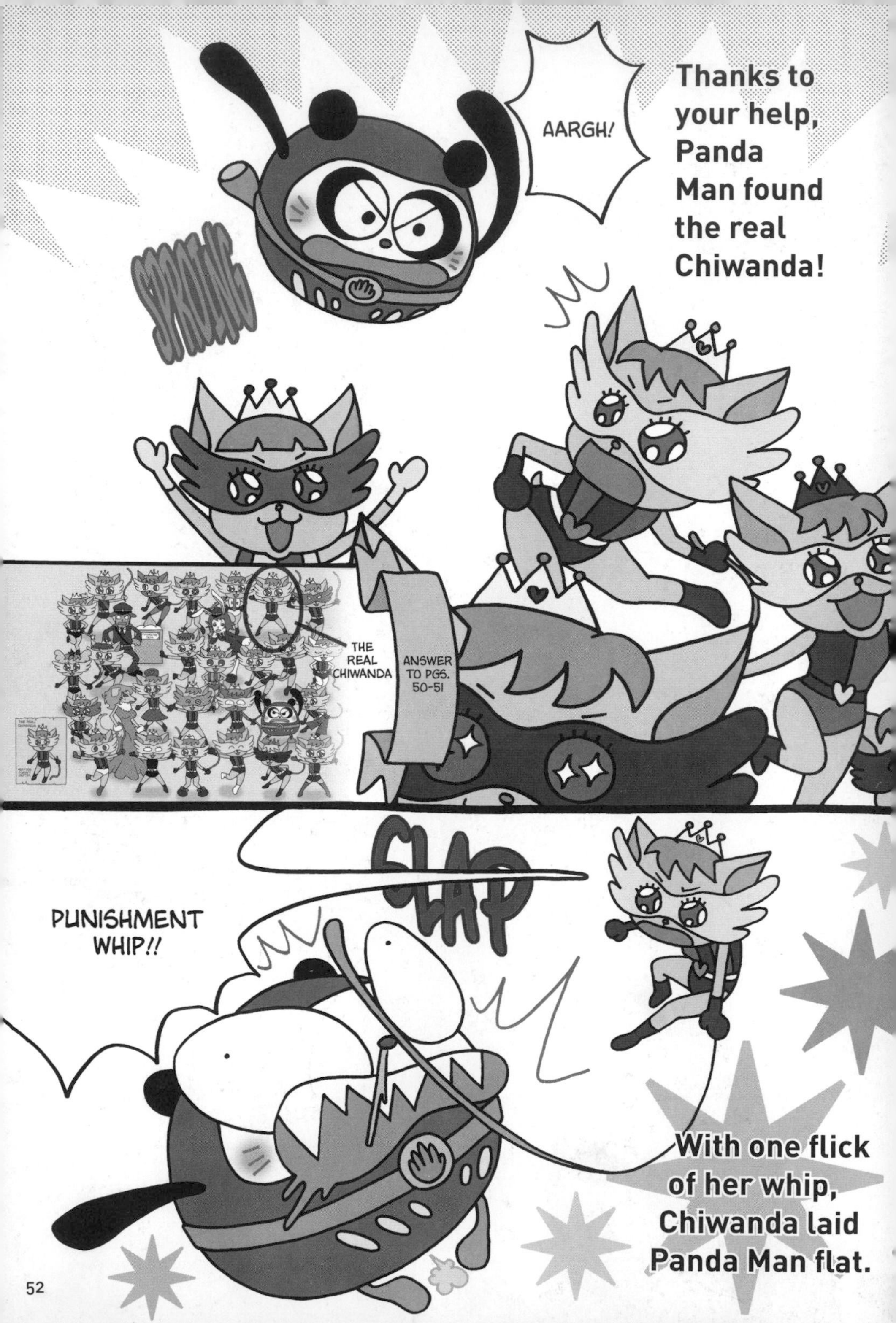
Thanks to your help, Panda Man found the real Chiwanda!
AARGH!
SPROING
ANSWER TO PGS. 50-51
THE REAL CHIWANDA
CLAP
PUNISHMENT WHIP!!
With one flick of her whip, Chiwanda laid Panda Man flat.

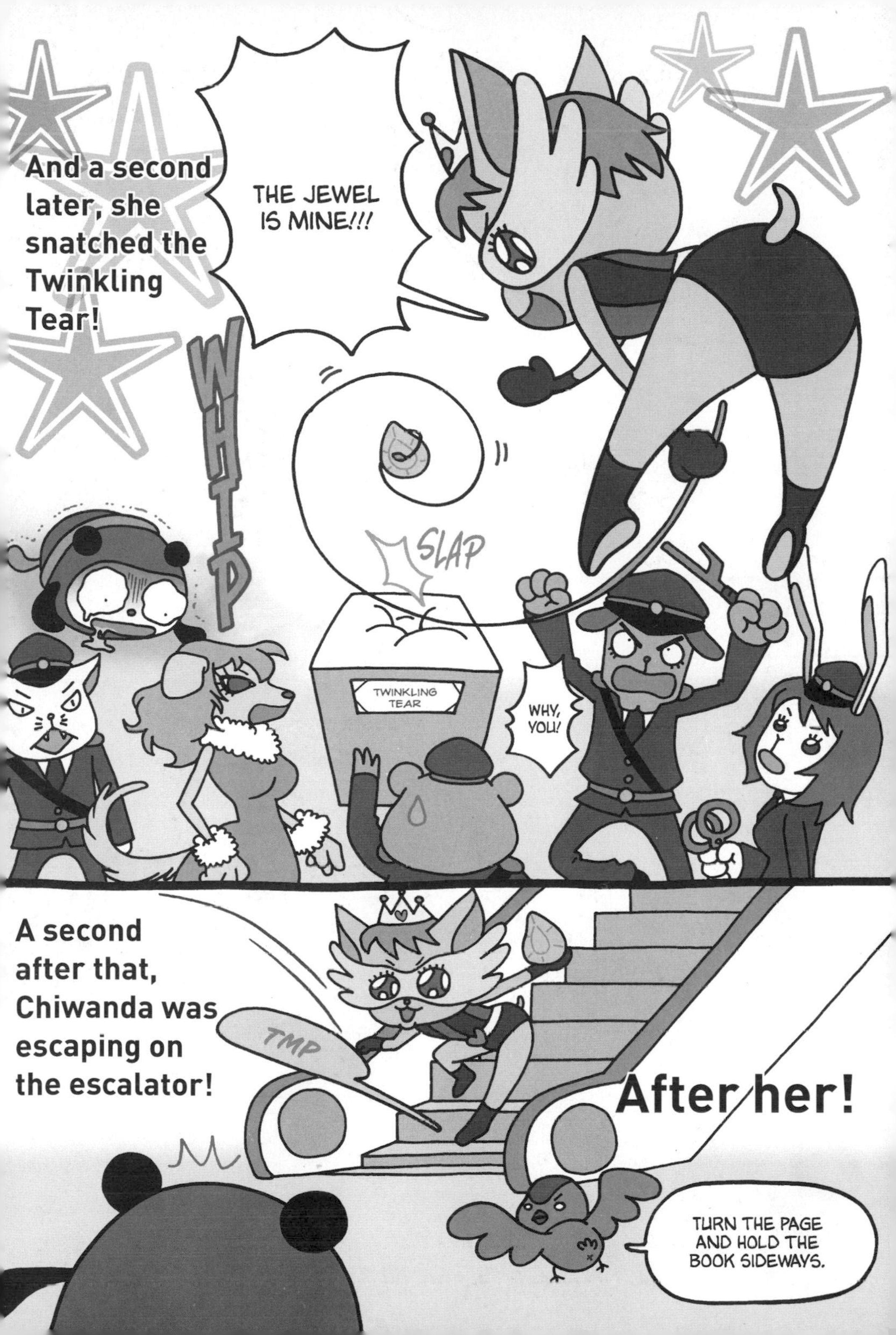
And a second later, she snatched the Twinkling Tear!
THE JEWEL IS MINE!!!
WHIP
SLAP
TWINKLING TEAR
WHY, YOU!
A second after that, Chiwanda was escaping on the escalator!
TMP
After her!
TURN THE PAGE AND HOLD THE BOOK SIDEWAYS.

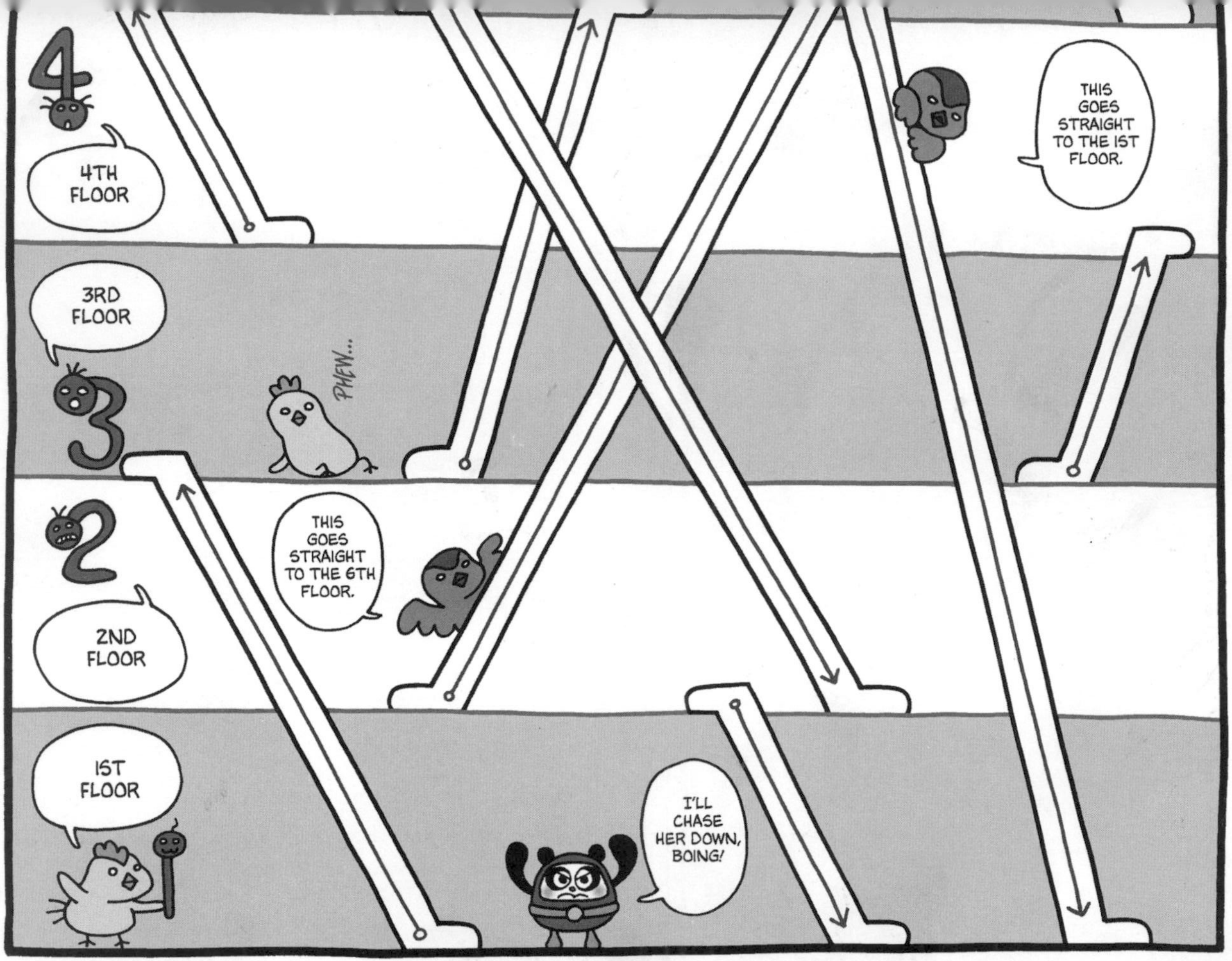
4TH FLOOR
3RD FLOOR
2ND FLOOR
1ST FLOOR
PHEW...
THIS GOES STRAIGHT TO THE 6TH FLOOR.
THIS GOES STRAIGHT TO THE 1ST FLOOR.
I'LL CHASE HER DOWN, BOING!

Which route should you take to catch Chiwanda? You can go up, down, and up again.

Help Panda Man get to the top by following the arrows!

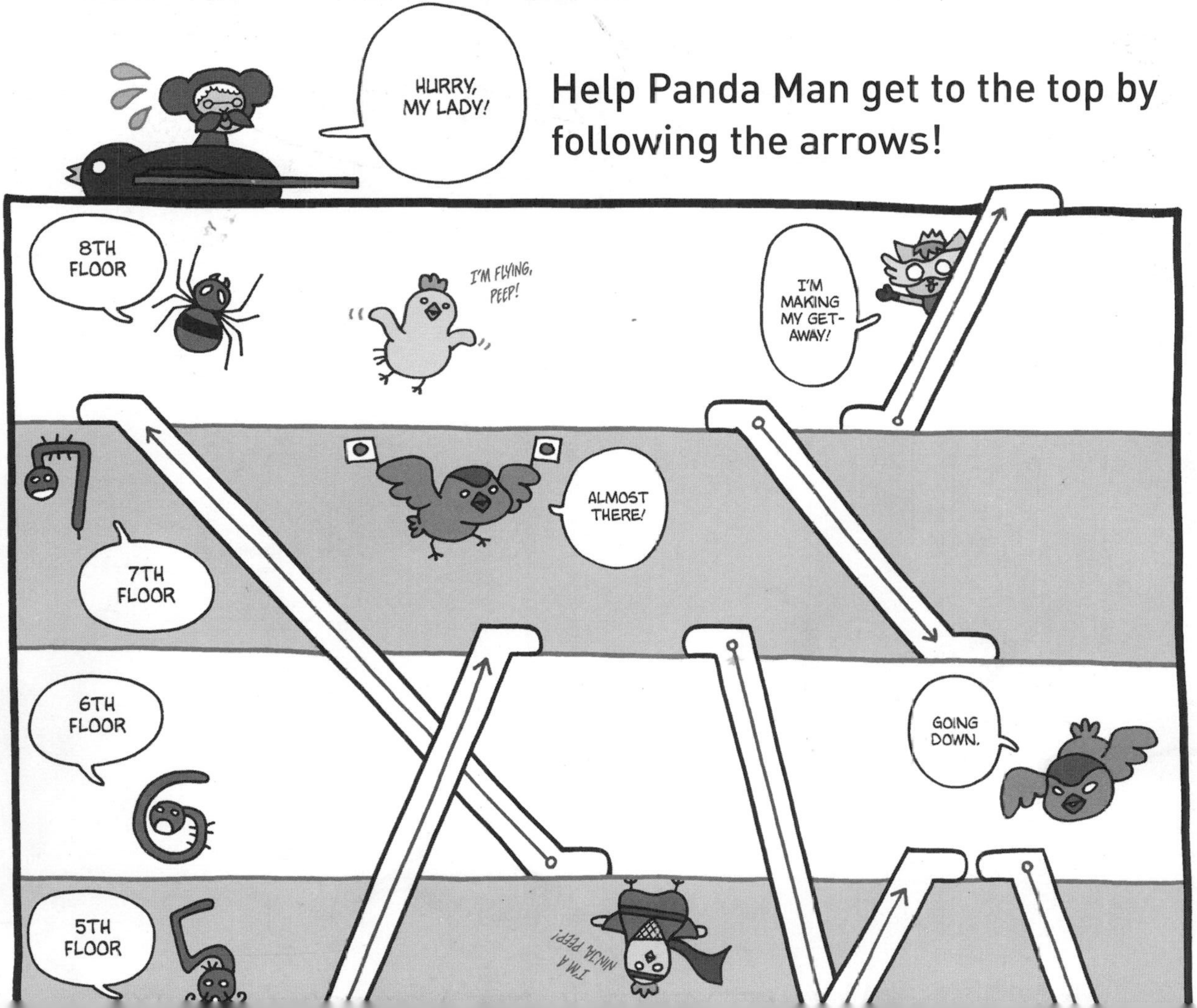
HURRY, MY LADY!
8TH FLOOR
I'M FLYING, PEEP!
I'M MAKING MY GET-AWAY!
ALMOST THERE!
7TH FLOOR
6TH FLOOR
GOING DOWN.
5TH FLOOR
I'M A NINJA PEEP!

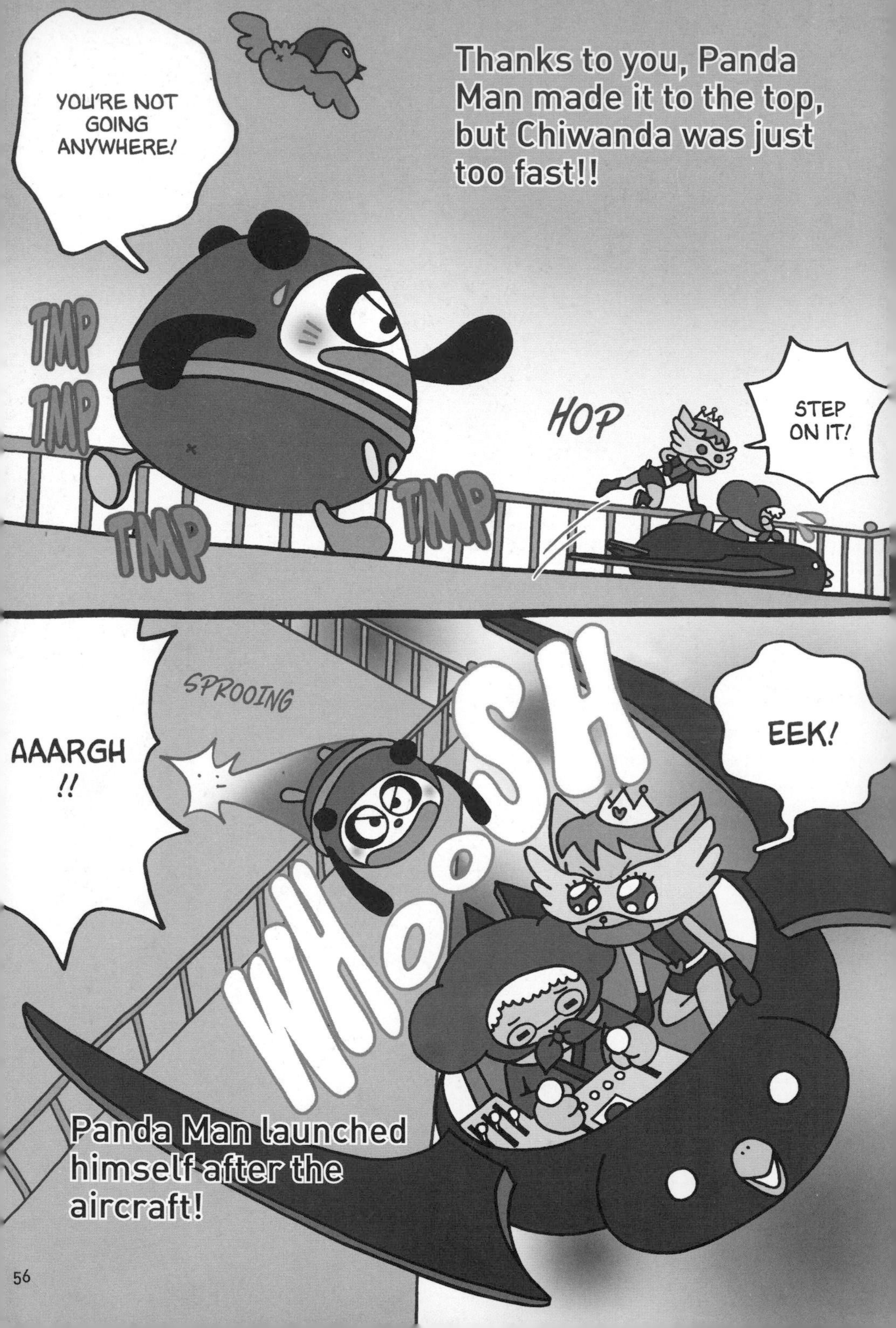

Thanks to you, Panda Man made it to the top, but Chiwanda was just too fast!!
YOU'RE NOT GOING ANYWHERE!
TMP
TMP
STEP ON IT!
HOP
TMP
TMP
EEK!
WHOOOSH
SPROOING
AAARGH !!
Panda Man launched himself after the aircraft!

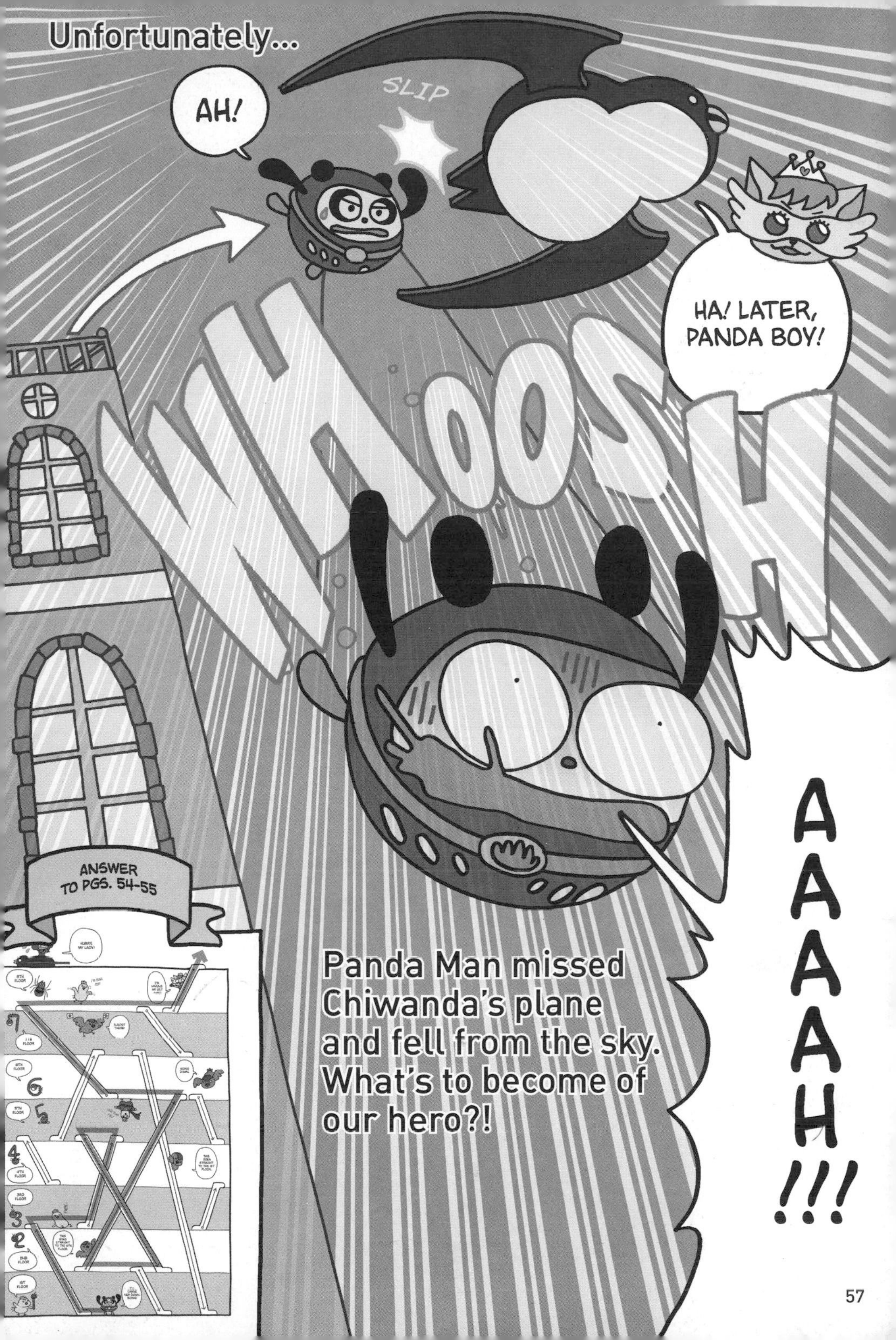
Unfortunately...
AH!
SLIP
HA! LATER, PANDA BOY!
WHOOSH
AAAAH!!!
ANSWER TO PGS. 54-55
Panda Man missed Chiwanda's plane and fell from the sky. What's to become of our hero?!

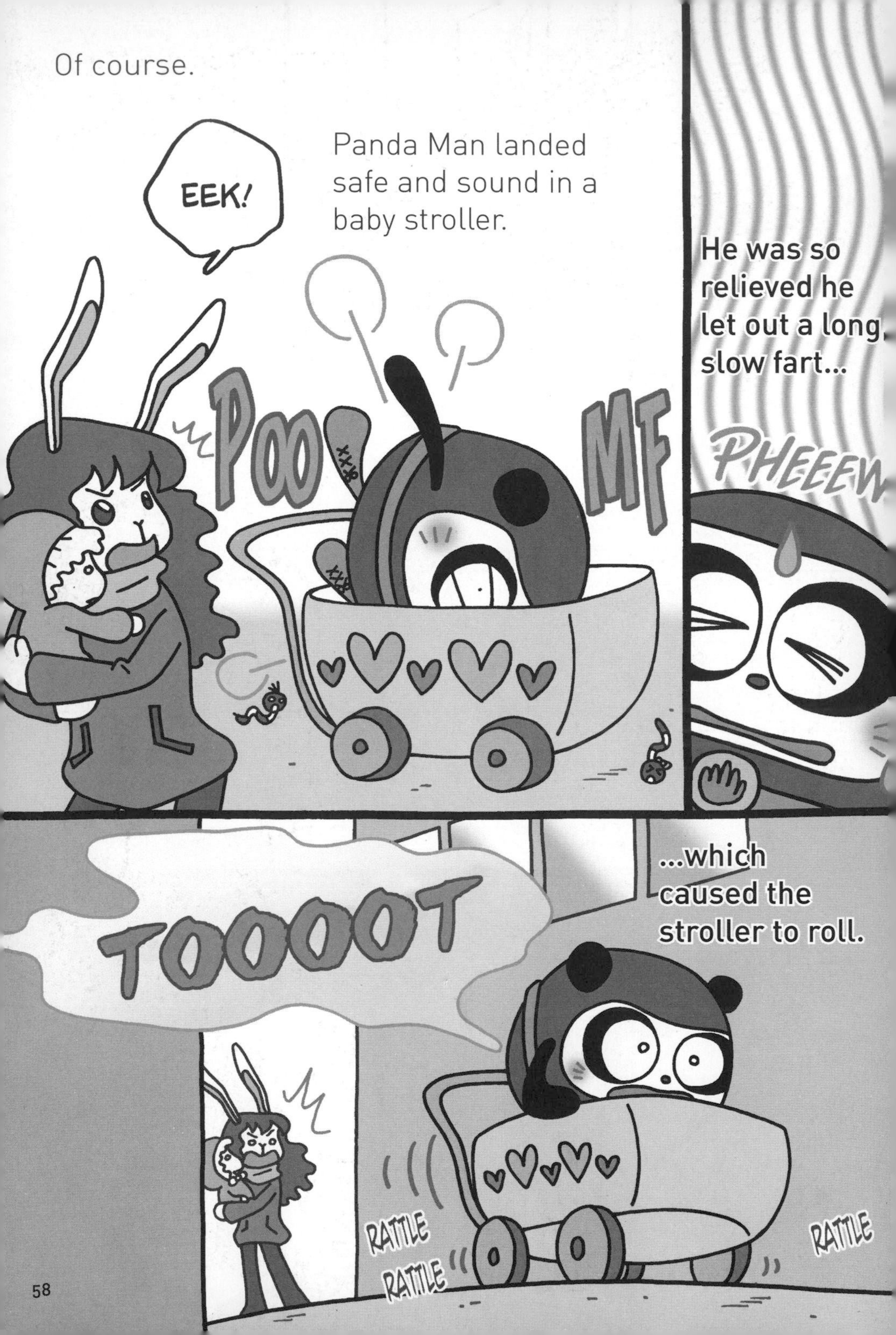
Of course.
EEK!
Panda Man landed safe and sound in a baby stroller.
POOMF
He was so relieved he let out a long, slow fart...
PHEEEW
TOOOOT
...which caused the stroller to roll.
RATTLE
RATTLE
RATTLE

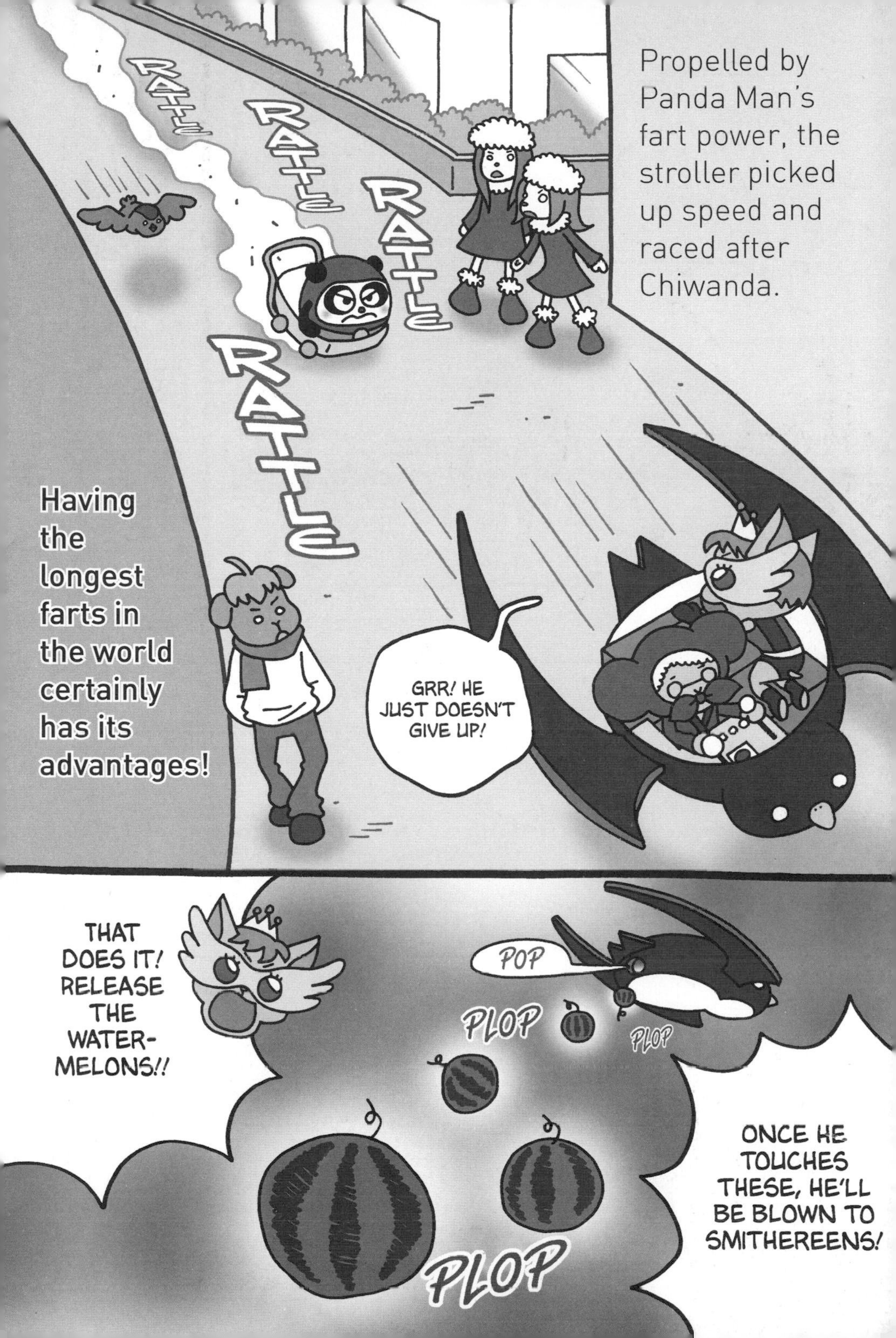
Propelled by Panda Man's fart power, the stroller picked up speed and raced after Chiwanda.
RATTLE RATTLE RATTLE RATTLE
GRR! HE JUST DOESN'T GIVE UP!
Having the longest farts in the world certainly has its advantages!
POP
PLOP
PLOP
THAT DOES IT! RELEASE THE WATER-MELONS!!
ONCE HE TOUCHES THESE, HE'LL BE BLOWN TO SMITHEREENS!
PLOP

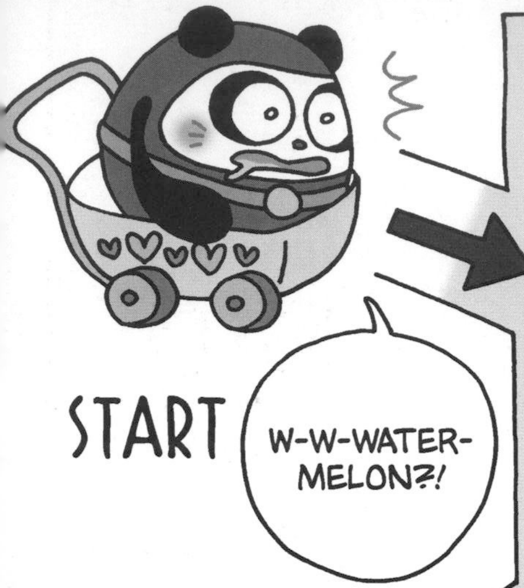
START
W-W-WATER-
MELON?!

Panda Man's super hungry, but he can't touch those watermelons! Help him stay on Chiwanda's trail while avoiding the watermelons!

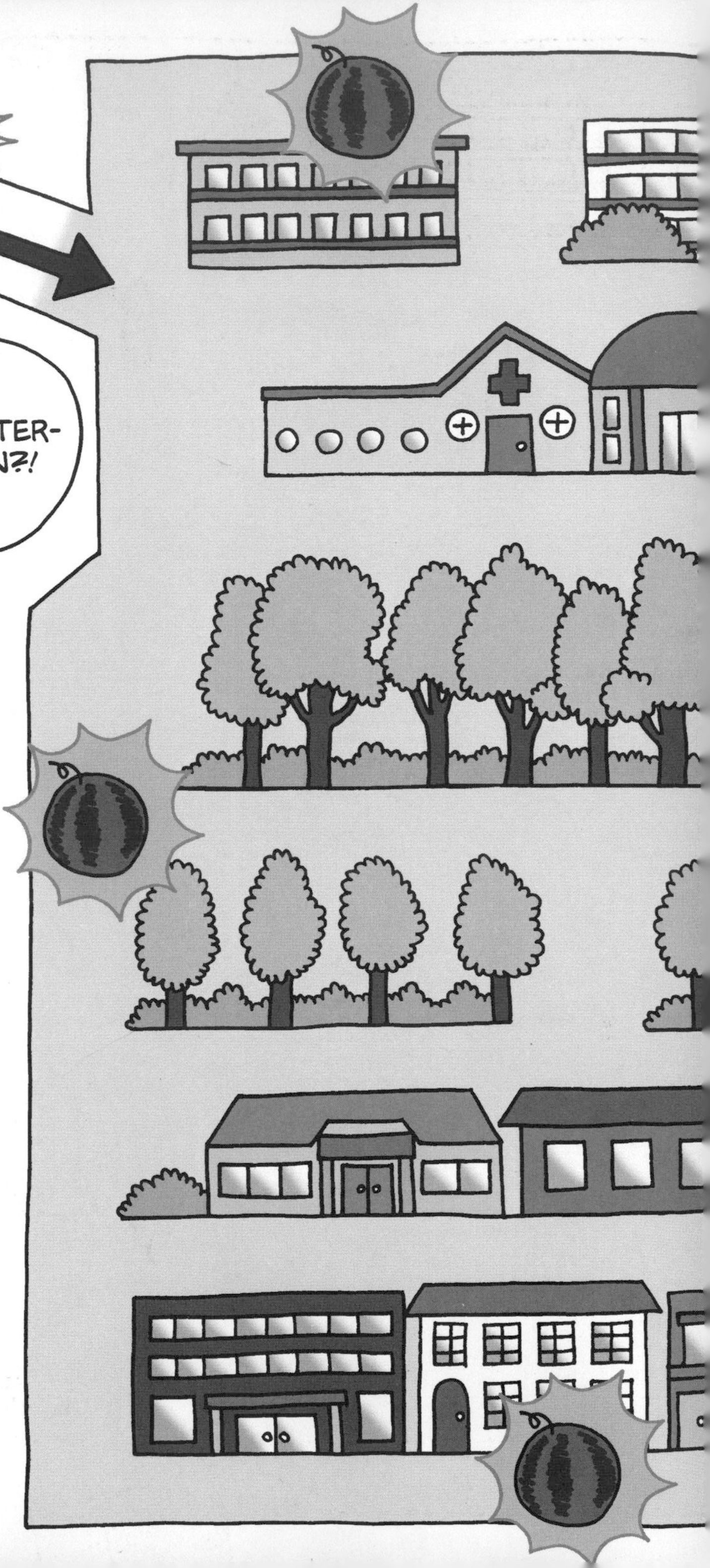

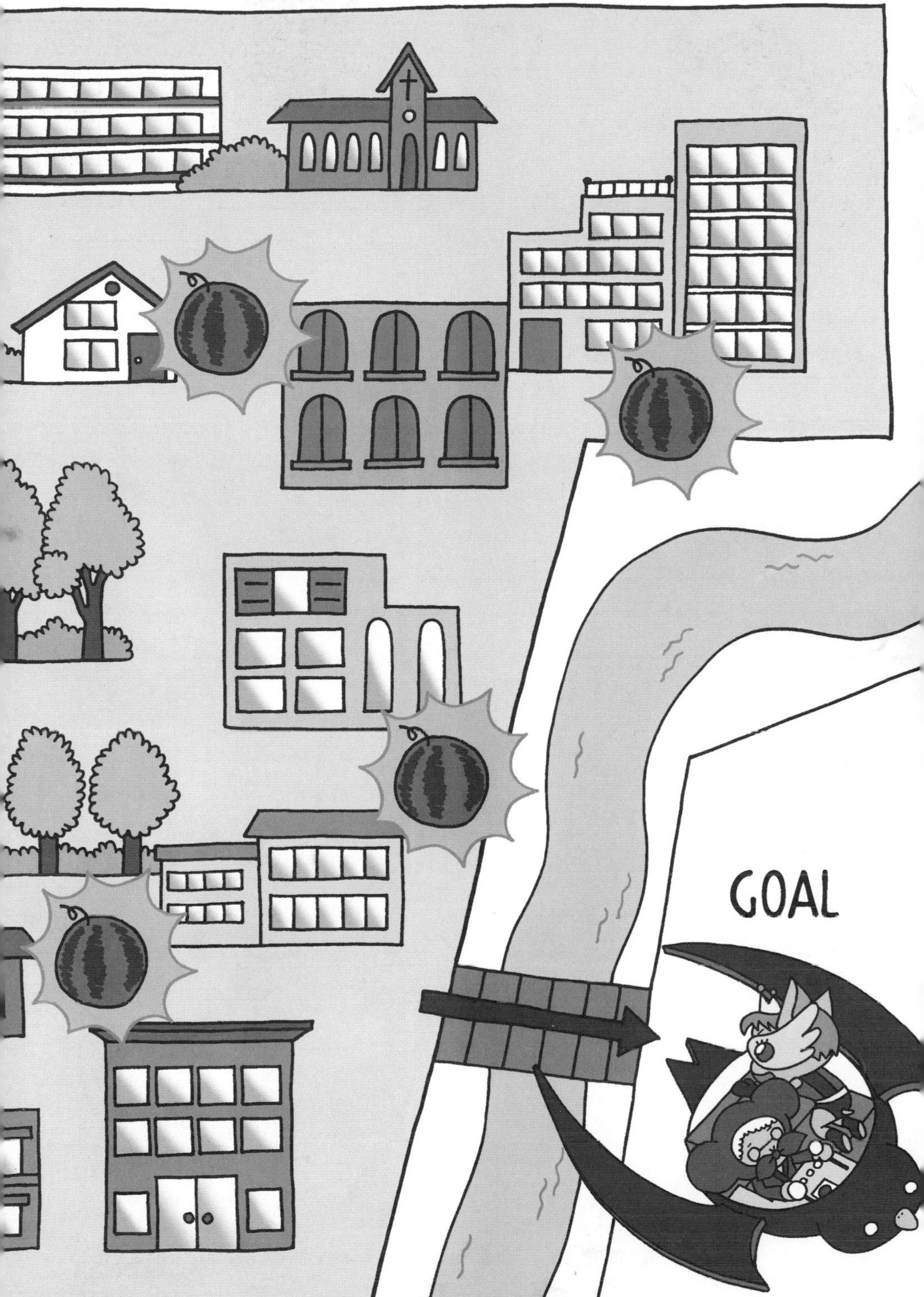
GOAL

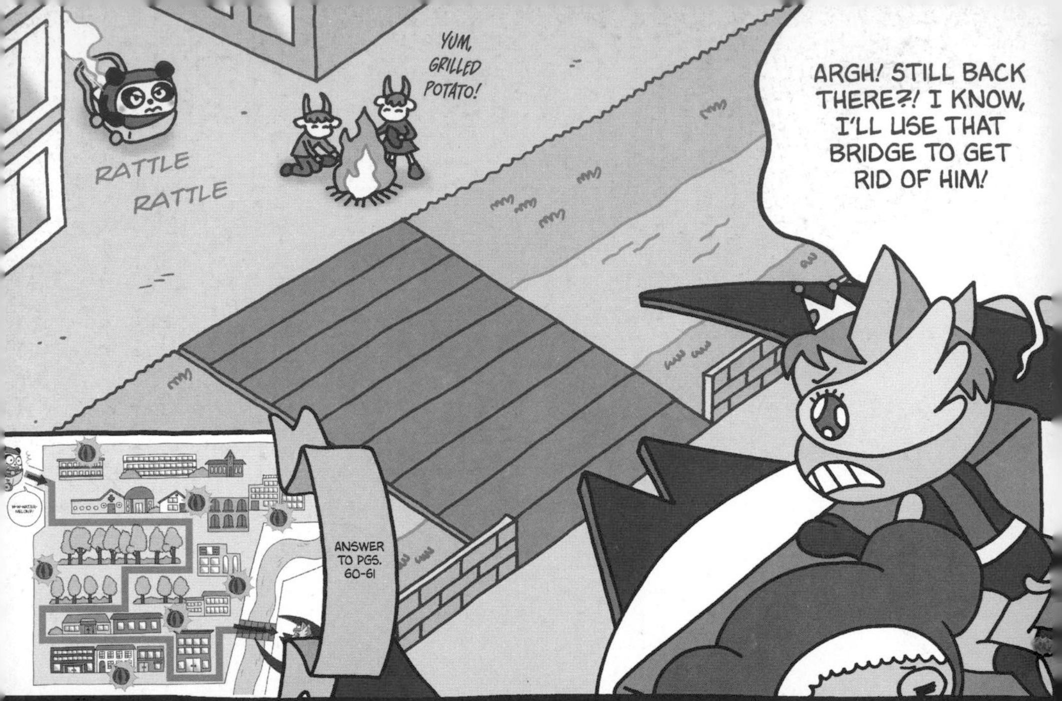
ARGH! STILL BACK THERE?! I KNOW, I'LL USE THAT BRIDGE TO GET RID OF HIM!
YUM, GRILLED POTATO!
RATTLE RATTLE
ANSWER TO PGS. 60-61

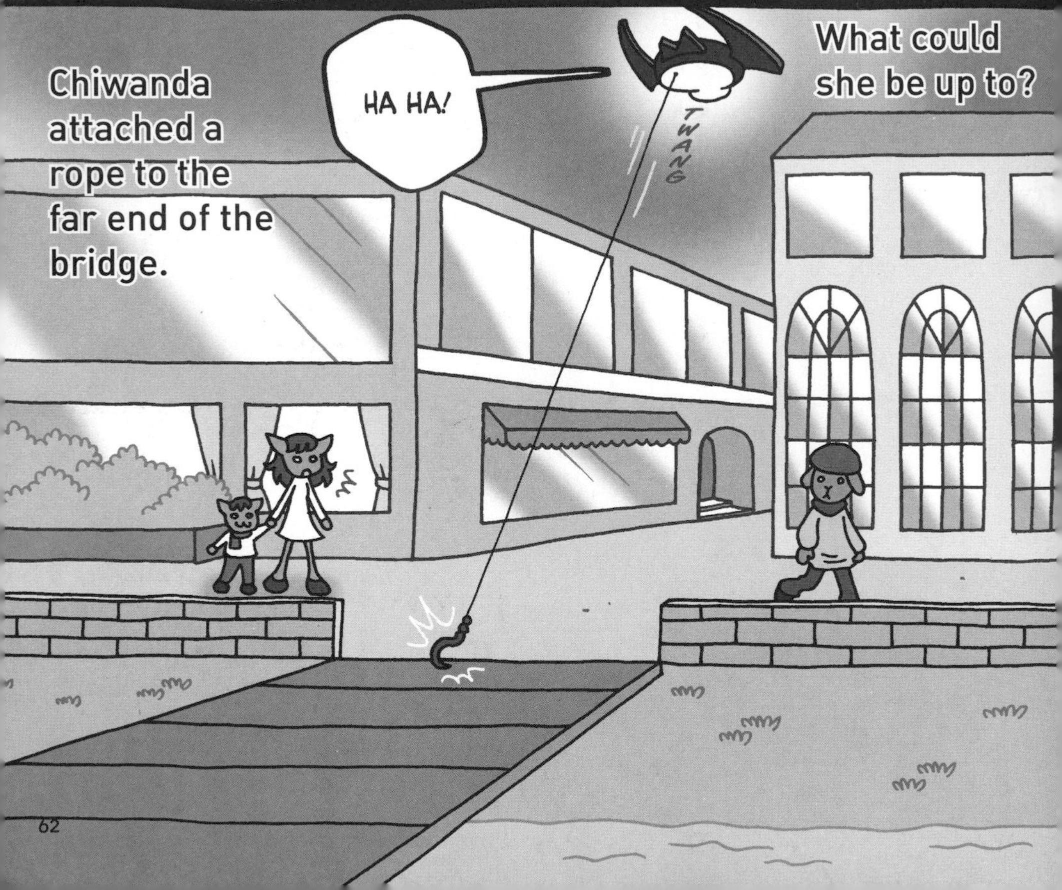
What could she be up to?
HA HA!
TWANG
Chiwanda attached a rope to the far end of the bridge.

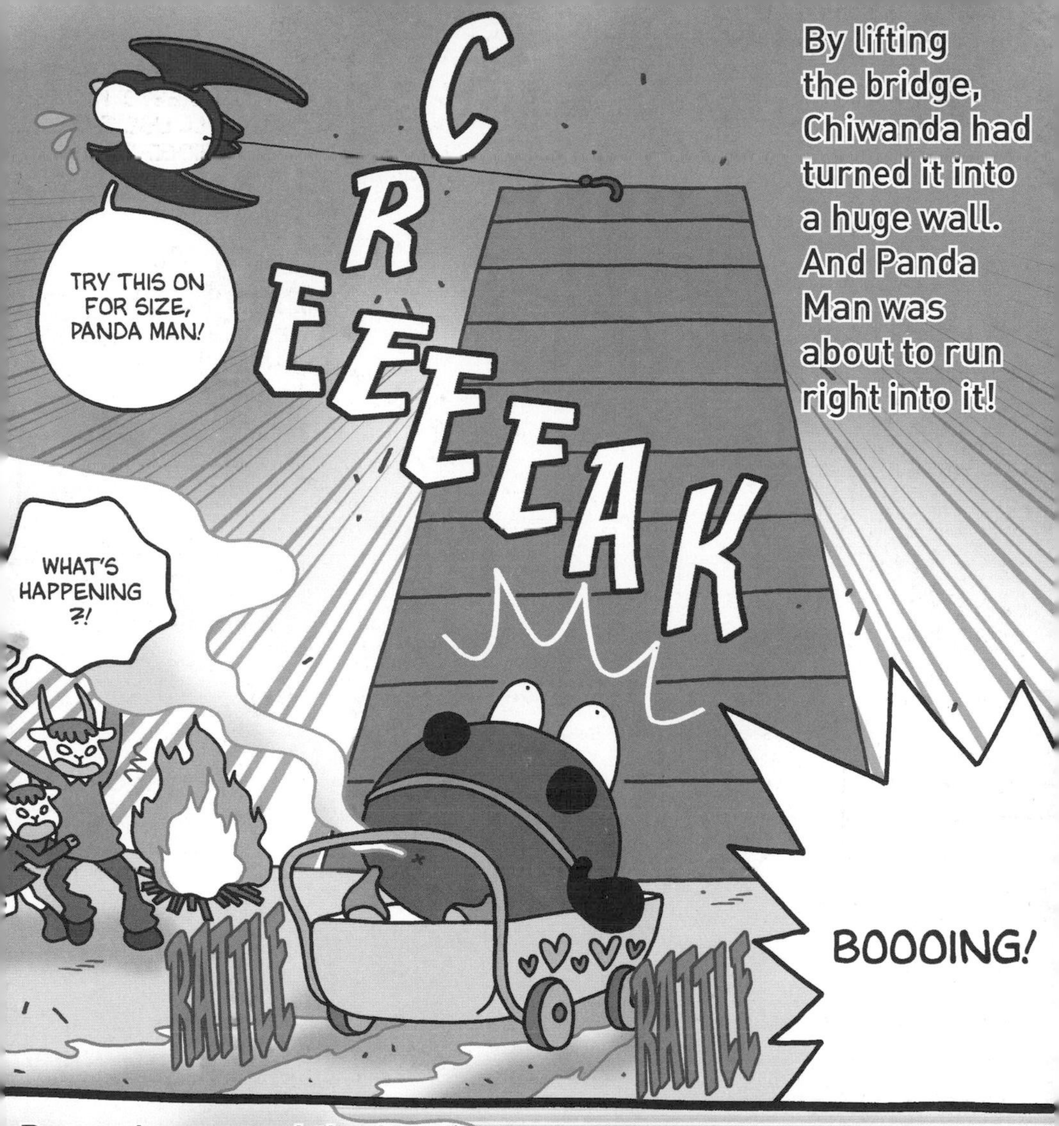
By lifting the bridge, Chiwanda had turned it into a huge wall. And Panda Man was about to run right into it!
CREEEEEAK
TRY THIS ON FOR SIZE, PANDA MAN!
BOOOING!
WHAT'S HAPPENING ?!
RATTLE
RATTLE

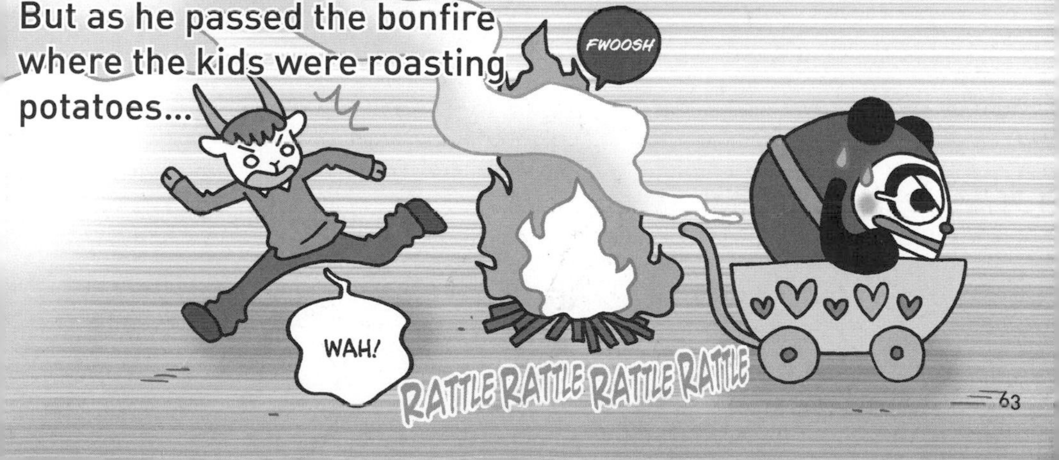
But as he passed the bonfire where the kids were roasting potatoes...
FWOOSH
WAH!
RATTLE RATTLE RATTLE RATTLE

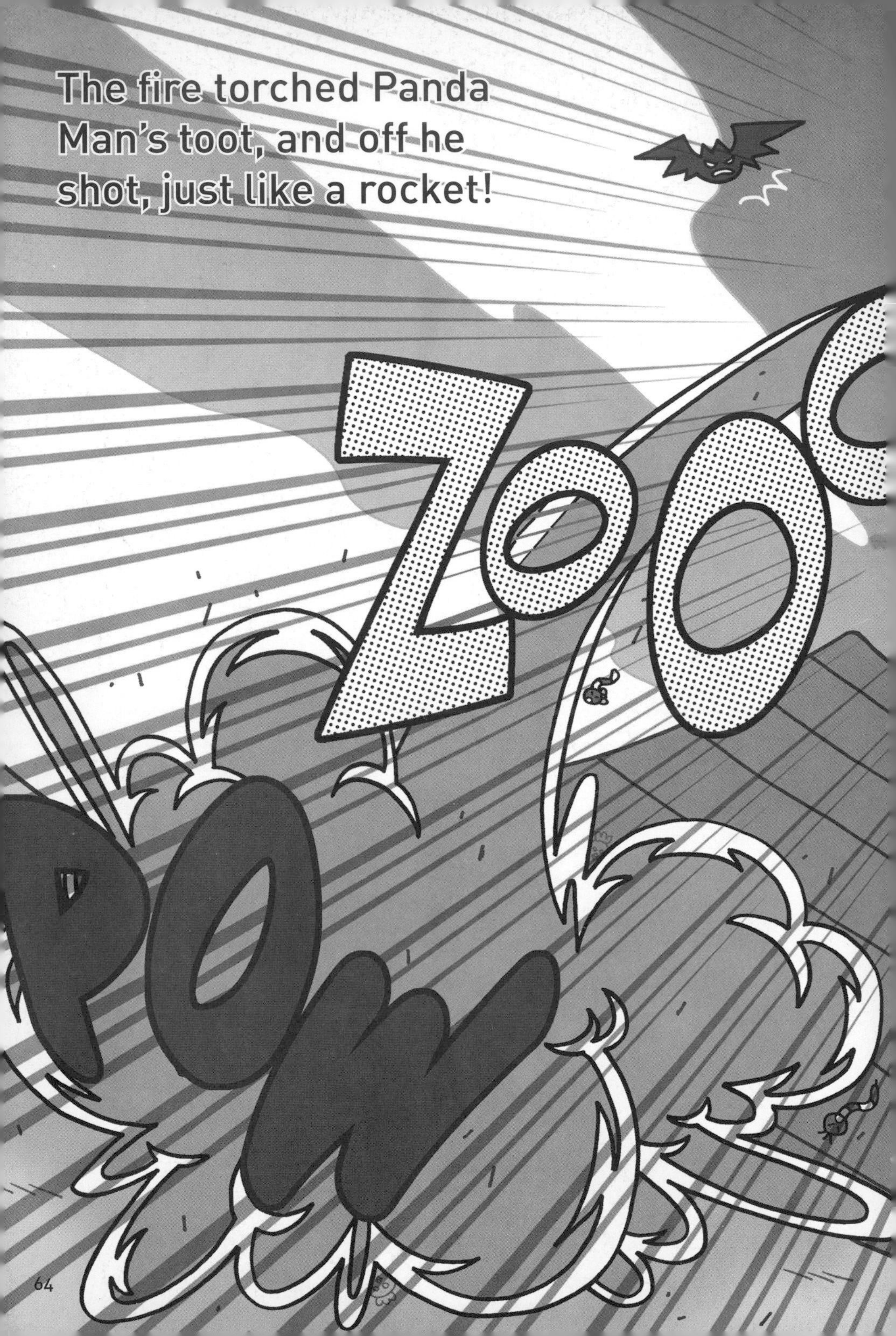
The fire torched Panda Man's toot, and off he shot, just like a rocket!
ZOO
POW

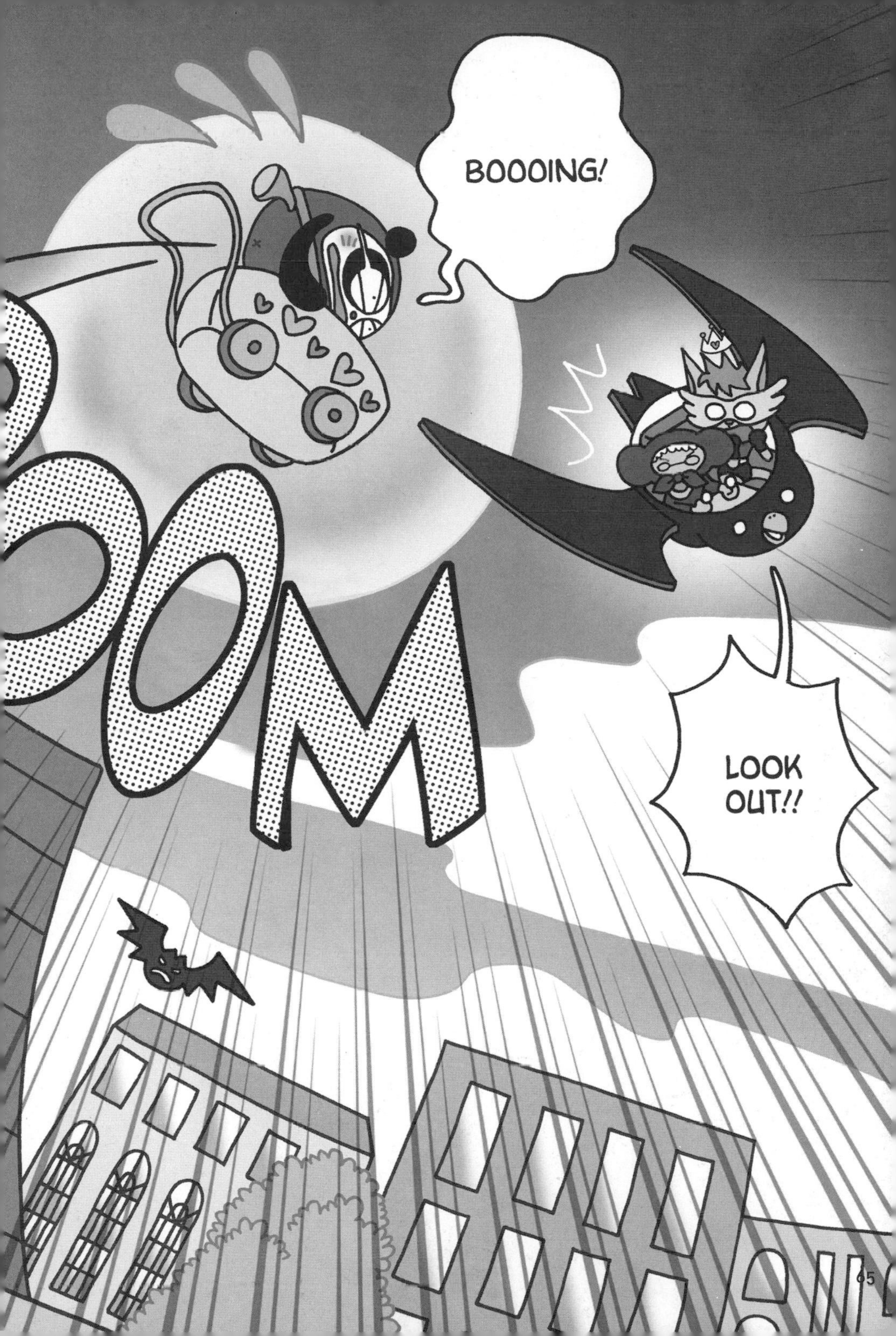
BOOOING!
BOOM
LOOK OUT!!

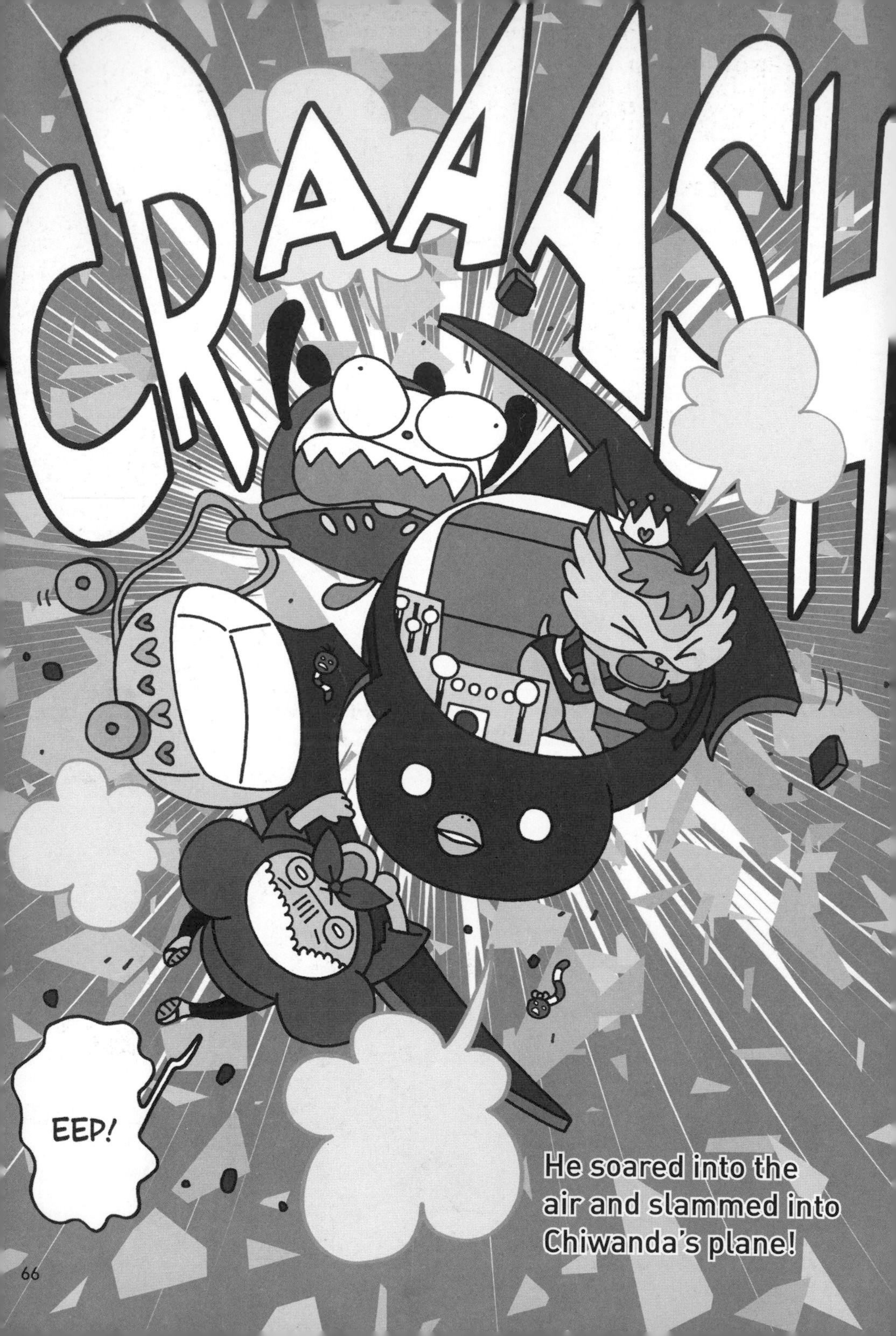
CRAAASH
EEP!
He soared into the air and slammed into Chiwanda's plane!

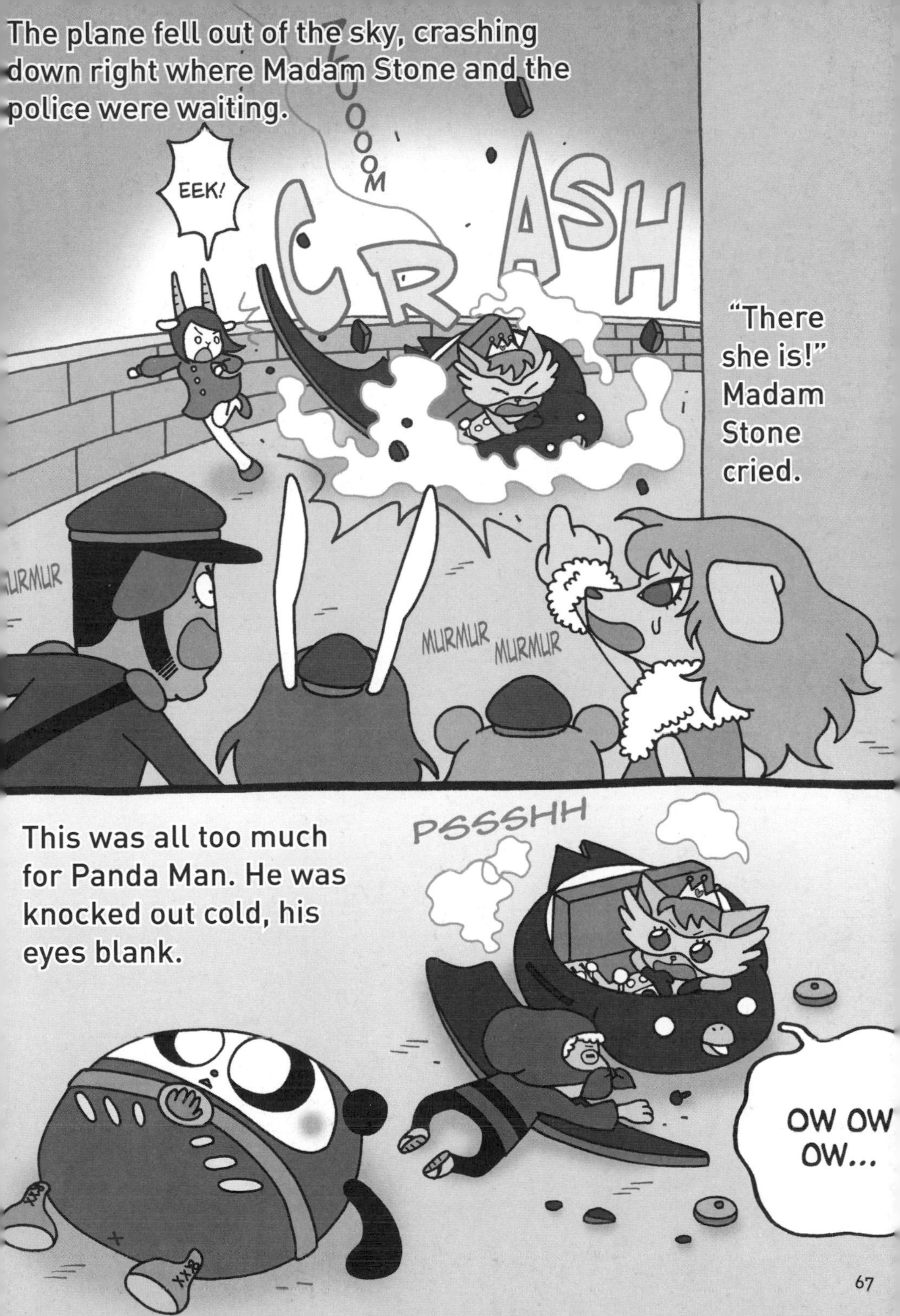
The plane fell out of the sky, crashing down right where Madam Stone and the police were waiting.
ZOOOOOM
EEK!
CRASH
"There she is!" Madam Stone cried.
URMUR
MURMUR MURMUR
This was all too much for Panda Man. He was knocked out cold, his eyes blank.
PSSSHH
OW OW OW...

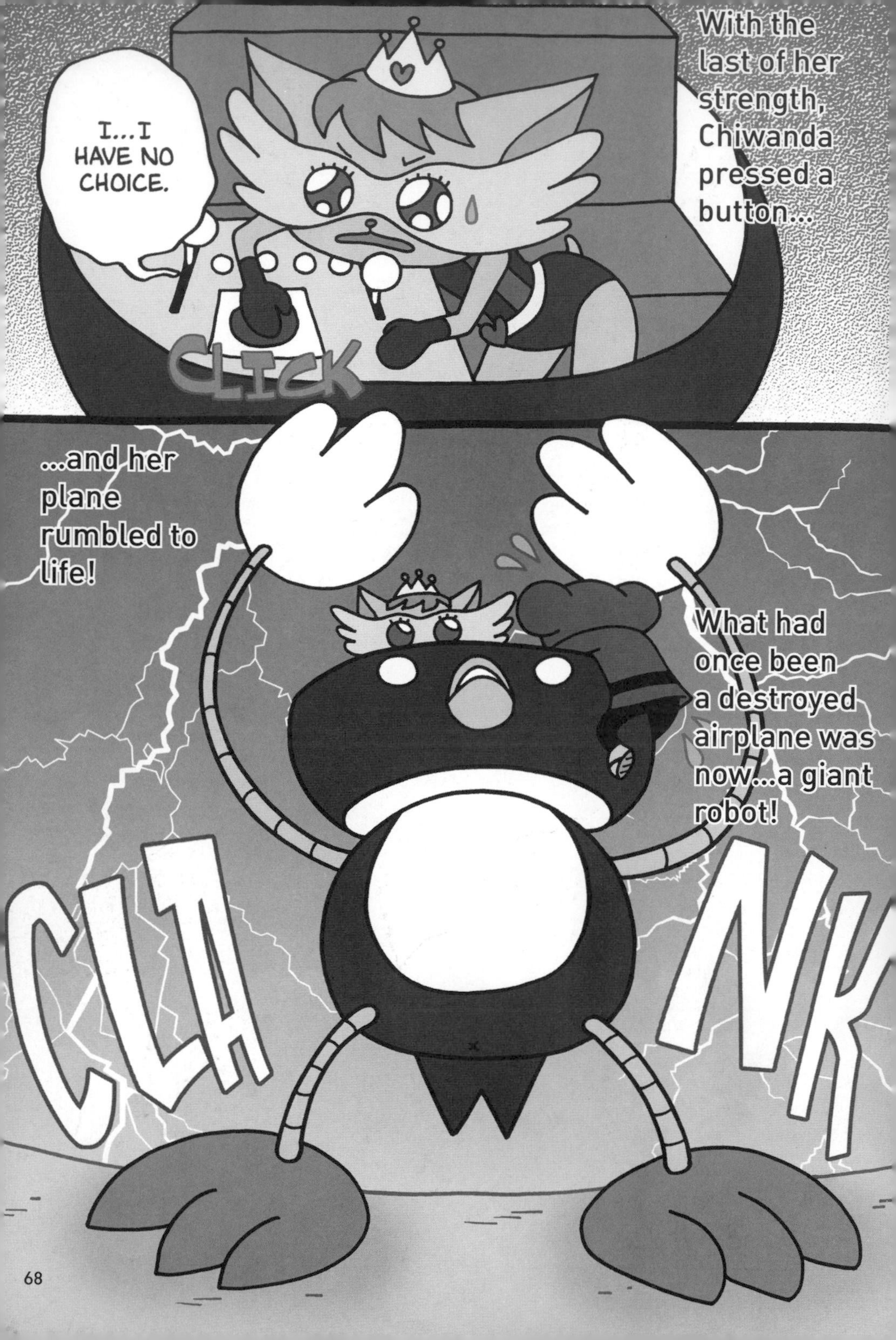
With the last of her strength, Chiwanda pressed a button...
I...I HAVE NO CHOICE.
CLICK
...and her plane rumbled to life!
What had once been a destroyed airplane was now...a giant robot!
CLANK

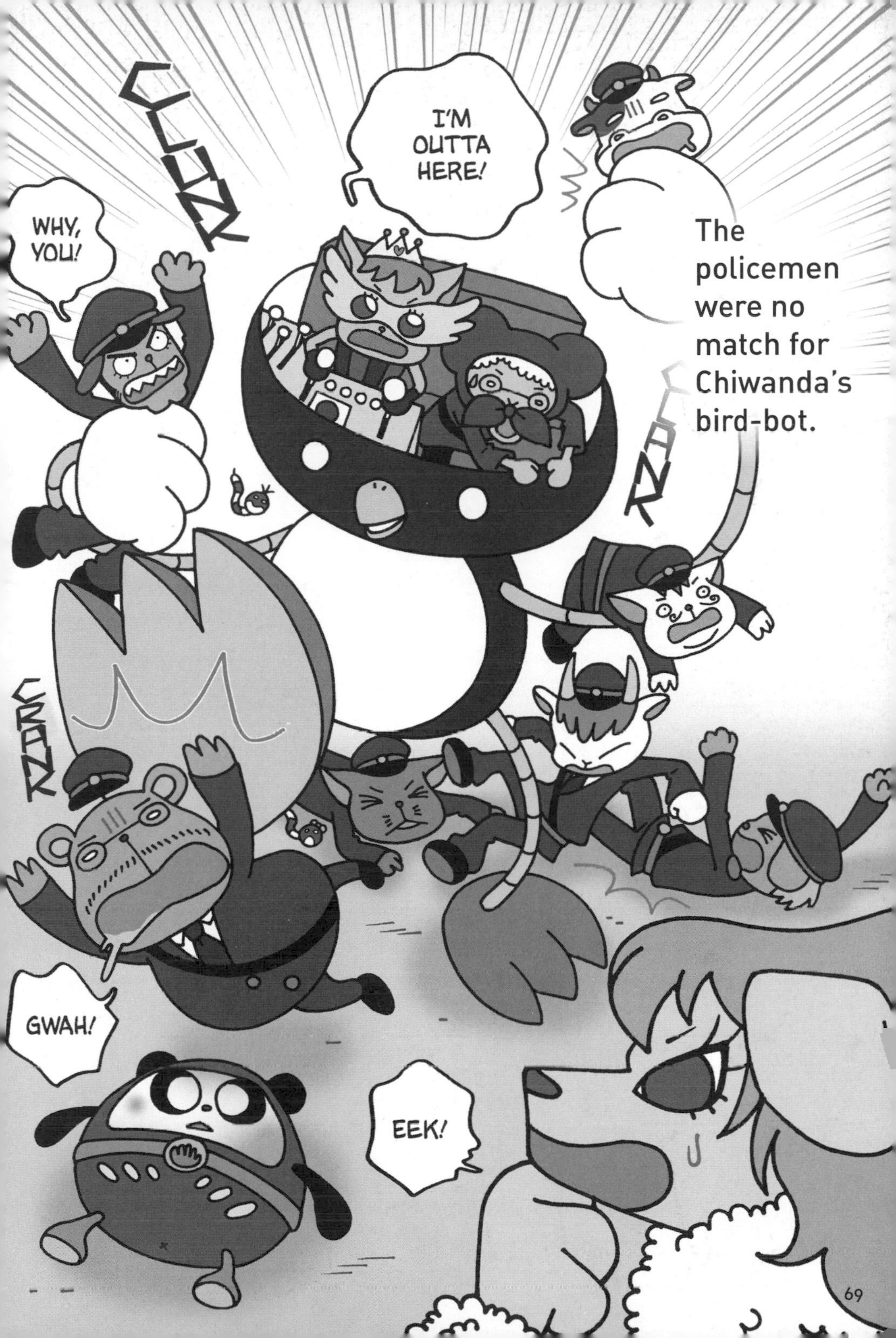
The policemen were no match for Chiwanda's bird-bot.
I'M OUTTA HERE!
WHY, YOU!
EEK!
GWAH!

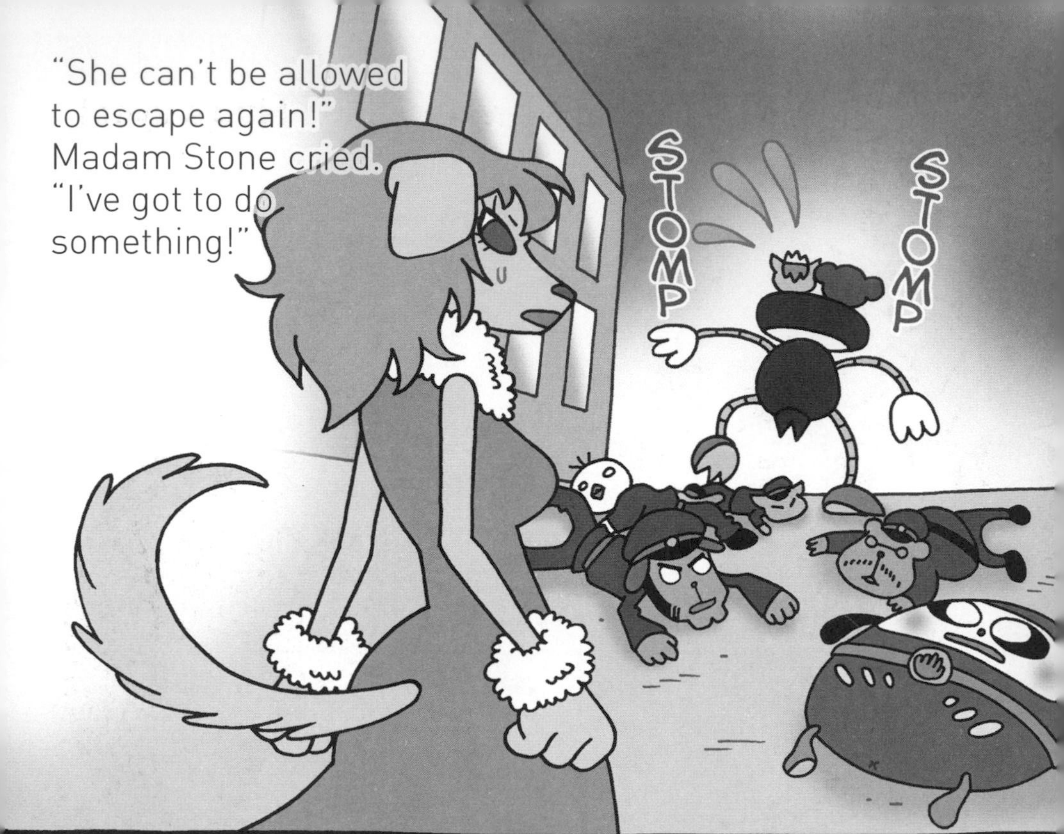
"She can't be allowed to escape again!" Madam Stone cried. "I've got to do something!"
STOMP
STOMP

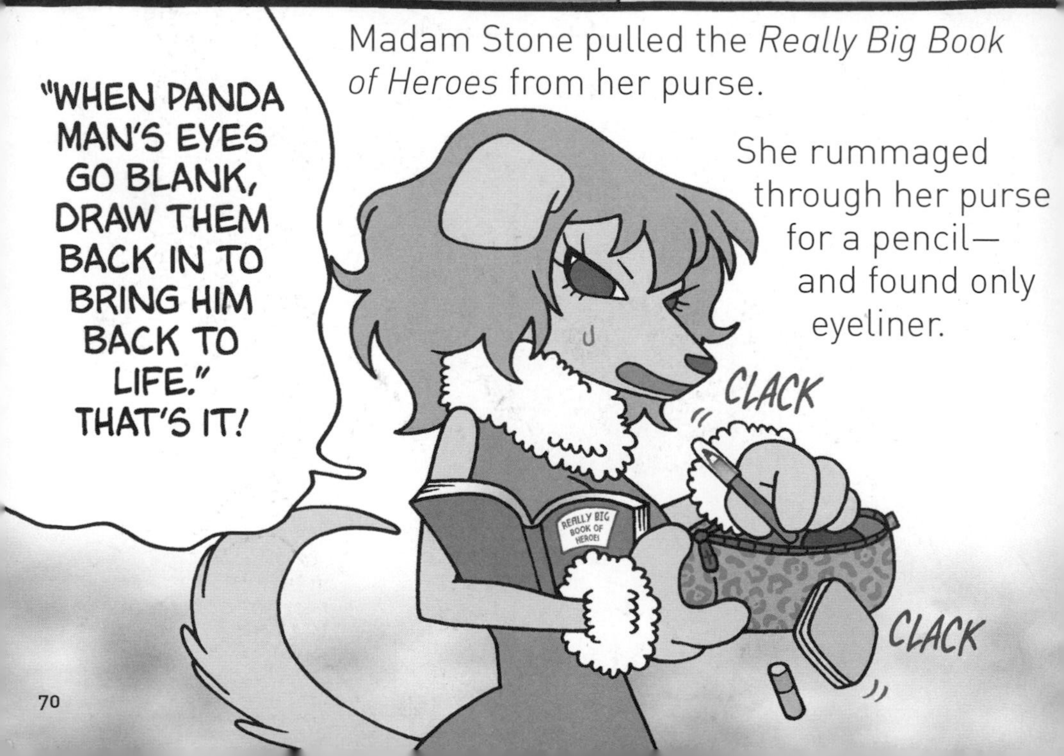
Madam Stone pulled the *Really Big Book of Heroes* from her purse.
She rummaged through her purse for a pencil— and found only eyeliner.
CLACK
CLACK
REALLY BIG BOOK OF HEROES
"WHEN PANDA MAN'S EYES GO BLANK, DRAW THEM BACK IN TO BRING HIM BACK TO LIFE." THAT'S IT!

It's up to you! Draw in Panda Man's eyes!

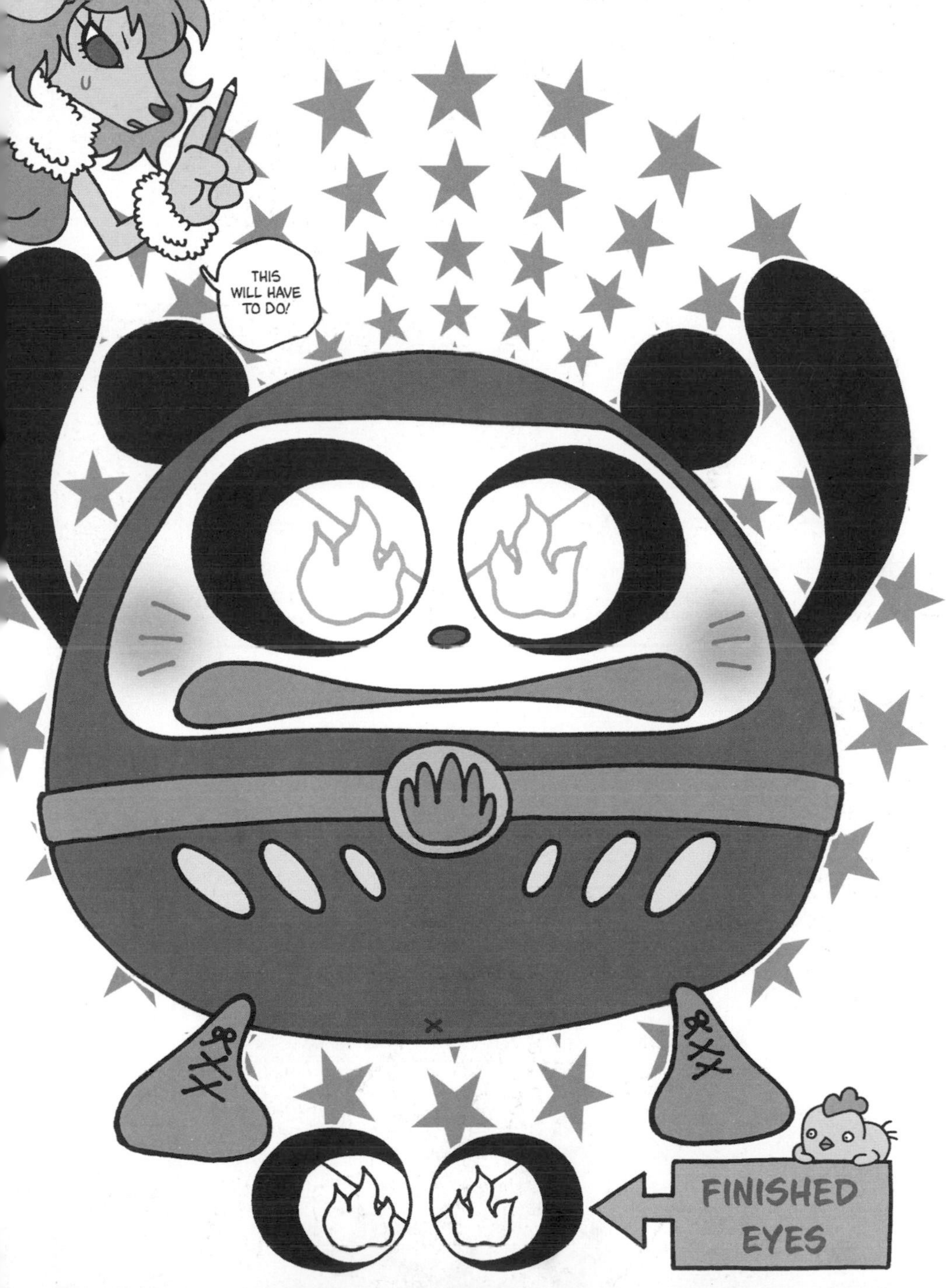
THIS WILL HAVE TO DO!
FINISHED EYES

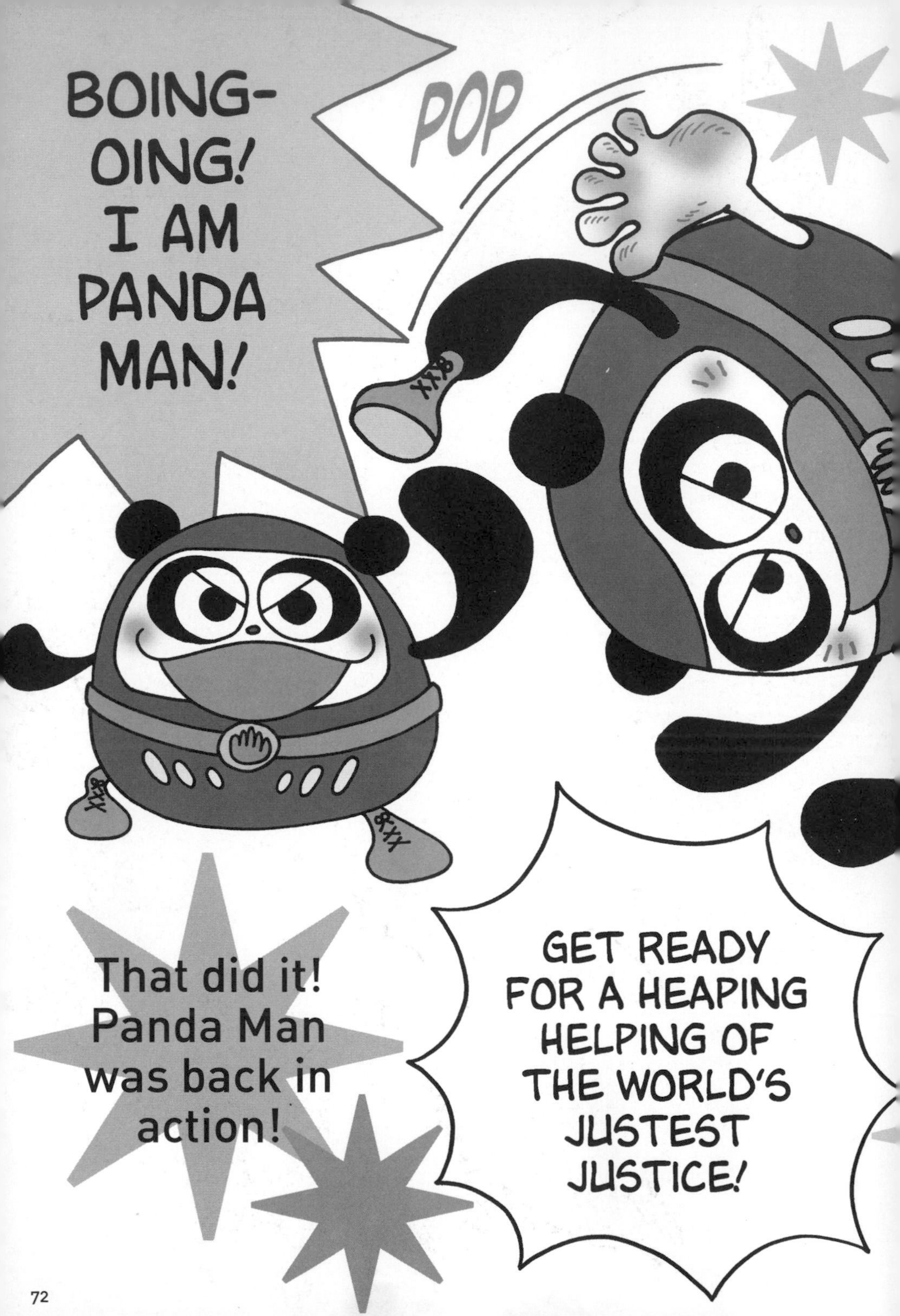
BOING-OING! I AM PANDA MAN!
POP
That did it! Panda Man was back in action!
GET READY FOR A HEAPING HELPING OF THE WORLD'S JUSTEST JUSTICE!

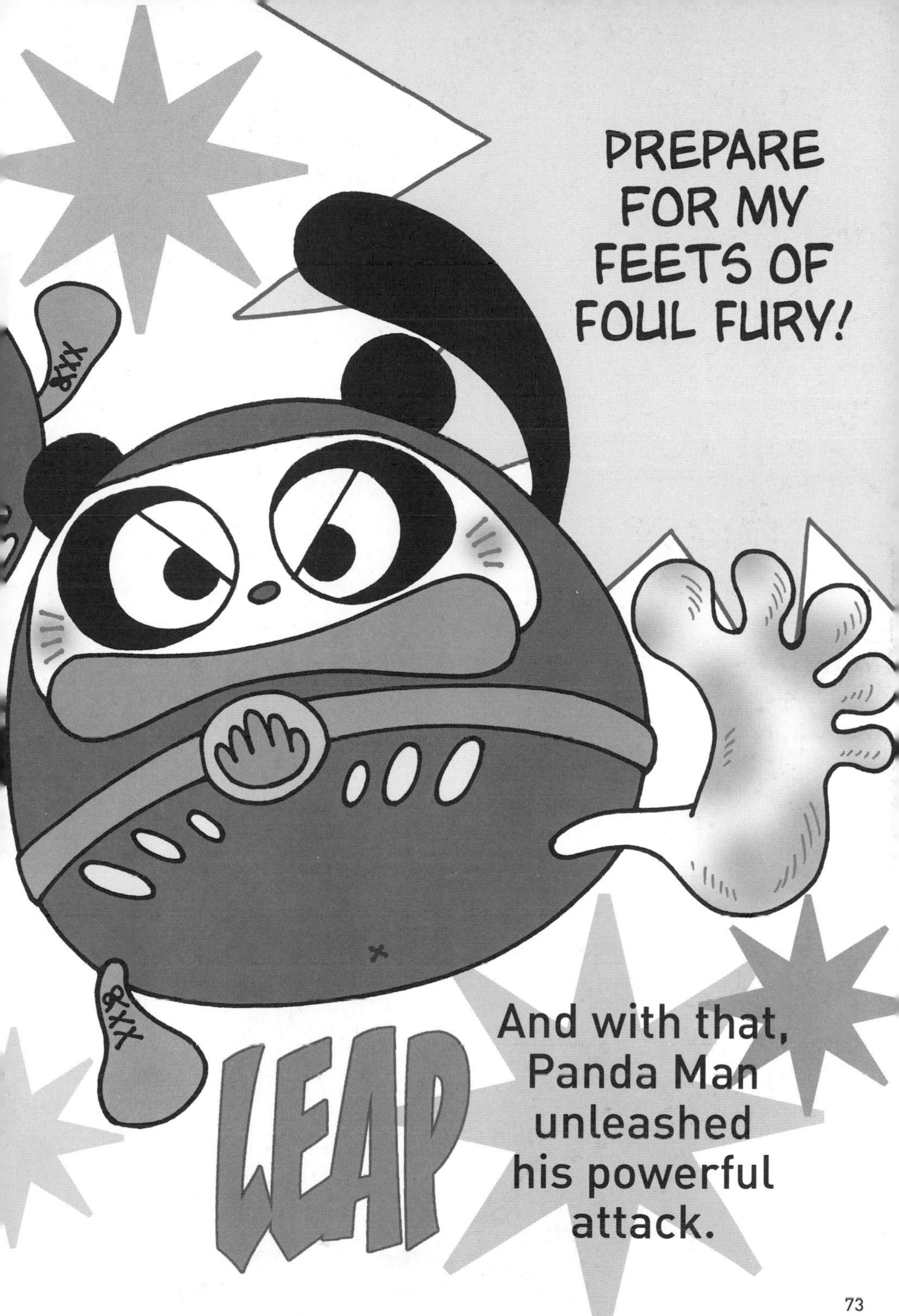
PREPARE FOR MY FEETS OF FOUL FURY!
LEAP
And with that, Panda Man unleashed his powerful attack.

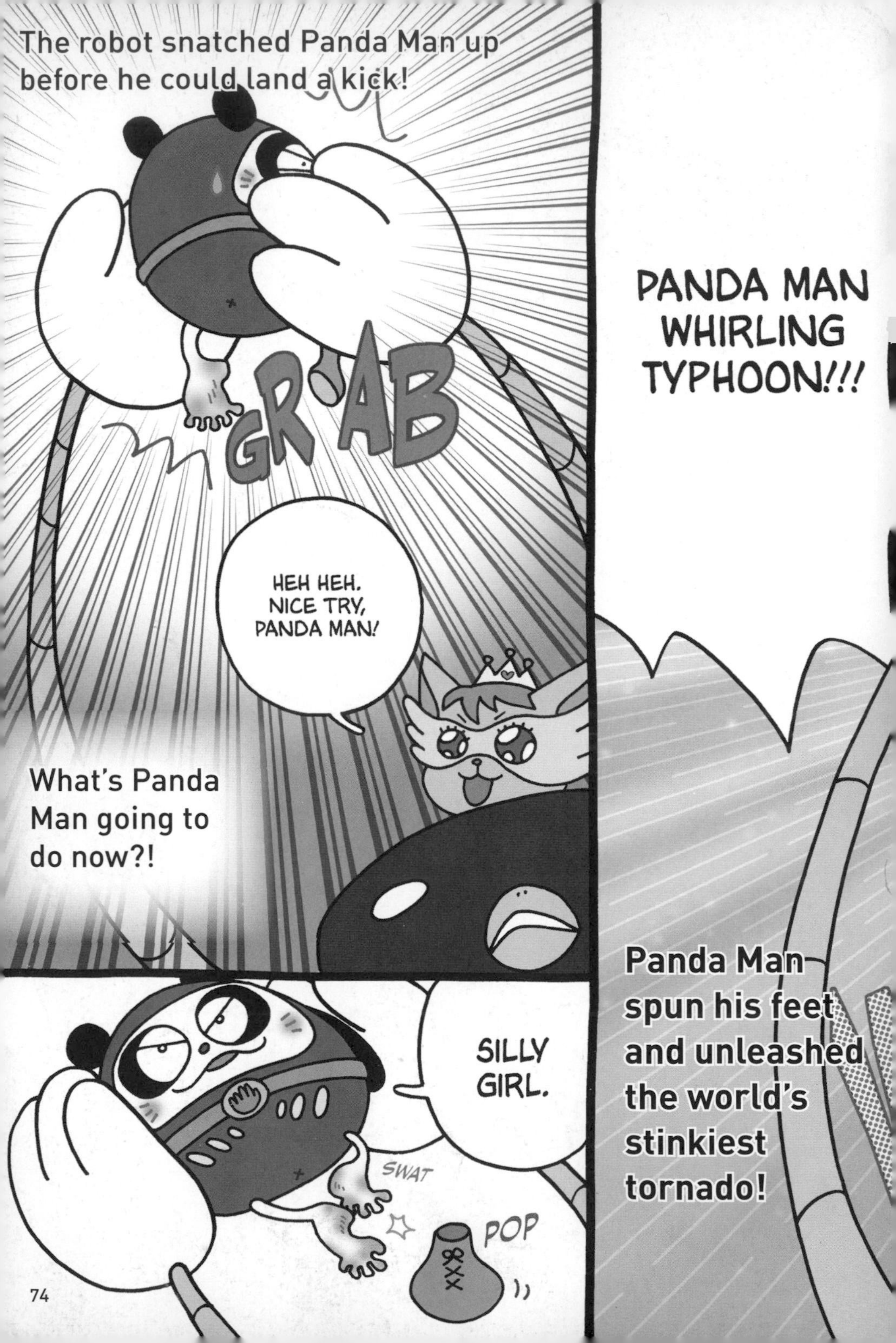
The robot snatched Panda Man up before he could land a kick!
GRAB
HEH HEH. NICE TRY, PANDA MAN!
What's Panda Man going to do now?!
SILLY GIRL.
SWAT
POP
PANDA MAN WHIRLING TYPHOON!!!
Panda Man spun his feet and unleashed the world's stinkiest tornado!

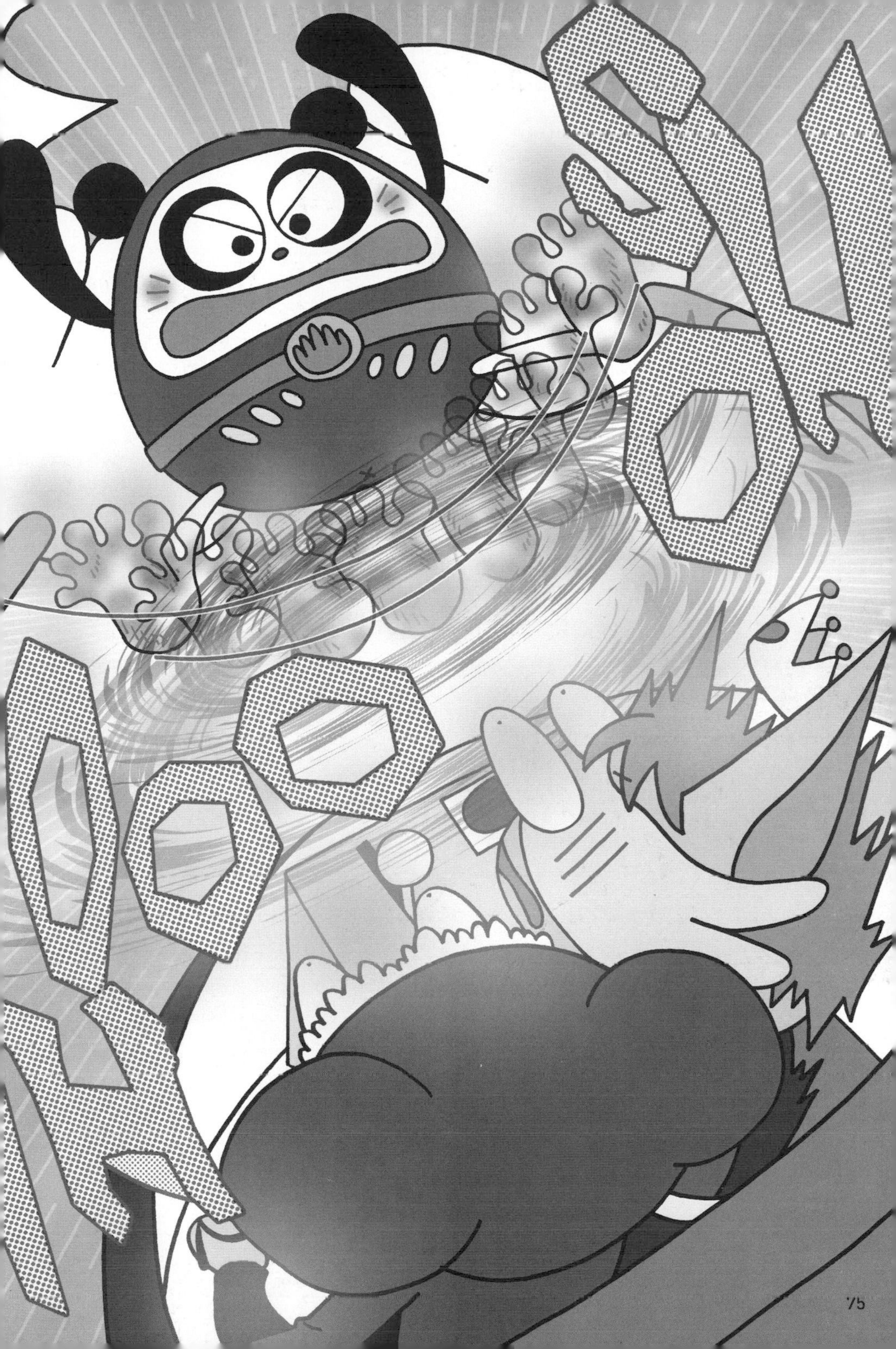

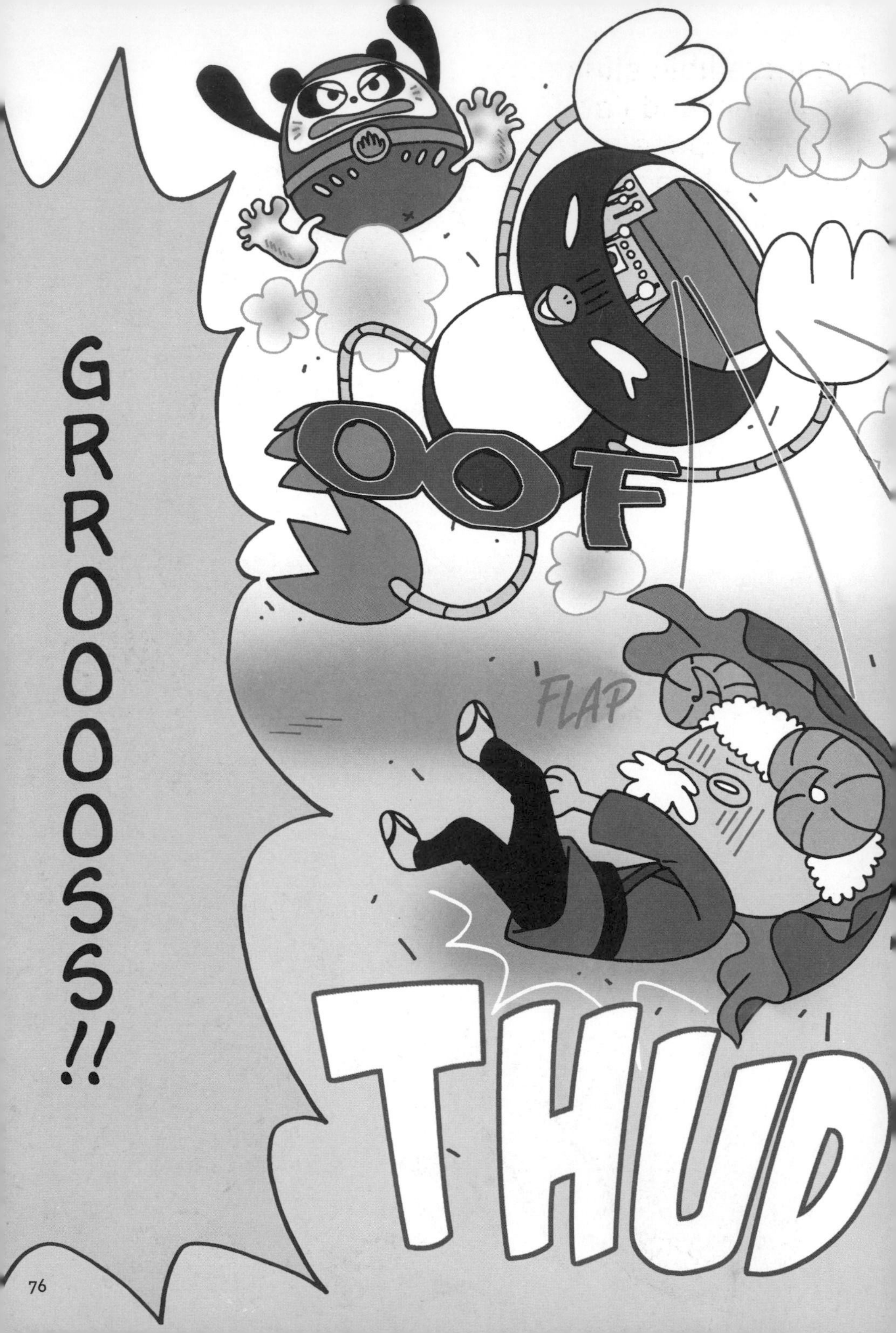
OOF
FLAP
THUD
GRROOOOSS!!

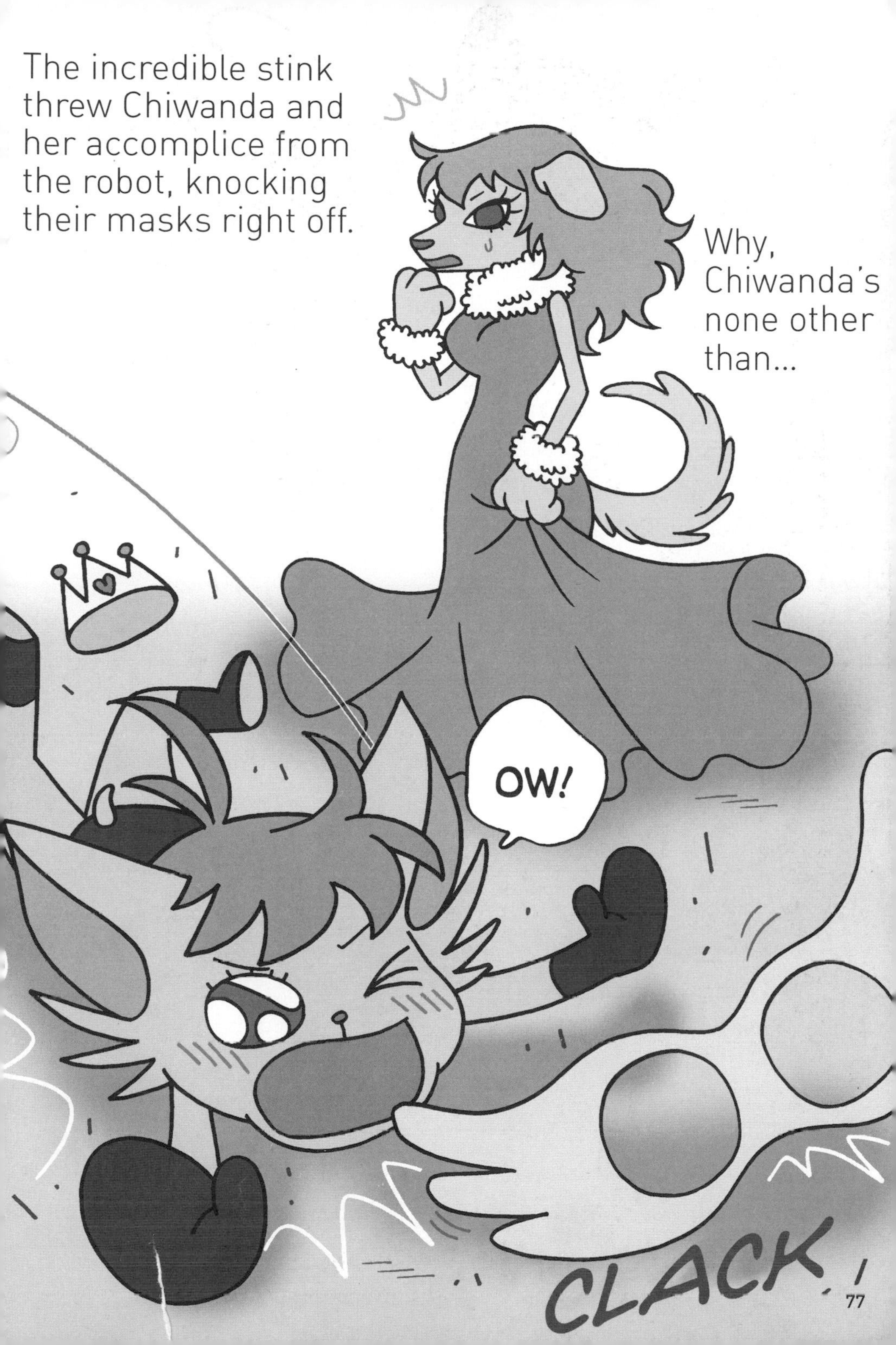
The incredible stink threw Chiwanda and her accomplice from the robot, knocking their masks right off.
Why, Chiwanda's none other than...
OW!
CLACK

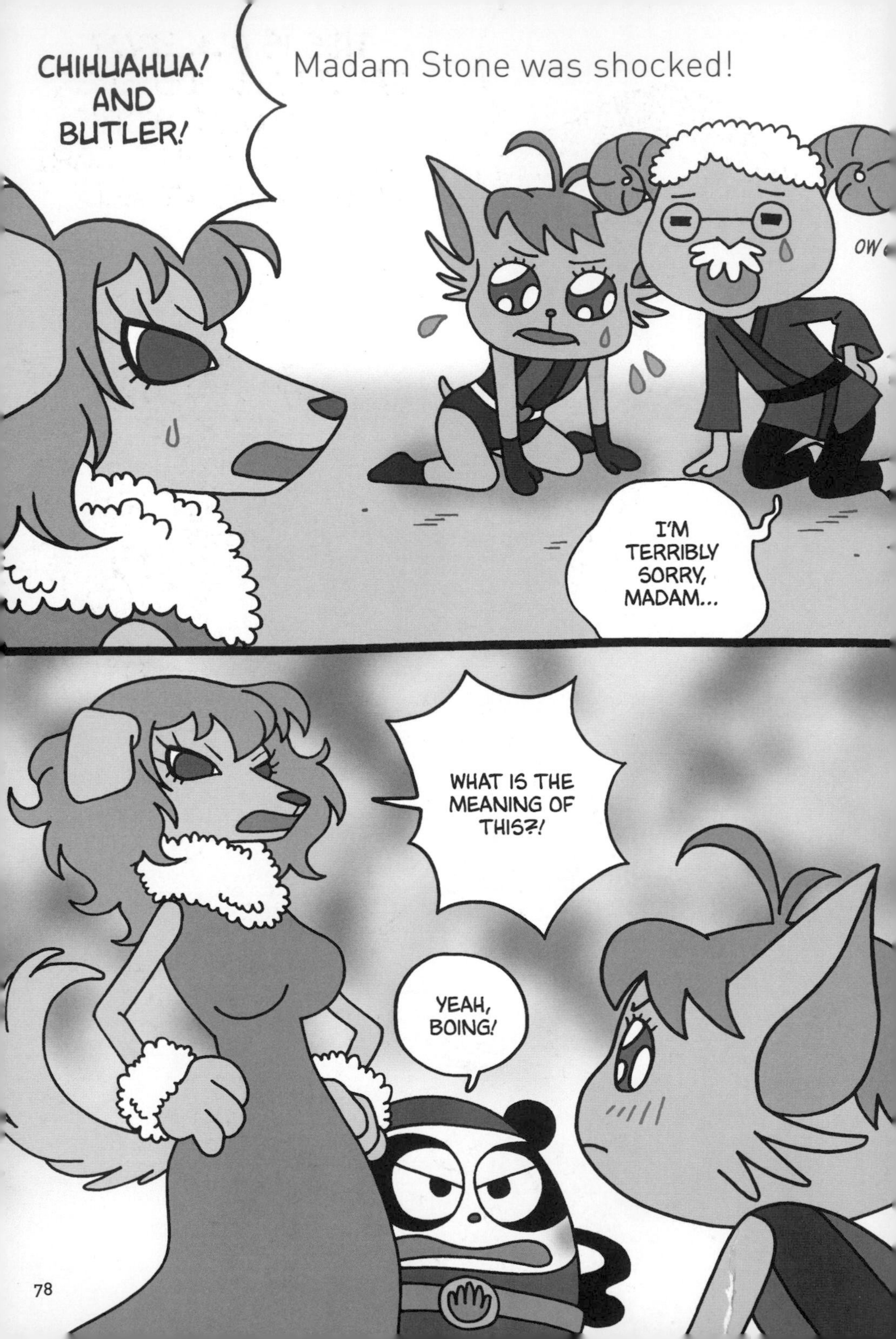
Madam Stone was shocked!
CHIHUAHUA! AND BUTLER!
OW
I'M TERRIBLY SORRY, MADAM...
WHAT IS THE MEANING OF THIS?!
YEAH, BOING!

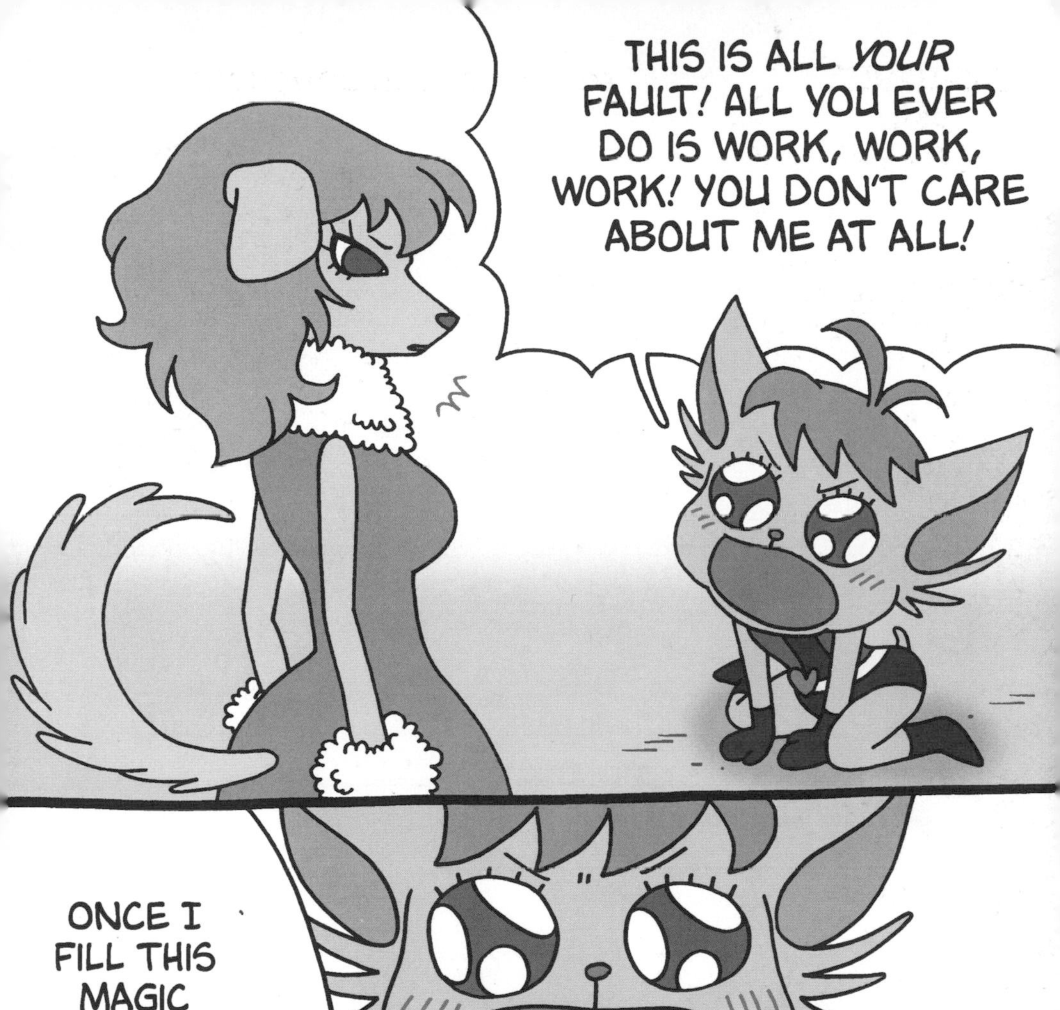
THIS IS ALL YOUR FAULT! ALL YOU EVER DO IS WORK, WORK, WORK! YOU DON'T CARE ABOUT ME AT ALL!

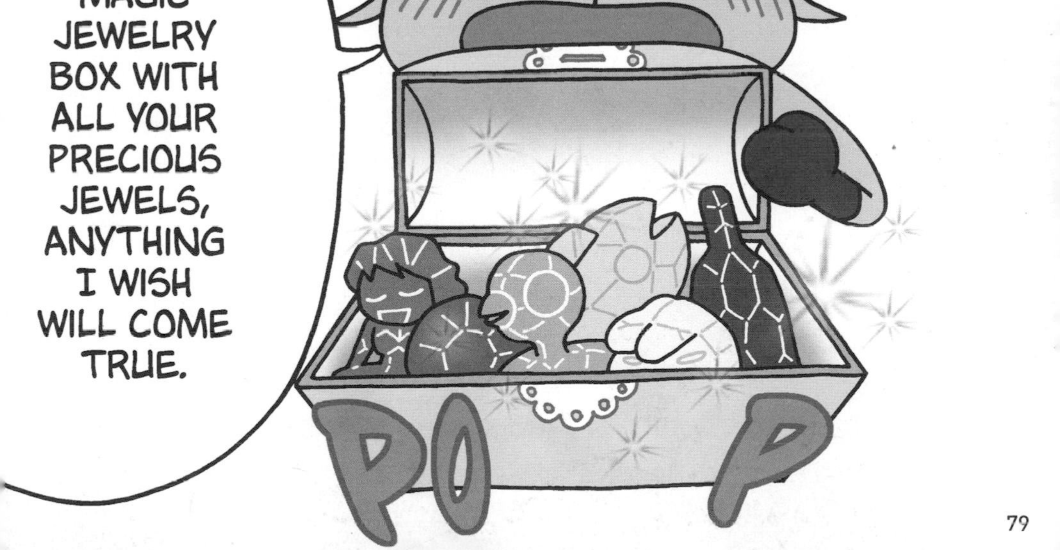
ONCE I FILL THIS MAGIC JEWELRY BOX WITH ALL YOUR PRECIOUS JEWELS, ANYTHING I WISH WILL COME TRUE.
POP

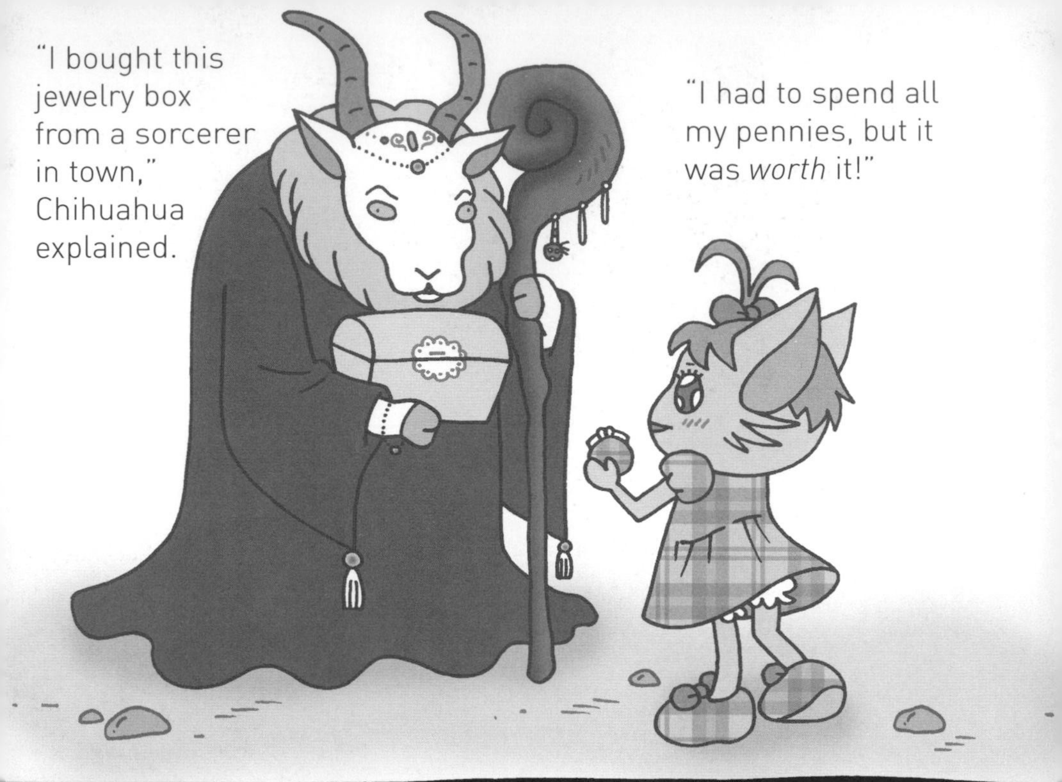
"I bought this jewelry box from a sorcerer in town," Chihuahua explained.
"I had to spend all my pennies, but it was *worth* it!"

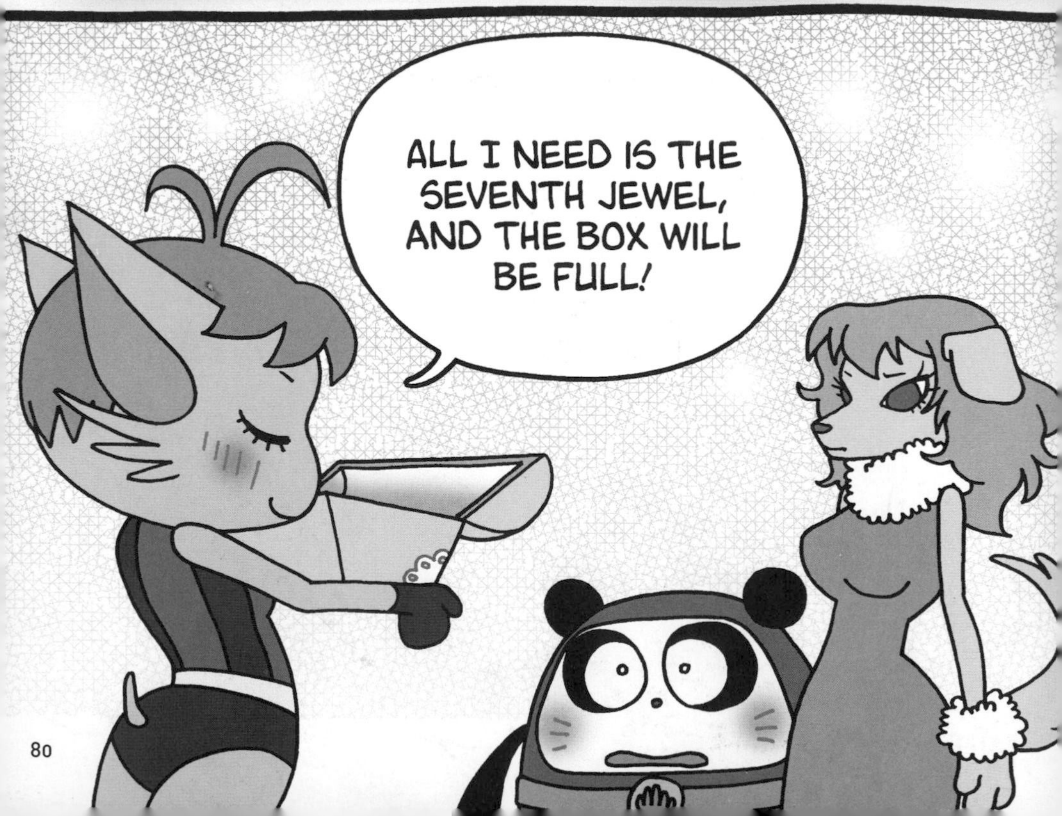
ALL I NEED IS THE SEVENTH JEWEL, AND THE BOX WILL BE FULL!

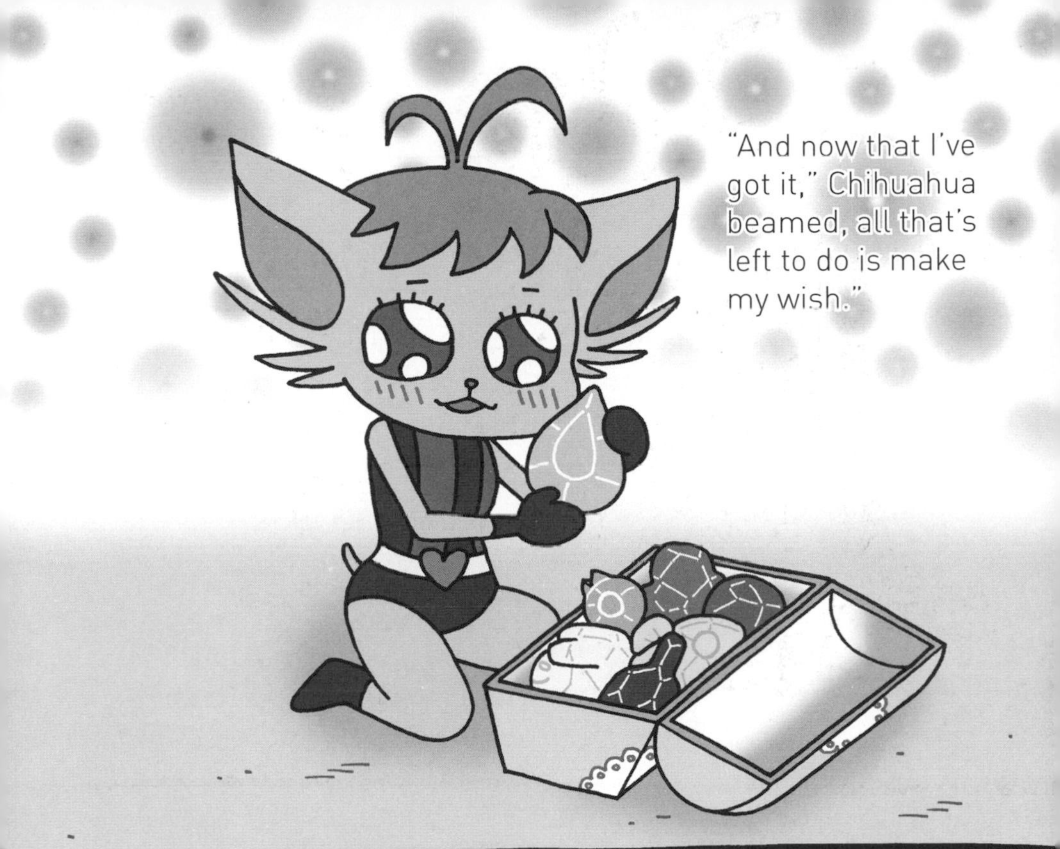
"And now that I've got it," Chihuahua beamed, all that's left to do is make my wish."

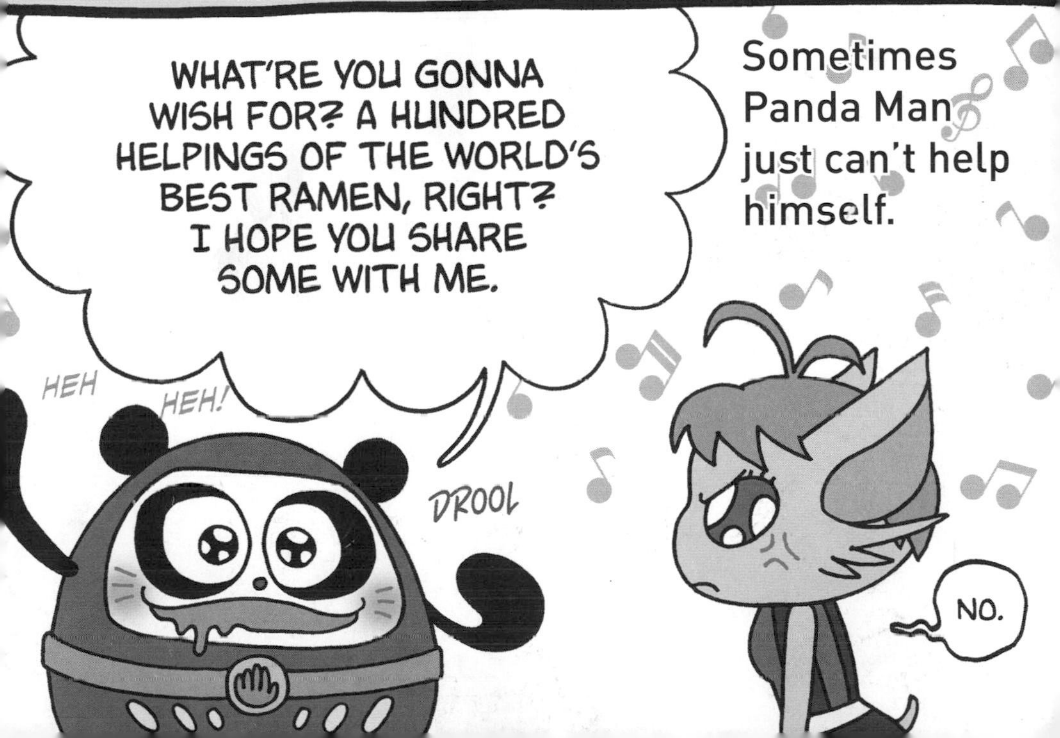
WHAT'RE YOU GONNA WISH FOR? A HUNDRED HELPINGS OF THE WORLD'S BEST RAMEN, RIGHT? I HOPE YOU SHARE SOME WITH ME.
HEH HEH!
DROOL
Sometimes Panda Man just can't help himself.
NO.

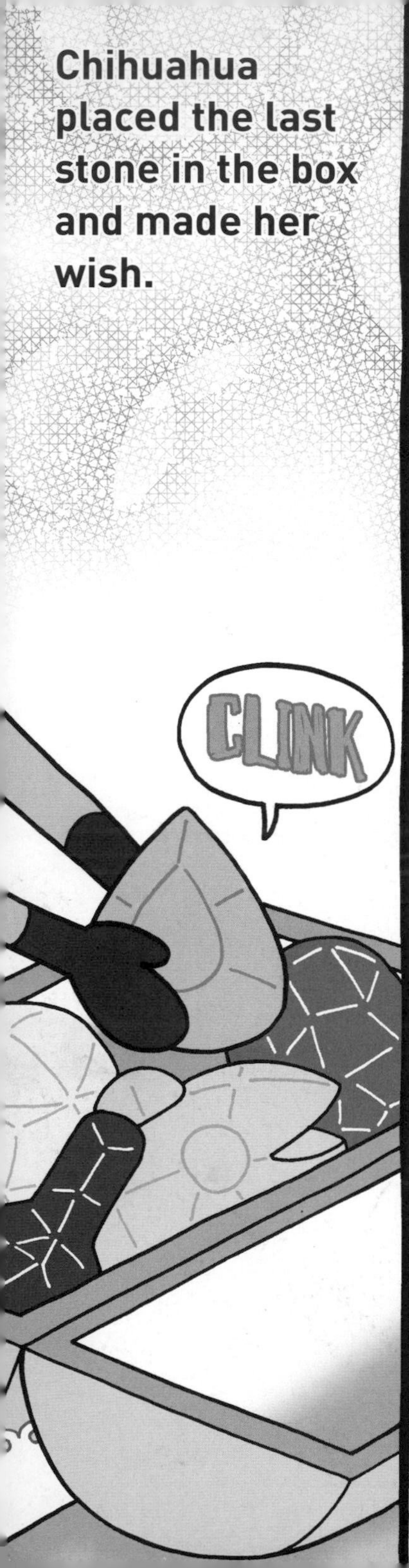
Chihuahua placed the last stone in the box and made her wish.
CLINK
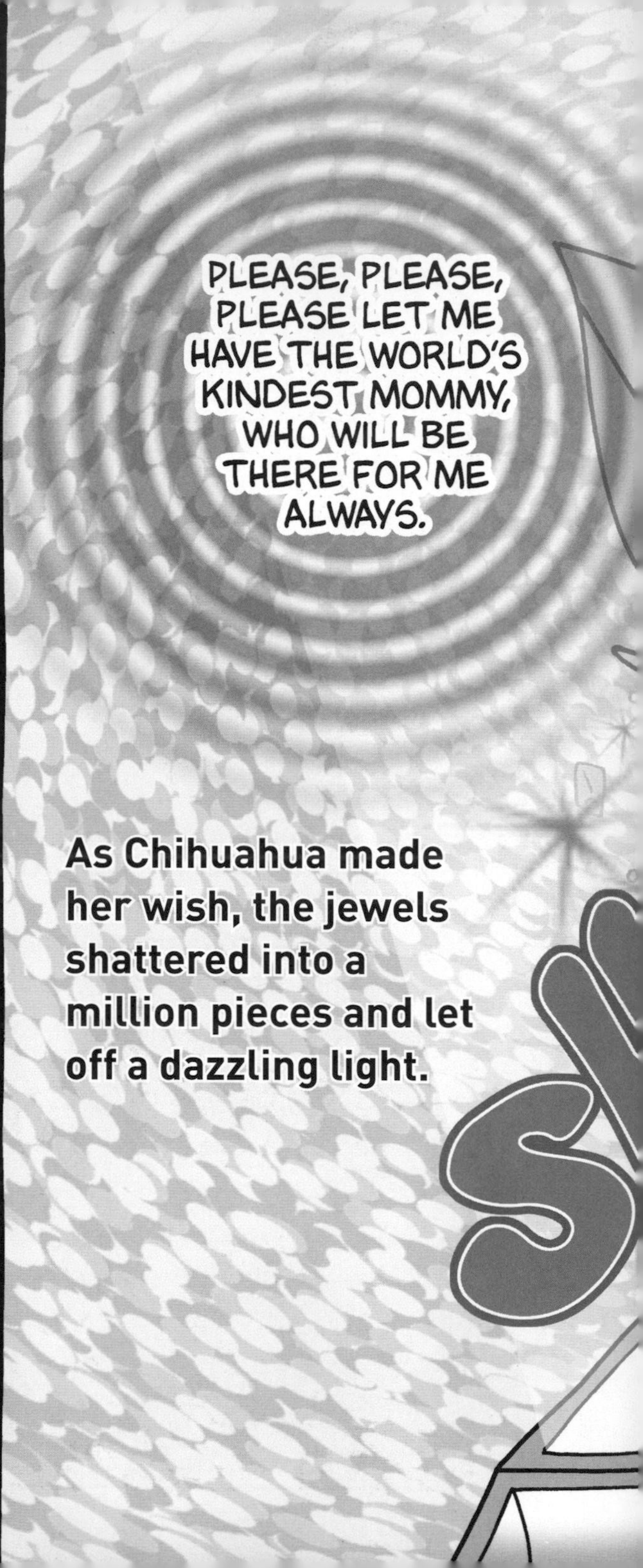
PLEASE, PLEASE, PLEASE LET ME HAVE THE WORLD'S KINDEST MOMMY, WHO WILL BE THERE FOR ME ALWAYS.
As Chihuahua made her wish, the jewels shattered into a million pieces and let off a dazzling light.

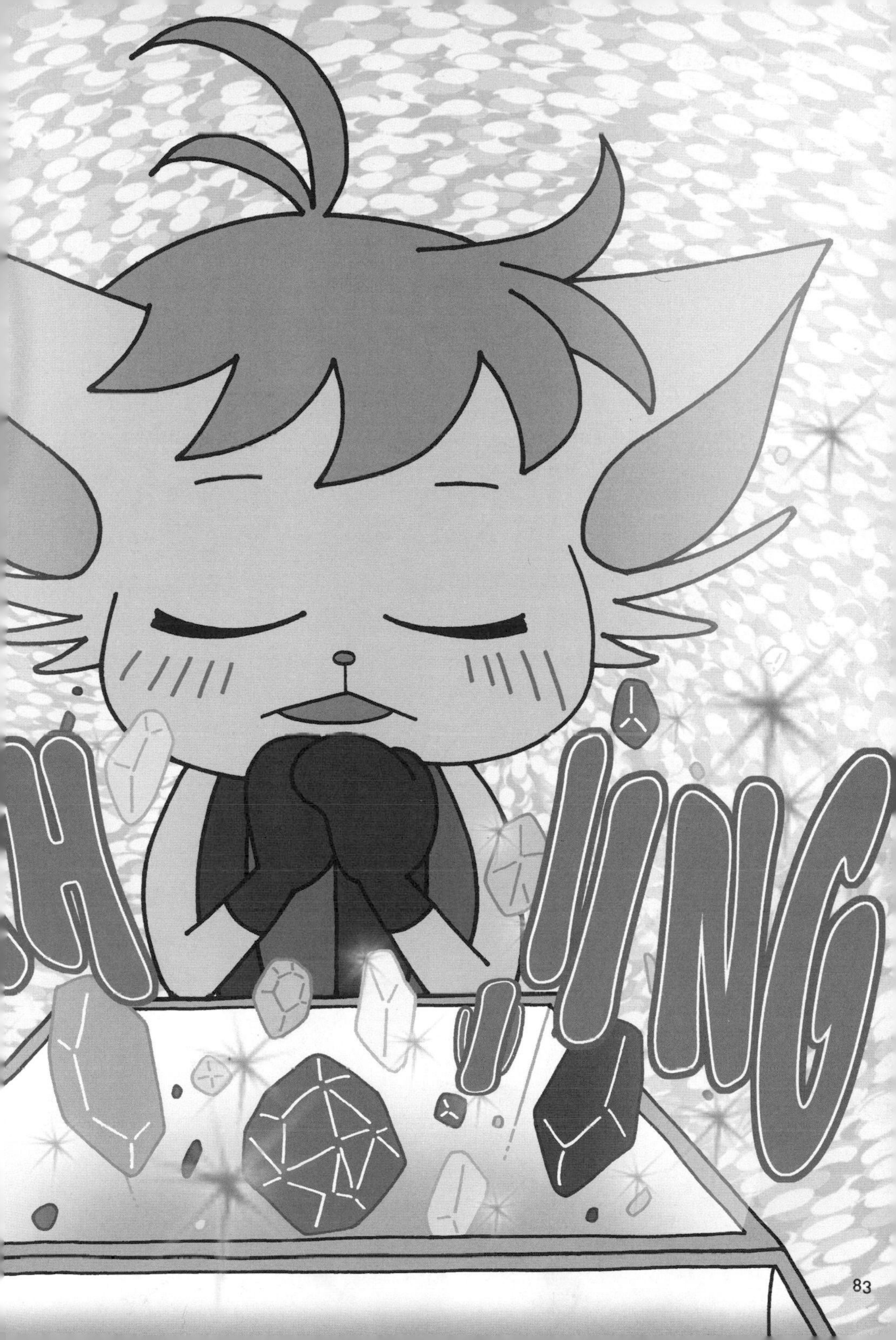
H'ING

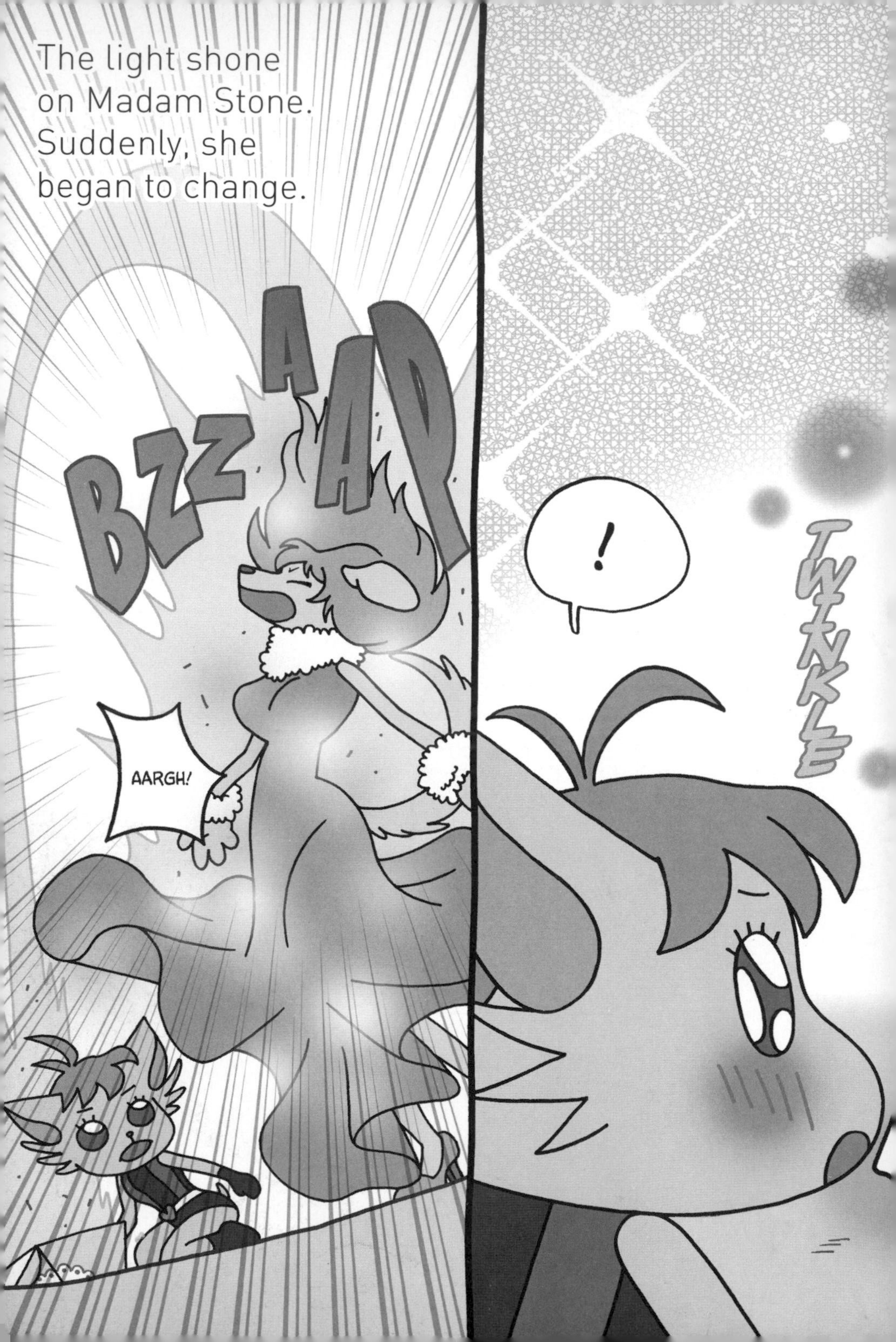
TWINKLE
!
The light shone on Madam Stone. Suddenly, she began to change.
BZZAAP
AARGH!

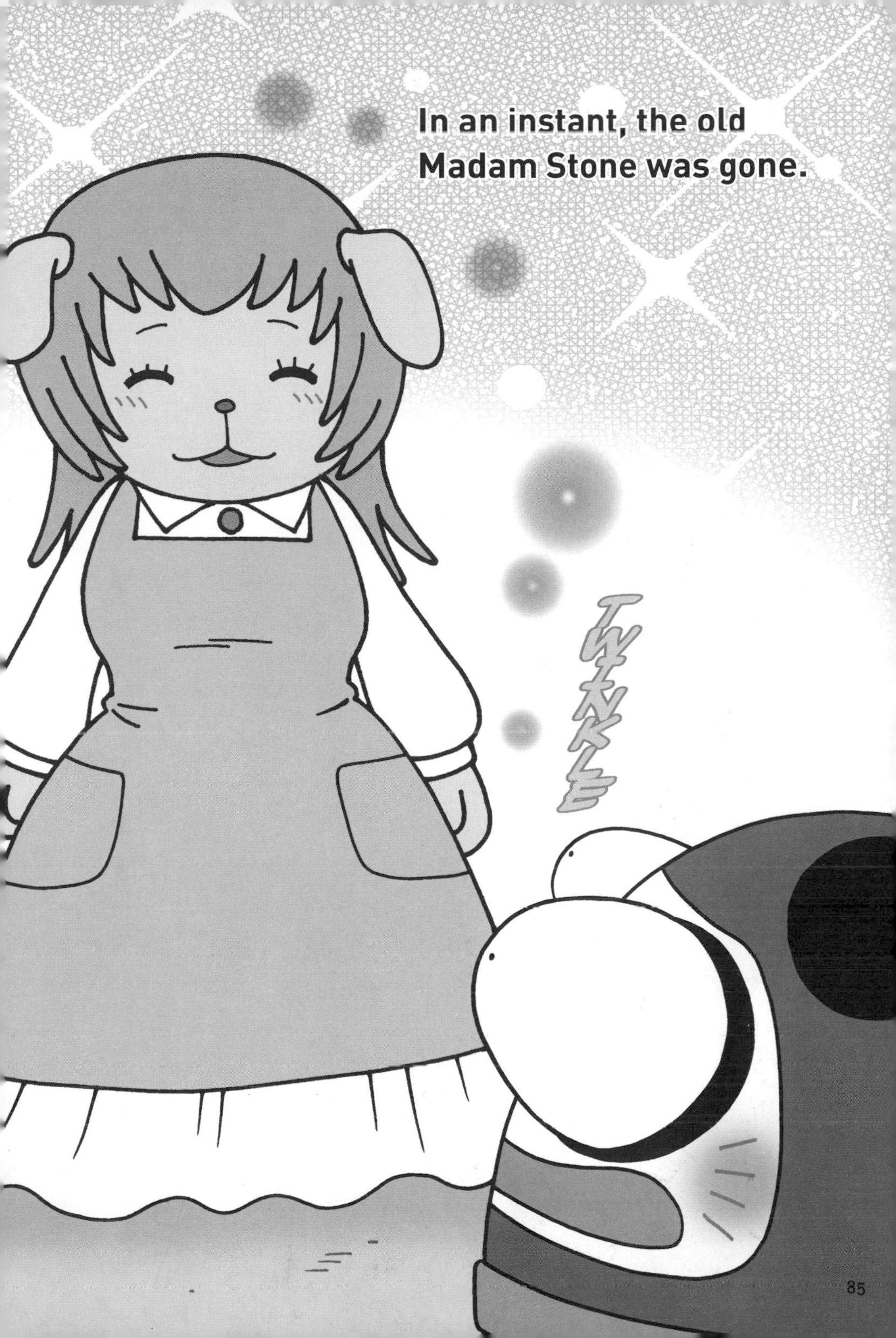
In an instant, the old Madam Stone was gone.
TWINKLE

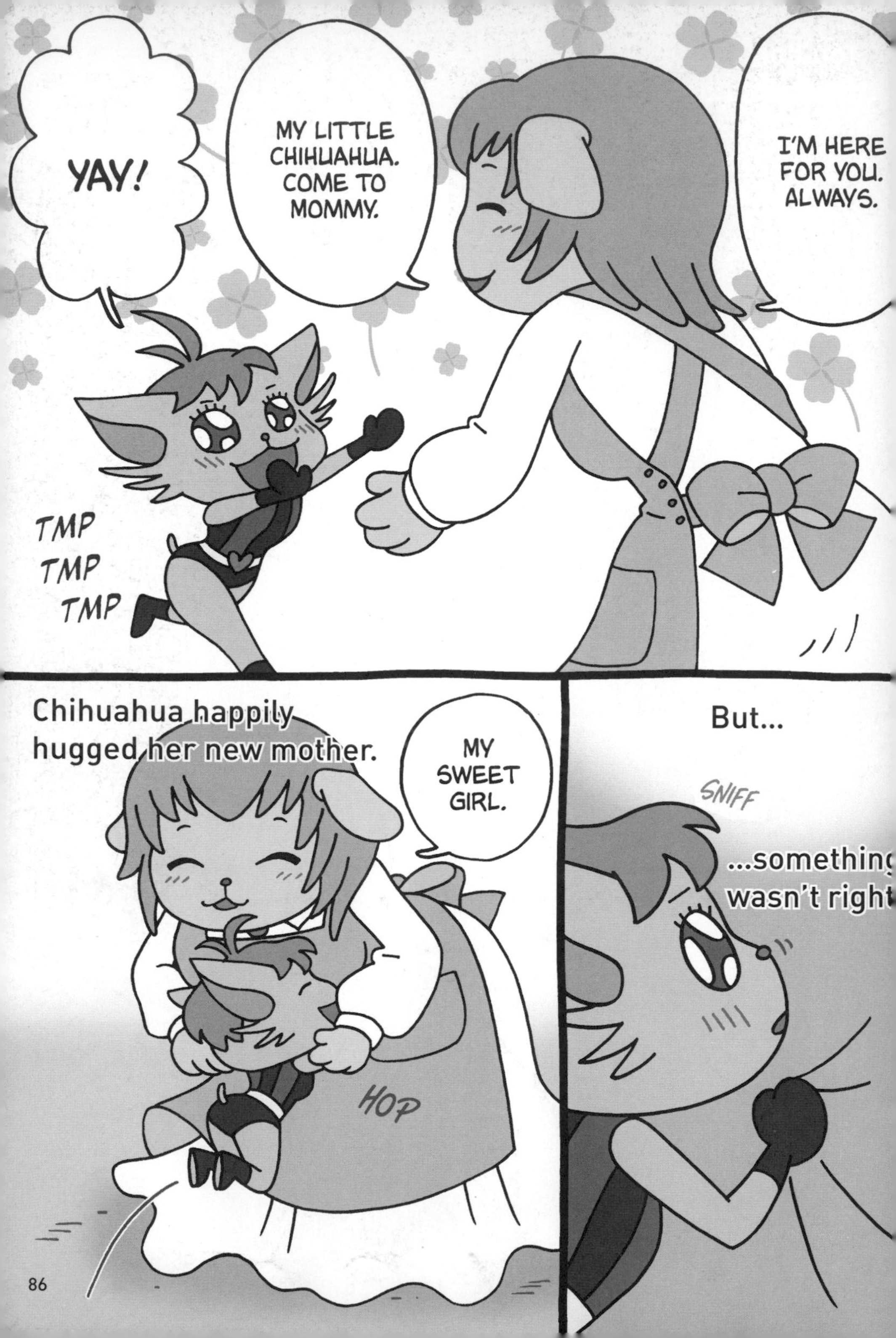
YAY!
MY LITTLE CHIHUAHUA. COME TO MOMMY.
I'M HERE FOR YOU. ALWAYS.
TMP TMP TMP
Chihuahua happily hugged her new mother.
MY SWEET GIRL.
HOP
But...
SNIFF
...somethin
wasn't righ

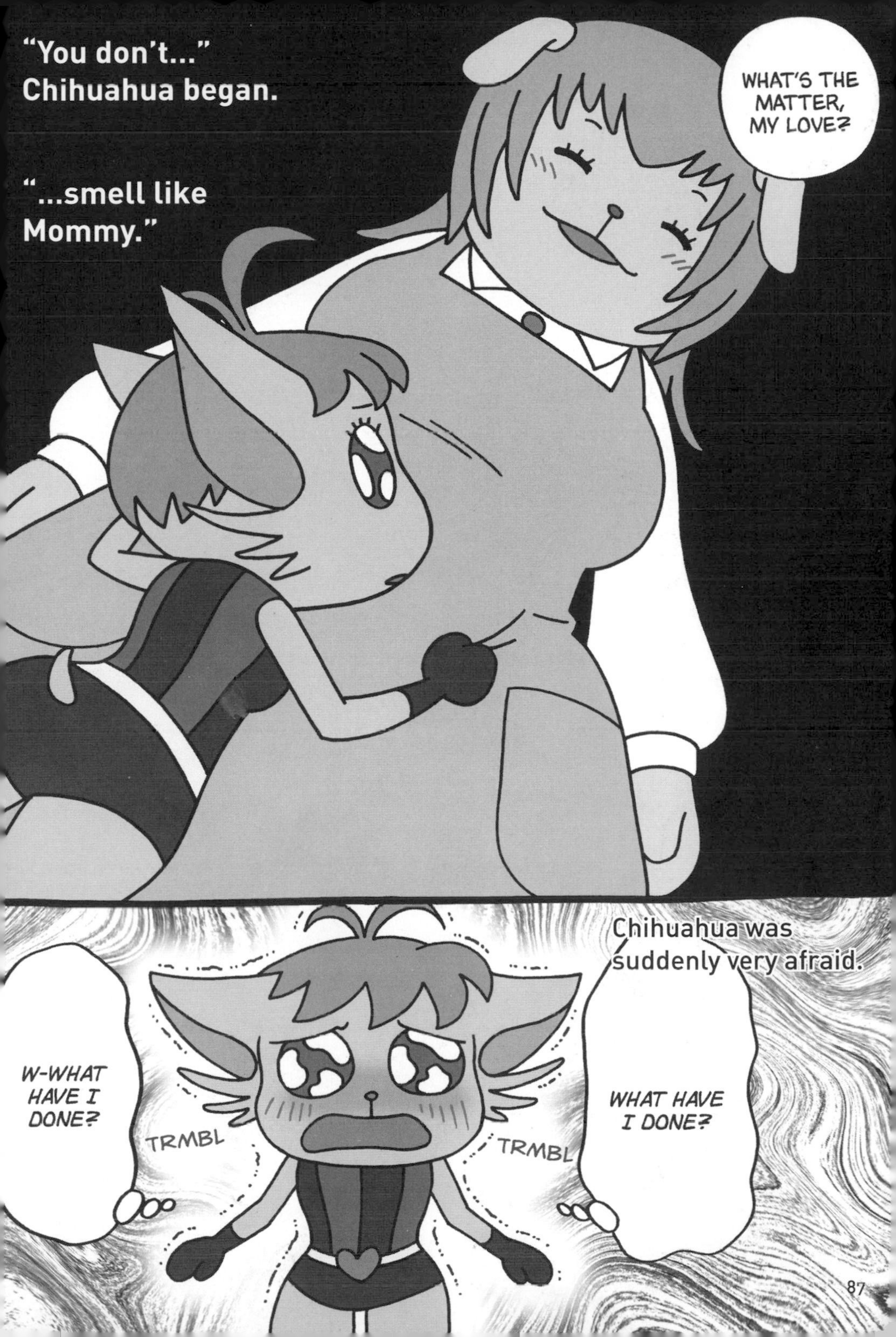
"You don't..." Chihuahua began.
"...smell like Mommy."
WHAT'S THE MATTER, MY LOVE?
Chihuahua was suddenly very afraid.
W-WHAT HAVE I DONE?
TRMBL
WHAT HAVE I DONE?
TRMBL

"I...I just wanted my mommy to be nicer," Chihuahua cried. "I wanted to eat dinner together and play in the park and shop and..." she sobbed. "But now...now..."

It soon became clear to Chihuahua that she had done a terrible thing.

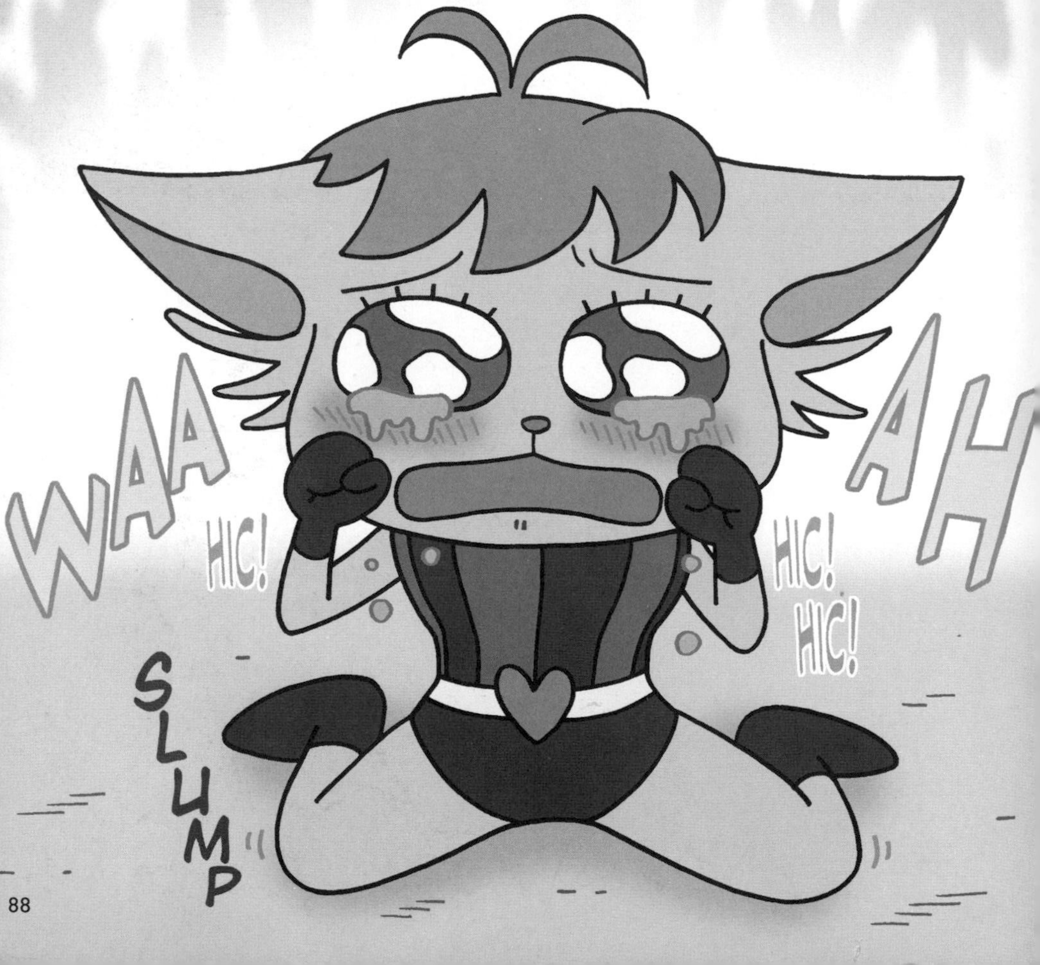
WAA
AH
HIC!
HIC!
HIC!
SLUMP

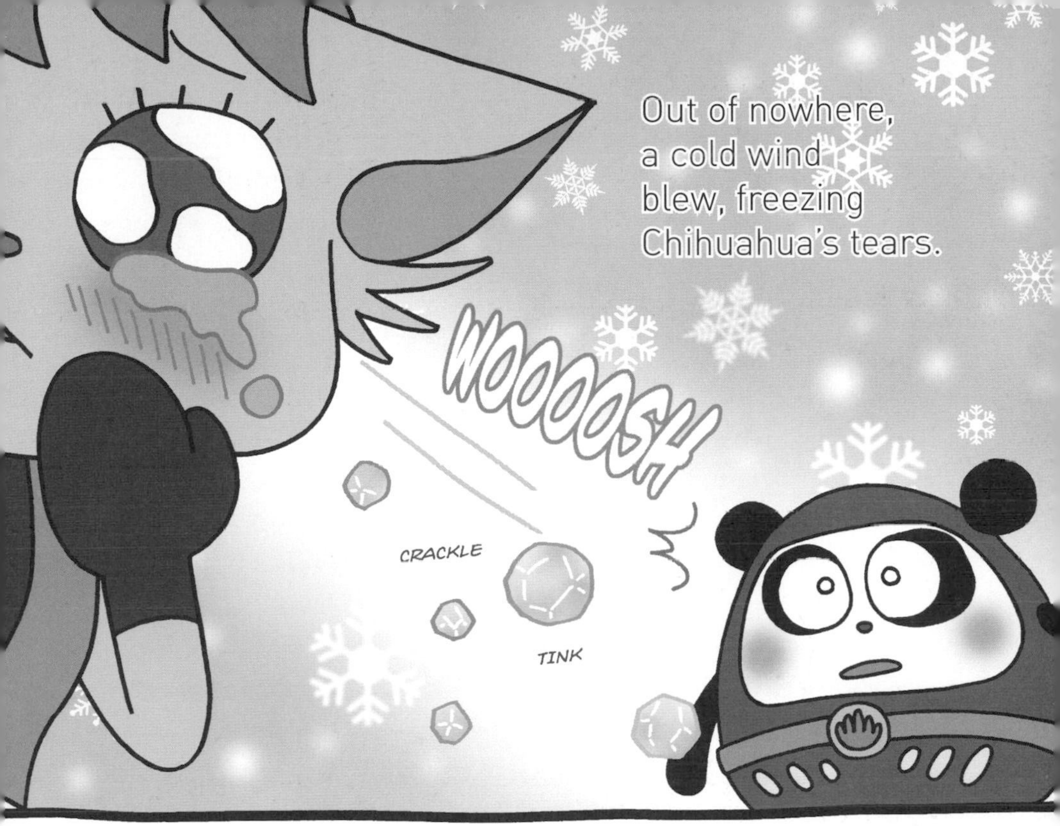
Out of nowhere, a cold wind blew, freezing Chihuahua's tears.
WOOOOSH
CRACKLE
TINK

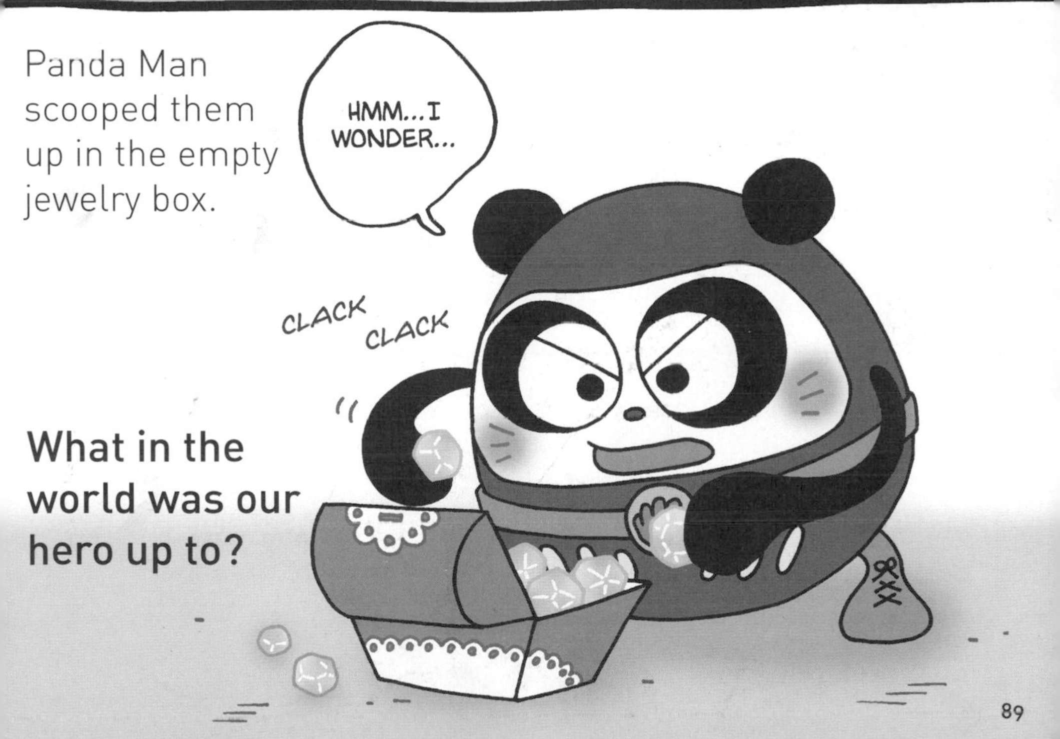
Panda Man scooped them up in the empty jewelry box.
HMM...I WONDER...
CLACK CLACK
What in the world was our hero up to?

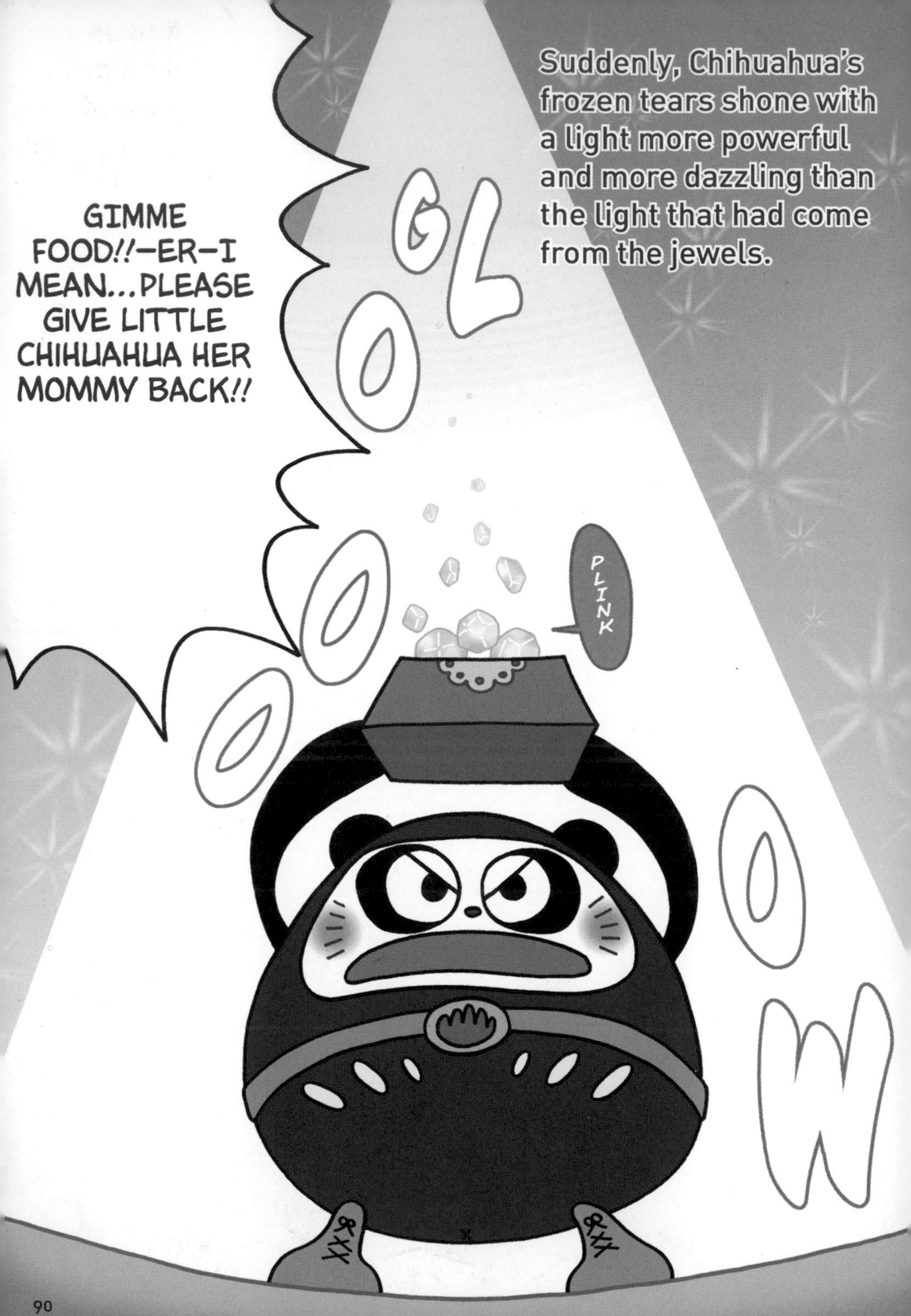
Suddenly, Chihuahua's frozen tears shone with a light more powerful and more dazzling than the light that had come from the jewels.
GIMME FOOD!!—ER—I MEAN...PLEASE GIVE LITTLE CHIHUAHUA HER MOMMY BACK!!
GLOOOOOOW
PLINK

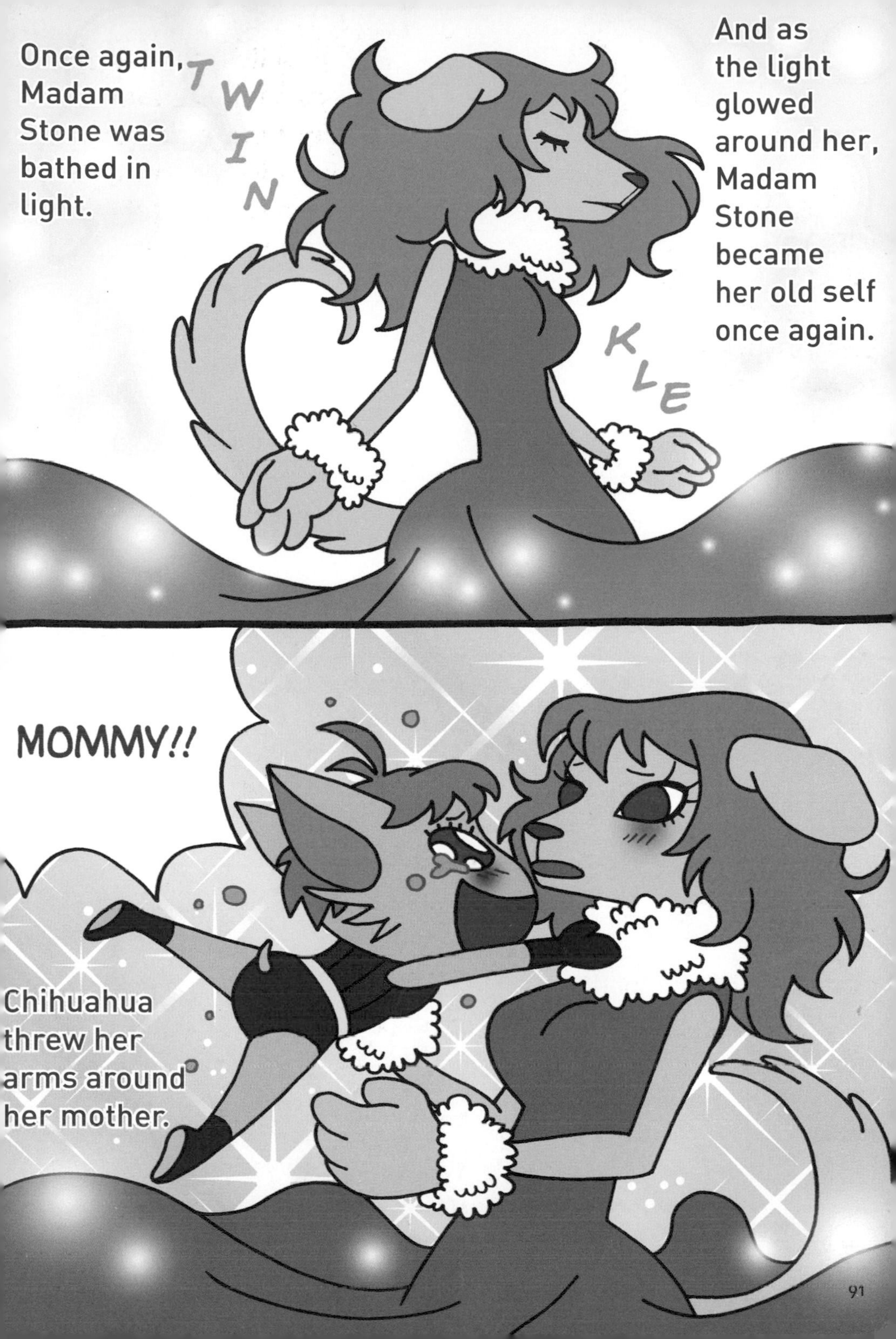
Once again, Madam Stone was bathed in light.
TWINKLE
And as the light glowed around her, Madam Stone became her old self once again.
MOMMY!!
Chihuahua threw her arms around her mother.

“Oh Chihuahua,” Madam Stone cried. “I’m sorry you were so lonely.” She hugged her daughter tight. “You’ll never feel that way again. I promise.”

“I love you, Mommy!” Chihuahua cried happily.

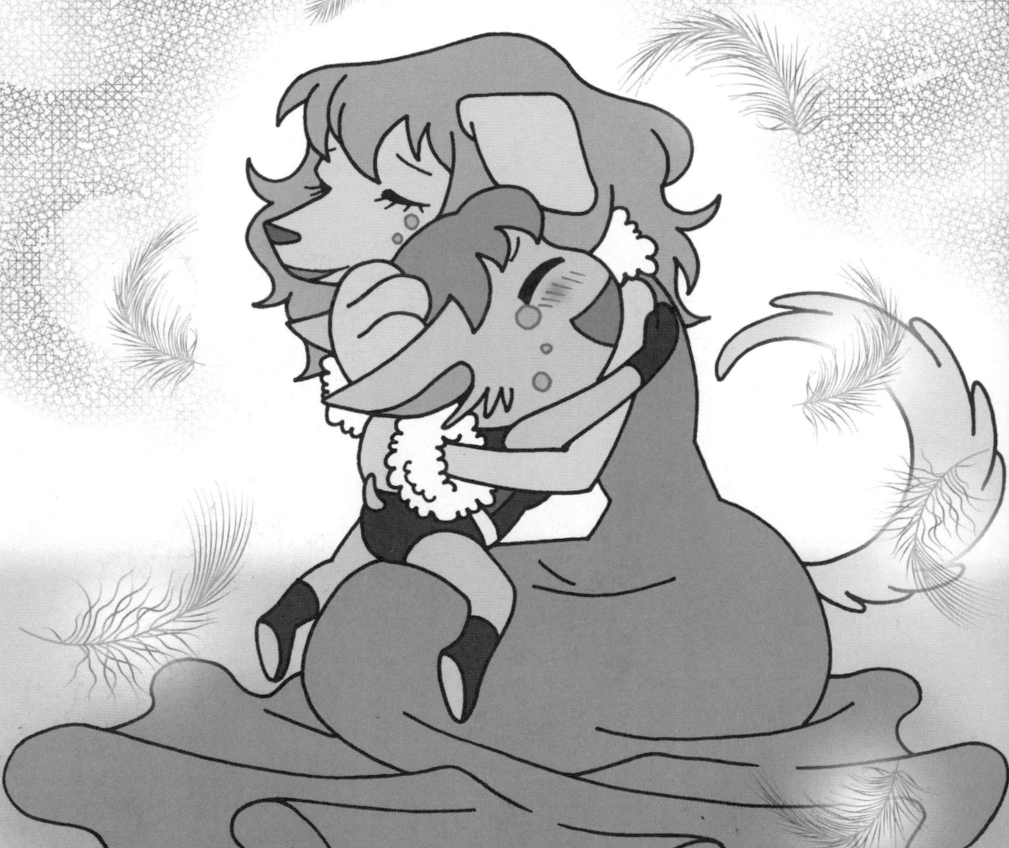

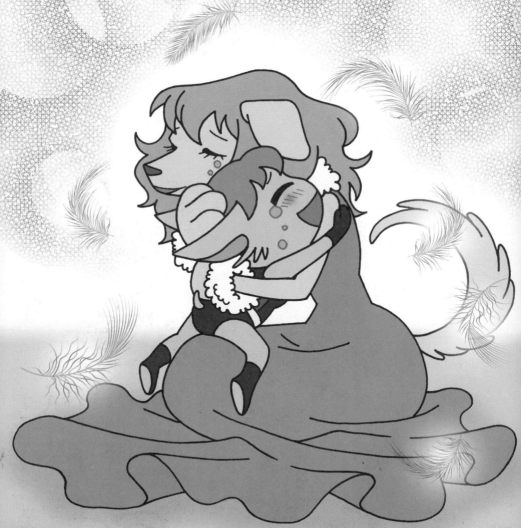

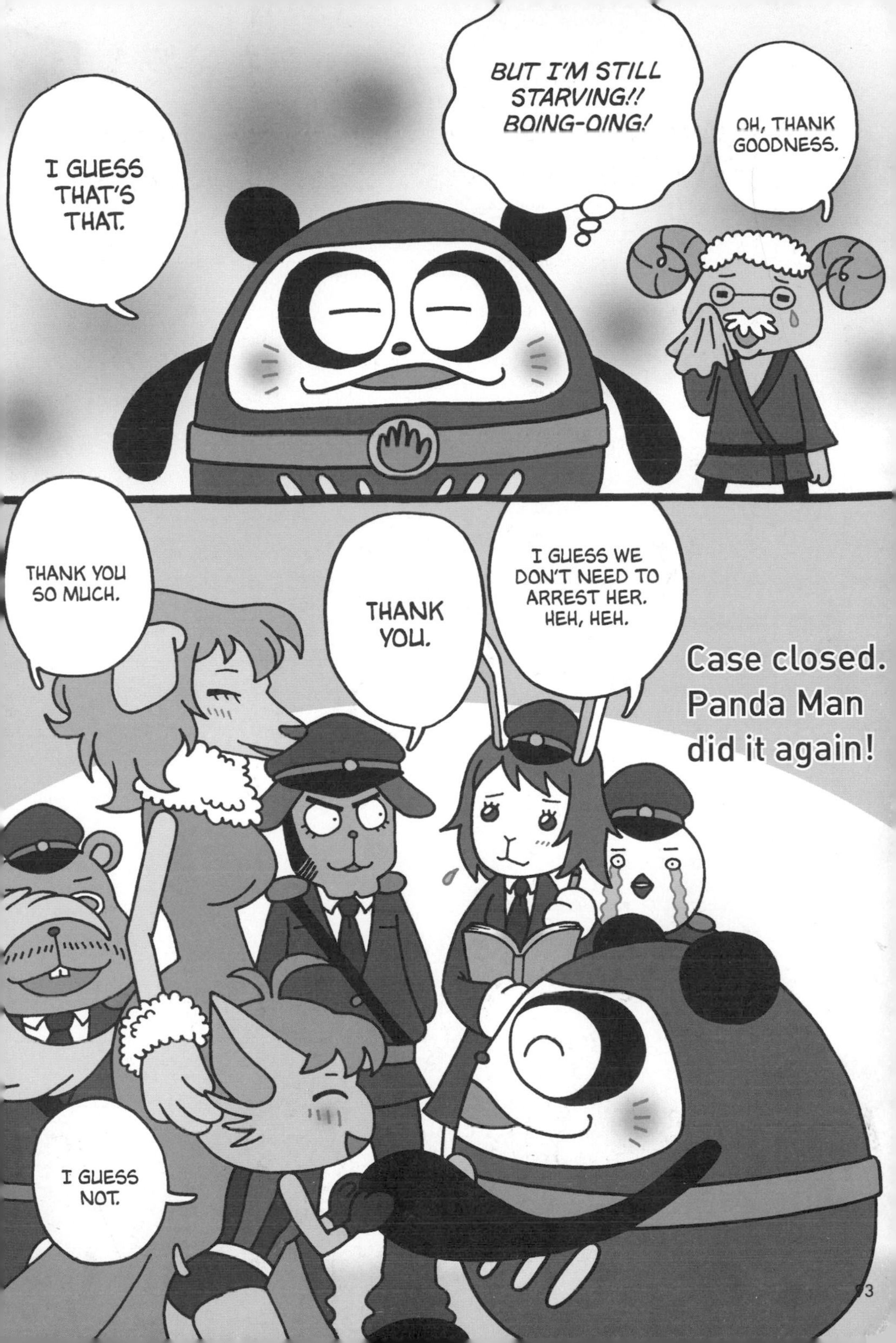
OH, THANK GOODNESS.
BUT I'M STILL STARVING!! BOING-OING!
I GUESS THAT'S THAT.
I GUESS WE DON'T NEED TO ARREST HER. HEH, HEH.
THANK YOU.
THANK YOU SO MUCH.
Case closed. Panda Man did it again!
I GUESS NOT.

That night, Panda Man, Chihuahua and Madam Stone enjoyed a steak dinner. Panda Man, of course, was happy to finally be eating. Chihuahua and her mother were just happy to be eating together.

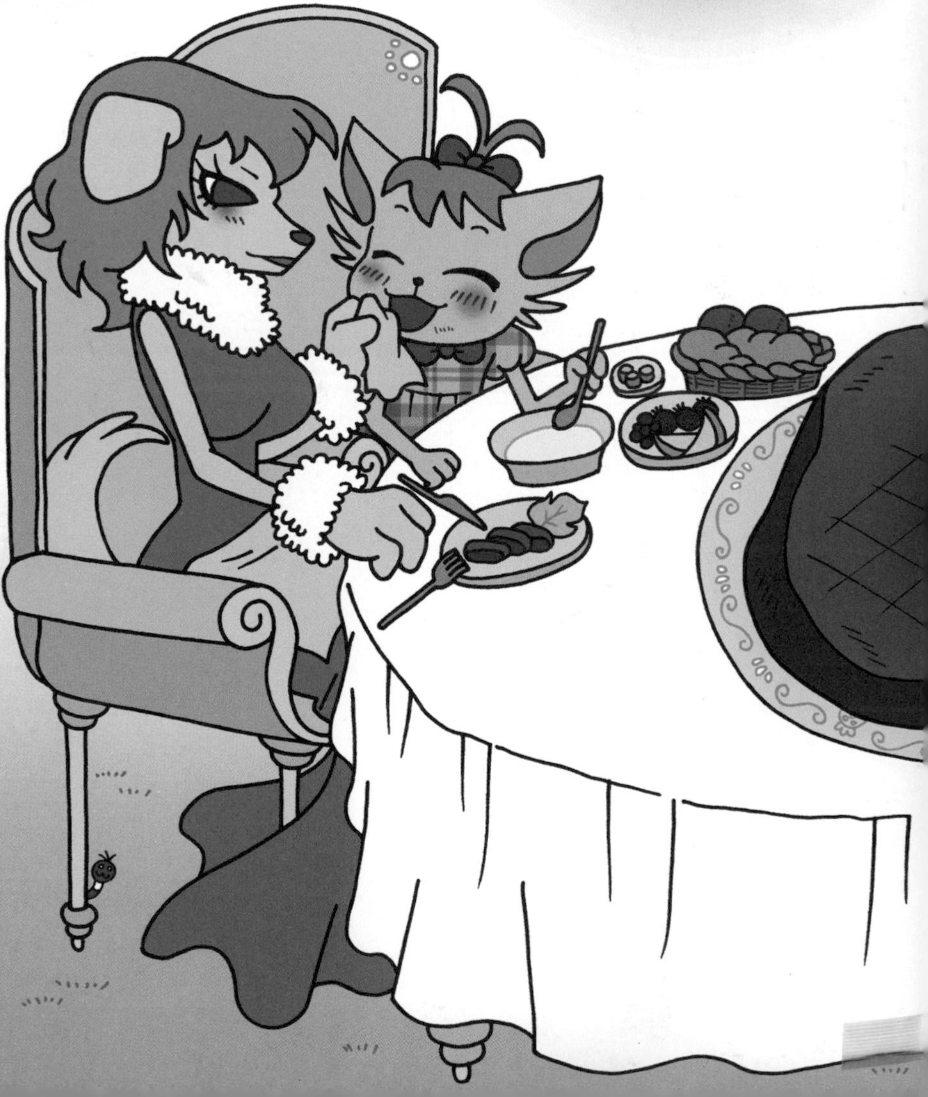

Panda Man opened wide and took a big bite of his steak.

Dinner is always better with family and friends.

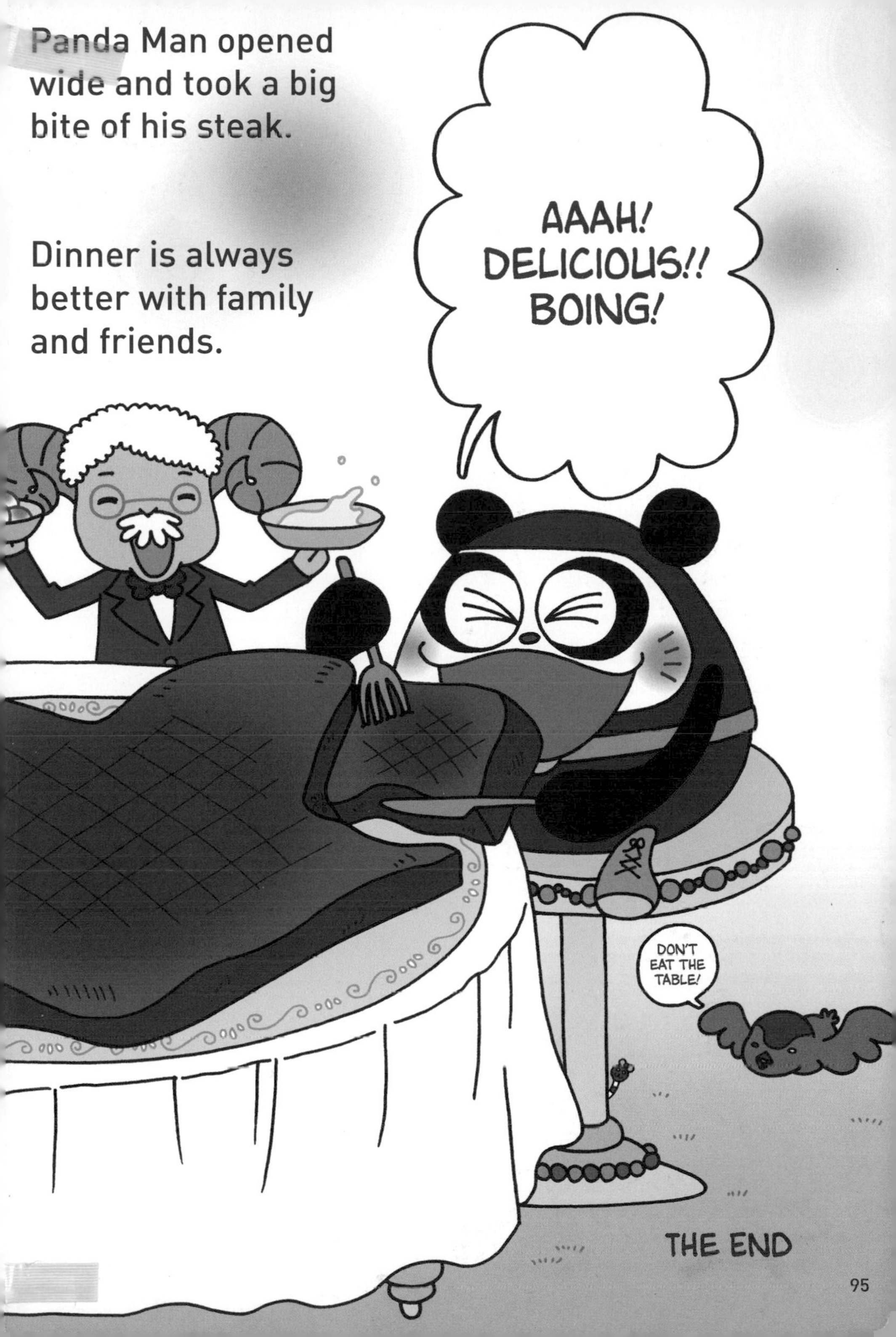
AAAH! DELICIOUS!! BOING!
DON'T EAT THE TABLE!
THE END

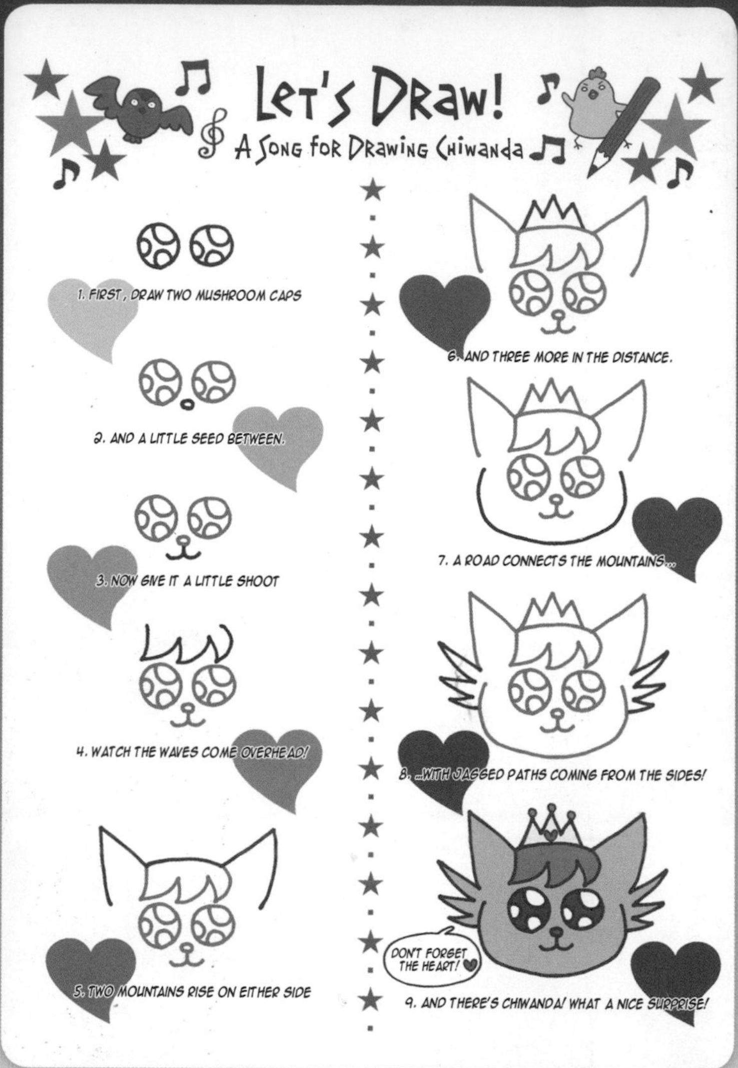

LET'S DRAW!
A SONG FOR DRAWING CHIWANDA
1. FIRST, DRAW TWO MUSHROOM CAPS
2. AND A LITTLE SEED BETWEEN.
3. NOW GIVE IT A LITTLE SHOOT
4. WATCH THE WAVES COME OVERHEAD!
5. TWO MOUNTAINS RISE ON EITHER SIDE
6. AND THREE MORE IN THE DISTANCE.
7. A ROAD CONNECTS THE MOUNTAINS...
8. ...WITH JAGGED PATHS COMING FROM THE SIDES!
DON'T FORGET THE HEART!
9. AND THERE'S CHIWANDA! WHAT A NICE SURPRISE!

Panda Man vs. Chiwanda

VIZ Kids Edition

Story by Sho Makura
Art by Haruhi Kato

Translation: Katherine Schilling
Touch-up Art & Lettering: John Hunt
Graphics & Cover Design: Yukiko Whitley
Editor: Traci N. Todd

First published in Japan in 2008 by SHUEISHA Inc., Tokyo.
English translation rights arranged by SHUEISHA Inc.

Printed in China

Published by VIZ Media, LLC
P.O. Box 77010
San Francisco, CA 94107

10 9 8 7 6 5 4 3 2 1
First printing, May 2011

www.vizkids.com